THE
ARROW CATCHER

BY JIM MATHER

ISBN: 1491011394
ISBN 13: 9781491011393

1

948. Boston sweltered. The weather had obviously decided to move directly from winter into the heart of summer, cutting out spring altogether. And it was only the second week of April. Even though it was late in the day and the sun drooped low in a cloudless, bleached blue sky, it was still hot enough to wilt every living thing beneath it.

Daniel, Victoria, and six-year-old Jonathan Lusk hurried up the scalding sidewalk, the soles of their shoes burning their feet by the time they reached their destination, the front porch of a slat-walled house on Harvard University's faculty row. As Victoria combed her son's hair and straightened his tie, someone inside put a record on and the smooth deep voice of Vaughn Monroe, singing *Dance Ballerina Dance,* poured out the open windows.

Daniel nudged his son. "What time you got?"

The boy studied the white gloved hands on his new Mickey Mouse watch. "The big hand is on the twelve and the little hand is on the seven. So... seven o'twelve," he announced, looking to his father for confirmation.

"Seven o'clock," his mother corrected.

Daniel pulled his son tight against his long legs and kissed his ash blond head. "I like seven o'twelve better," he said, a sparkle in his eyes. "You want to ring the doorbell, Mr. Seven O'Twelve?"

Jonathan stabbed the button with his pudgy index finger, then ran back to hide behind his dad's legs. Victoria Lusk turned to shoot her husband a look. "I cannot believe I let you talk me into this!" The door opened behind her. Without skipping a beat, her face lit up as it swung towards their hosts, Benjamin and Esther Levy. "Ben!" she gushed, "Esther. Thank you so much for inviting us!" Mrs. Lusk bent forward to kiss Benjamin Levy on his large fleshy lips. "And a happy birthday to the birthday boy!" Ben eagerly puckered to accept the kiss but Victoria angled her chin at the last instant, giving him only her makeup-covered cheek. "Is there anything I can help you with?" she asked, just to be polite.

"Tons," said Esther. "Our Sarah is near helpless and my Rachael was asked out on her first date, tonight of all nights!"

"A gorilla must have escaped from the zoo," Jonathan whispered to his father, making him chuckle.

"Wonderful," moaned Victoria as she and Esther Levy disappeared into the mass of Harvard professors and their families packed into the small living room. The men were all attired in suits and ties, ladies in cocktail dresses. All held flared martini or tulip-shaped whiskey sour glasses as smoke curled up from the cigarettes or pipes in their fingers or lips. "Come on, people!" came Esther Levy's school yard voice. "This is supposed to be a party!"

Soon, Peggy Lee's earthy *Manana* filled the room again with music.

A chubby buck-toothed boy in short pants slipped off the sofa. He slurped noisily from a paper cup filled with foamy orange punch as he crossed to where the two remaining Lusks stood just inside the door. "How come you got here so late?" asked Dwayne Ackerman, a pale orange mustache tracing his upper lip.

"We're not late," said Jonathan. "We're right on time, see," he said, cocking his wrist and exposing the dial of his watch.

"We got here at six," Dwayne whined, a smirk on his face. "We had a special meeting, just for the chosen people."

"I don't care," said Jonathan, and meaning it. Who would want to be on any team that chose Dwayne Ackerman or sit through a meeting in such a warm, stuffy room.

The song ended and Peggy Lee's voice dissolved into an insistent scratch. "Will someone please put on something else?" hollered Mrs. Levy from inside the kitchen.

The sweeping sound of violins soon rose above the din. Everyone stopped talking and turned towards the music.

"What is this?" demanded Daniel.

Jonathan's head snapped around. It was his father's rare angry voice.

"You promised that if we came…"

As Dr. Levy took his father's elbow and led him out of earshot, everyone in the room, even Dwayne, sang along with the man on the record. Jonathan tried to sing along too but quickly realized he didn't even know what language it was in. "What is this song?" he asked.

"*Hatikvah*," Dwayne hissed, as if he were some kind of idiot. "Our new national anthem."

"That's not our national anthem!"

"For Israel, stupid, our new country."

Jonathan's face flushed. He was about to tell Dwayne he was happy to learn he had another country and the sooner he moved there, the better. But he was stopped by a nearby woman, who angrily shushed them.

Dwayne took another slurp from his paper cup. "Had any punch yet?" he whispered. "I've already had five."

"Who made it?"

"Mrs. Levy, but it's good."

Jonathan wormed his way through the forest of rigid legs to the far wall, where a folding table had been set up next to the fireplace. Like the mantle and the rest of the room, the table had been decorated in white and blue crepe paper. Jonathan scanned his options. One plate was filled with neat rows of crackers and cheese; another of olives, bell pepper slices, and carrot sticks. But most appealing was a large crystal bowl filled with a frothy punch. He eased a ladleful into a paper cup and sipped. It tasted like a melted 50-50 ice cream bar, his favorite. In one swallow, he drained the cup, wiped his mouth on his sleeve, and helped himself to a refill.

On a Slow Boat to China started on the record player and Jonathan glanced back to see if his father liked this song better than he had the last. He seemed his old self again, smiling and joking with Dr. Levy.

"Eat. Eat," prodded Mrs. Levy as she set down a fresh tray of food. "Have one of Mrs. Engel's wonderful sandwiches or one of my Sarah's delish celery sticks."

Jonathan eyed the tray of small sandwiches. They were cut into the shapes of hearts, circles, and diamonds and laid out in a precise, military-like formation. Each sported a small toothpick flag with thick blue bars on a white field and a blue star at its center. He sniffed and inspected the assortment before him. The diamonds were filled with a mushy gray meat and smelled metallic, like the liquid Geritol his mother made him drink each morning. The hearts oozed oily orange fish eggs and smelled like his dead goldfish. The circles were open-faced bagel halves piled high with sour cream and salmon. All rejects.

He reached for one of the celery sticks, filled with a neatly leveled layer of smooth peanut butter, when a tray of glasses hit the floor and shattered behind him. Jonathan spun to see his mother, standing next to the ruined wet glitter of what had been a tray of full martini glasses, her eyes fixed on the front door.

"Stay out of this, Dr. Lusk! This is not a faculty matter!"

Jonathan couldn't see who was yelling. But the man's voice had a familiar accent. He craned his neck to get a better look. "Dr. Makram!" he said as he started for the front door. His mother grabbed him midstep. "But Mom, maybe Saied's with him."

"Stay here!" she commanded.

Although he was one of his father's good friends and a fellow professor at Harvard, his mother had never liked Yusuf Makram or his wife or even his son. "Do not call him that," she would say whenever he referred to Saied as his best friend. "They are little more than Palestinian riff raff." But Saied *was* his best friend. He liked Dr. Makram too. He had always been nice, taking him and Saied out for burgers, fries and milk shakes whenever his father insisted he be allowed to spend the night with them.

"If it involves faculty and could end up requiring disciplinary action, it is a faculty matter," Jonathan heard his father say, his voice calm and steady as always.

"Then censure him," Makram yelled, pointing at Levy. "He takes part in the murder and rape of Palestinian men, women, and babies. And what about betrayal of friends?" he said, staring Daniel in the eye. "Is that a faculty matter?"

"Come on, Yusuf. You know that isn't true."

"A friend would not be here with this Jewish pig."

"It's a birthday party," Daniel argued calmly, "just as we attended for Saied."

Makram's dark eyes turned away and carefully swept the room for something.

"Have you been drinking?" asked Daniel, sniffing the air.

"Why do you insult me further? Is it not insult enough that you are here?"

"I can smell it."

"If you smell anything," Yusuf said, gesturing towards Levy, "it is surely your host. He reeks of death and the blood of women and small children."

"It'll smell a lot better as soon as you scram!" Levy shot back.

The Palestinian balled up his fists.

"Look, Yusuf," said Daniel, stepping between Makram and Levy. "Nothing good's going to come of this. Go home before any more damage is done... please. We can talk about it in the morning."

Yusuf's black eyes flashed in recognition at something across the room. He pushed his way through the stiff, hostile crowd to the fireplace with Levy on his heels. Makram set down his red leather briefcase and snatched a wicker basket from off the mantle. It was near to overflowing with checks and cash, mostly twenties and fifties.

He read the first check. "Pay to the order of the State of Israel! What are these, birthday presents?"

Daniel appeared shocked. He fixed his gaze on Levy for an answer.

"How many dead children, how many dead wives will this purchase?" Makram said, ripping up a fistful of money and checks and throwing it in Dr. Levy's face. When he reached for another handful, a bystander punched Makram full in the face, snapping his head back.

"And you're not raising money to murder innocent Jewish women and children?" said the man. "Money from American Arabs paid one of your animals, Abu Kishk, to blow up a bus full of women and children and old grandfathers outside Kfar Sirkin. His own people bragged about it!"

Daniel yanked out his handkerchief and reached for the Palestinian's bloody nose. Makram slapped his hand away.

"You are supposed to be such a brilliant boy," Makram blurted at Daniel, not caring that blood was flowing over his lip and into his mouth. "Chairman in but three years. A Nobel Prize." He shrugged. "Well, I am not a chairman. I have no Nobel Prize. Yet I am not blind to the savagery of these pigs, while you claim ignorance! I mistakenly thought you a friend, not just of mine but all peoples, and yet here you are drinking and breaking bread with murderers!"

"For the last time, Yusuf," said Daniel, "I sympathize with your people. I can't imagine what it would be like, having your land taken from you. But Ben's people haven't even had a home to be taken away... for centuries. It's unfortunate the UN decided to give them yours. I'm sure they would have preferred California, right?" Daniel offered jokingly as he nudged Dr. Levy, trying to lighten things up. But no one found any humor in it.

Makram jabbed a finger hard into Lusk's chest, leaving a bloody fingerprint on his white shirt. "You would not be making sport of it if it was your wife there now, instead of mine. Do you know what they do to our women?"

"Please, Yusuf, we've gone over this before."

"The pretty ones, they kill while raping them, thrusting their daggers into their hearts at the moment of ecstasy to heighten their sadistic pleasure. The old and not beautiful, they..."

A group of men fell on Makram. A punch looped out of the roiling mob. Someone cried out in pain. The raw violence so close sent Jonathan scurrying under the folding table to hide. Beneath the bottom edge of the flimsy crepe, he watched the men's feet performing a strange, disjointed dance, punctuated by grunts and curses. "Get this piece of crap out of my house!" Dr. Levy shouted. A shoed foot shoved a red leather briefcase under the table, right beside where Jonathan sat. Then the circle of shoes stumbled towards the front of the house amidst more grunts and curses.

Jonathan waited for a bit, expecting someone to come back for the briefcase. When no one did, he grabbed the handle and crawled out. "Dad!" he yelled, holding it up. "What about this?"

Daniel snatched the case from his hand and rushed outside. Through the front window, Jonathan could see his father stride towards the street. He hoisted the briefcase into the air and yelled at someone.

A brilliant flash. A deafening, house-buckling explosion. Bits of glass and wood and a scalding wind hit Jonathan's face and chest as some unseen force slammed him against the wall. The room began to spin sickeningly, faster and faster. He reached out to steady himself but the table was gone and he fell. His head throbbed. The back of his throat was raw. He felt sure he was about to throw up.

Loud, agonized moans enveloped him, punctuated by screams of pain. Jonathan tried to see what was wrong with them but the room was too full of smoke and dust. And there was an odd, pungent odor in the air that smelled like fireworks.

The house creaked, its walls tilting at a surrealistic camber as if about to collapse. "Mom," he tried to scream but it came out in a raspy whisper.

As Jonathan struggled to his feet, his head felt light, forcing him to take a knee. Then everything went dark.

It seemed only a second before he opened his eyes again. But it had clearly been longer. He was lying on his stomach, his cheek resting in a wet black puddle almost as big as his chest. A bad, metallic taste filled his mouth. He pushed himself up but the effort made him vomit again, enlarging the black pool. It was then that he noticed it wasn't just the bloody vomit that was black, everything in the smoky room seemed to have lost its color.

"Mom!" he whispered, his throat raw.

A ghostly figure tottered stiffly, eerily out of the smoke. Fear swept through Jonathan's small body, making him forget the ache in his throat and the pulsating pain in his head. The figure inched slowly nearer until he could make it out. It was his mother, but it was not. The dress was like the one she had been wearing, but it was torn and dirty. A thousand cuts peppered her pale arms, legs, and face. A deep red gash ran across her cheek from her nose to her ear. But it was her bloody eyes that drove him away.

Part of Jonathan wanted his mother's arms around him, making everything better. But another part screamed to put distance between him and whatever she had become.

"Where are you?" cried Victoria, her voice desperate.

"I'm...right here," he whispered.

She spun, her hands grasping at the sound. But her dead eyes, wide and bulging, were too much for him and Jonathan jumped back, slamming into the wall. His mother staggered towards him, her arms waving in front of Jonathan's face like thick snakes. He was trapped.

Her hand brushed his hair and she lunged for her son. Jonathan dropped to the litter-strewn hardwood floor and scrambled on hands and knees around his mother's feet. Without looking back, he ran rubber-legged out through what had been the front wall and into the pitted front yard.

"Dad!" he yelled, ignoring the pain in his throat.

He listened. There was only the distant wail of sirens heading his way. "Dad!"

2

After their long stay at Boston's Beth Israel Hospital, Jonathan and his mother didn't go home as he expected. Instead, the taxi took them to a downtown hotel.

While Victoria Lusk, her eyes hidden behind dark glasses, her face behind a black lace veil, rummaged through her purse for money to pay the driver, Jonathan took his first look at the four-storied building that was to become their new home.

There wasn't much to set the hotel apart from the rest of the bland buildings lining both sides of the busy street. As with the others, all of its street-level walls were papered in a patchwork of worn circus, boxing, election, and revival posters. Even its massive picture windows, one of its two distinctive features, were so thickly filmed in gray smoke that nothing inside could be seen clearly. His eyes gravitated onto its elaborate sign that hung halfway up the front of the tan brick building and spanned its entire width. Much of the gold paint had faded or flaked but its elegantly scrolled letters could still be read – *Hotel La Fleur*.

"Hot…el Laf…," started Jonathan, trying to sound it out.

"Lenox, sweetheart," his mother piped in. "Hotel Lenox."

That didn't look right but she was a better reader than he was so it let it drop. "Have you seen this place before?" he asked.

"Your father and I stayed here on our honeymoon."

"Here?"

"Room 742," came Victoria's voice from behind her veil. "It would have been ten years next April. The manager was kind enough to book us into the same room."

The driver lugged their suitcases inside while Jonathan helped his mother navigate the wide sidewalk, strewn with cigarette and cigar butts, broken glass, dog droppings, and something that looked suspiciously like dried vomit.

A rotund doorman rose unsteadily from a rickety folding chair. His girth and the strain of standing seriously tested the stitching in his shiny black pants and soiled red blazer, both of which looked several sizes too small for him. As Jonathan and Victoria neared the entrance, the man tipped his hat and opened one of the *La Fleur's* double bronze doors.

"Do the doormen still look as sharp as they used to?" Victoria asked her son.

He had no idea. The only doormen he had ever seen were at the fancy hotel in Norway, where they stayed when his father received his Nobel Prize. This guy didn't look or smell anything like them. "Maybe," he said, not wanting to tell her what he really thought, especially with the man was standing so close. Plus his answer wouldn't be what his mother wanted to hear and, for the first time since the explosion, she was in her airy-voiced party mood.

An immense glass chandelier hung from the lobby's two-story high ceiling, dominating the room. Jonathan stopped and craned his neck to get a good look at it. "Are we at the front desk, sweetheart?" Victoria asked.

"Almost," he said, leading her the rest of the way to the counter, where a bored Asian man read a racing form. As his mother worked out the details of their stay, Jonathan's hazel eyes went back to the chandelier. There was something odd about it. Half of its bulbs were burned out, he quickly noticed, giving it a lopsided look. Or maybe it was lopsided.

The room reeked of the sharp odors of dust, musty carpet, stale food, and old people. The place was filled with them. Some slept. One paced back and forth, talking to himself. Several played games – checkers, dominoes, chess, or cards. The rest slept, read magazines or newspapers, or listened to a ballgame on the radio.

The clerk dinged his bell and an old pinch-faced man in a hotel uniform limped over. Jonathan's eyes fixed on the stiff prosthetic limb that was the man's right leg.

"Why don't you take a photo, it'll last longer," spat the bellhop, sending the boy's eyes in a different direction. The man wrestled their luggage onto a rickety cart. Then he manhandled it roughly across the room and into the small elevator, where his good foot tapped impatiently as Jonathan helped his mother inside.

The instant the bellhop jabbed one of the buttons, the elevator shot upwards so abruptly that Jonathan and his mother almost fell before their ascent slowed to a creep. As they rose, the man's head angled to the side, trying to see what was hidden behind Victoria's black veil. *Why don't you take a picture? It'll last longer*, Jonathan wanted to tell the one-legged jerk but held his tongue.

After what seemed like several minutes, the elevator stopped abruptly, rocking everyone and everything inside. "This is it," the bellhop announced, as if they hadn't figured it out already. He shoved the cart roughly past them and into a dimly lit hallway, where he hurried stiff-leggedly all the way to an end room. The number on the door read 327.

"This isn't room 742," Jonathan said, when he and his mother caught up.

"Only got four floors. Ain't no 742," the man said, unlocking the door and muscling the cart inside.

"You must be mistaken," Victoria insisted.

"Yeah, right," hissed the bellhop, "I only been here fifteen years, lady. Guess there's another three floors I ain't discovered yet."

Victoria's thin arm searched the air for her son's hand. "Take me back to the elevator."

The bellhop grabbed her trailing arm a little too energetically and she yanked it free. "Why don't you just stay here 'til we get it straightened out," he said, probably afraid he was about to lose what looked like his biggest tip in a long time.

"Fine," she said after some thought. "But I expect a speedy visit from your manager."

The man tossed their suitcases onto the bed, cleared his throat, and waited. When Victoria didn't move, he touched her hand with the key.

"Oh," she said, embarrassed, "my husband always handled these things." She dug around in her purse until she found something and handed it to him.

"You sure you want me to have all this?" he said, looking down disgustedly at her nickel tip. "I wouldn't want to bankrupt you or anything." He was still muttering as he slammed the door behind him.

Their room was fancier but not much bigger than Jonathan's bedroom had been back home. A small chandelier, a replica of the one in the lobby, hung from the ceiling, its glass bangles yellowed with age and dimmed by dust and fly carcasses. Ponderous purple drapes smothered the only window, blocking out all outside light.

A chipped rosewood double bed occupied the near third of the room. Most likely, it had once had a canopy but all that remained were the four corner posts. A matching mirrored rosewood dresser and nightstand sat nearby. In the far corner, a rosewood end table was pressed up against a gray wingback chair.

Jonathan drew back the drapes to discover what was outside. Dust rained down, filling the room with a fine, nose-tingling mist. He rubbed a peephole in the dirty glass with his finger and peeked out. But all that was visible through the tiny circle of clear glass was one lane of the street below, where a police car pulled up and two policemen hurried out. He ran the sleeve of his jacket across the pane to widen his view and see what was going on.

"The sunlight feels so good," his mother said, feeling her way over from the bed. "Is there a chair?"

Jonathan shoved the wingback chair over and his mother eased down into its soft frayed fabric. When she did, she apparently called "dubs" because from that point on she seldom left the chair except to sleep or go to the bathroom.

Their first few days at the Hotel La Fleur were exciting for Jonathan. He jumped out of bed each morning, curious to see what the kitchen had made them for breakfast. Morning, noon, and night, the bellhop pushed a small cart down the hallway and left a tray of food just outside their door.

And there was so much he needed to figure out. Which handle was for hot and which for cold on the tub and sink? Which switches turned on the old Packard Bell radio and how did he find his favorite shows? The nurses had given him a bag filled with crayons, coloring books, and Little Golden Books, so he had lots of stuff to read and color.

But over time, he gradually grew sick of their room. He had had more freedom at the hospital, he complained. "I can't stay inside anymore, Mom. I got to go out and look around."

"You know that is not possible, sweetheart," she said. "I cannot leave and there is no one to accompany you."

"I'm not a baby. I don't need anybody to watch me," he said, standing up as straight as he could.

"I said no."

"What about one of my friends coming over, then? Joey or Richie."

"We have talked about this before. No one is seeing me like this, but especially not their mothers. Now since you have nothing better to do, I want you to jump into the tub."

"Jump in the tub. Jump in the tub. I can't ever do anything I wanna do. I hate it here!"

"You cannot have visitors and you most certainly cannot go outside! Do you enjoy hurting me?" she asked, starting to cry, the tears leaking from under the dark glasses she never took off.

"I don't care," he said, tired of her crying too. "You shouldn't have made us come here. We should've gone home like everybody said!"

"Please do not do this to me, Jonathan. I could not possibly live in that house again. I will buy us a new one, I promise, with a pool and big backyard, just as before."

"Why can't we do it right now?"

"Because your father did not leave a will. We cannot do anything until the court makes me the legal owner and Mr. Mason can sell our old house."

"Yeah, but when'll that be? A year?"

"Hopefully just a few more days. Now, into the tub."

Jonathan sat on the side of the bathtub as it filled, swishing water around with his hand.

"That is my sweet boy!" his mother called.

Since she obviously couldn't tell if he actually took a bath or not, Jonathan decided he wouldn't take one again. Each night, he sat on the floor and played in the water with one of the makeshift boats he fashioned during the day. "Thank you, sweetheart!" she had called from her chair the second night. "You are becoming such a good little man!" And she never became any the wiser.

Besides being wrong about his supposed daily baths, she was also wrong about their moving into a new home anytime soon. After a month had passed, she no longer even talked about it. His father had always been the one to get things done or done right. His mother had always described herself as the *delegator* and his father the *implementer*. His dad said that that meant she told him what to do and he did it. Now there was no implementer.

The doctors had been wrong too. Instead of getting better, his mother had gotten worse. Most days, she didn't even seem to know he was there. All she did was sit in her chair, staring through her dark glasses at the window as if she still could see. Jonathan spent a goodly portion of his days actually looking out the same window, watching the endless stream of fascinating people parading up and down the sidewalk four floors below.

"You wouldn't even miss me if I did go outside!" Jonathan snapped, getting no response from his mother. The brown crayon in his small hand flew back and forth as he crudely filled in the Lone Ranger's chaps, not caring if he stayed inside the lines or not. He was sick of coloring. He was sick of reading the Little Golden Books he now knew by heart. The only things he had to look forward to anymore were his radio shows. "Kukla, Fran, and Ollie" during the week and "The Buster Brown Show" on Saturday mornings. But each only lasted an hour, leaving him with ten to twelve boring hours to kill.

Summer had started early that year and winter seemed intent on not being outdone. It was the early arrival of snow that brought things to a head. All day long, Jonathan had watched fat snowflakes drift down past their window and collect on the window sill. He loved the snow.

The next morning, he silently eased on his jacket and mittens, then tip-toed to the end table beside his mother's chair and picked up their room key. He lay on the bed, roasting as he awaited the bellhop's familiar footsteps to thud thump their way up the hallway with their lunch tray. Thankfully he didn't have to wait long.

"I'll get it, Mom," he yelled when he heard the rattle of plates and the quick rap on the door. He opened the door, slid the tray inside, and ran joyfully down the hallway.

The lobby appeared as if nothing had changed since he and his mother passed through it several months earlier. The same wrinkled, gray-haired old men and blue-haired old women, or people who looked just like them, filled the worn sofas and chairs. Some played cards in slow motion. One slept, still sitting up. Others cupped their ears and leaned as close as they could to the radio to hear a baseball game. Nothing to do there either, Jonathan concluded.

Outside, the recent snowfall had made the place look a lot cleaner than it had when they arrived. Even though it was still early in the day, neon signs were already glowing along the street. He could make out those for a movie house, a hot dog shop, even one with a naked girl sitting in a martini glass. He had no idea what kind of store that could be.

Jonathan strolled down the sidewalk, passing old bums who stood in groups of three and four, warming their hands over trashcan fires, drinking what looked like red soda pop from long-necked bottles they kept hidden in paper bags. He came to a man lying in the middle of the sidewalk. Everyone just walked around him as if he weren't there so he went around him too.

Beneath the naked-woman sign, a man dressed in a bright yellow suit, hat, and overcoat was yelling at everyone who walked by, trying to get them to go inside. "Come here," said the man, crooking a finger at Jonathan, and nodding toward the bright red door behind him. Jonathan froze. He had been warned repeatedly about talking to strangers, and this guy was definitely strange.

"Come on," the man coaxed. "I'll give you a free peek at something you'll never forget, something that will change your life forever, little man." The barker opened the door a crack and caught a quick glimpse inside. "Wowza!" he said, bobbing his bushy eyebrows.

Jonathan's curiosity overwhelmed his mother's warnings. Besides, she was afraid of everything, he told himself, as he cautiously approached the door. The man pushed it open just wide enough for him to get a peek inside. The pink lighting was weird, the bodies entangled and moving oddly; it took a few seconds before Jonathan could make out what he was looking at. His eyes flared and he scooted away so fast the man slapped his knee and laughed until tears ran down his cheeks. "Didn't I tell you?" he said. "Now you know what makes this big old world go round and round, little man. There ain't nothing goes on that ain't connected to that right there!"

Jonathan hurried back towards the hotel but by the time he reached the pizza shop he stopped. There was no one to run to, not any longer. Since the explosion, his mother wasn't the same mom she had been before. It was almost like she had died at the Levys'.

With his eyes locked on the barker, he made a wide arc around the man and continued on, getting a big belly laugh as he went. He passed a barber shop, a liquor store, and a place that sold some kind of foreign food before coming to a store with all kinds of interesting stuff in its windows. There were pistols and rifles, mortars, switchblade knives, giant bullets, watches and old coins. A pair of false teeth chattered noisily. A long-necked plastic bird rocked back and forth before dunking its head into a glass of blue water.

A bell tinkled as Jonathan entered the shop of wonders. The clerk glanced up from his newspaper just long enough to see it wasn't a serious shopper, then went back to his reading.

The aisles were cluttered with piles of old army and navy gear: leather pilots' helmets, gas masks, web belts, parachutes, fold-up shovels, canteens, cans of Sterno, and small jars of pills to disinfect water. The sharp odor of mothballs, rough wool, and gun oil filled the air.

The bell jingled behind him but Jonathan was mesmerized by a World War II embalming kit.

"You Jonathan?" asked a blue-uniformed policeman.

"How'd you know?"

"Your ma's worried sick," he said in a rough voice. "You ought'a be ashamed of yourself, scaring your ma like that." He grabbed Jonathan's ear and dragged him outside and back towards the hotel.

When the boy saw his mother standing on the snowy sidewalk up ahead, he knew he was in even worse trouble than he feared. Her body twisted and contorted, her arms clawing the air as if she were drowning. "Jonathan!" she screamed so loudly he could hear her from a half block away. "Jonathan!" A jolt of fear shot through him. It was like he was back at the Levys'.

Victoria Lusk was dressed in her long fox coat with the collar pulled up to her chin. Her bright red lipstick had been applied in only the general vicinity of her mouth, badly missing her lips completely in spots.

"Here he is, ma'am," the policeman said, shoving Jonathan up against her.

Victoria clutched her son. She kissed him over and over, smearing lipstick and white makeup across his head and the side of his face. Jonathan wanted to tell her he was sorry, but he could feel the tears welling up and was sure that if he said anything, he would start crying.

The big policeman helped Victoria back inside. "Let me give you a little something for your assistance," she said as they waited for the elevator to arrive. Her hands patted her shoulders, searching for something. "Did you steal my purse?" she asked.

"You didn't have one with you, ma'am," he replied calmly. "And besides, we're not allowed to accept anything. Reuniting mother and child is payment enough."

Victoria's knees buckled and her body went limp. The policeman reached out to catch her but not quickly enough and she landed hard on the tiled floor, pulling Jonathan down with her. "I'm sorry, Mom," he cried, scooting around and cradling her head in his arms.

Not one of the old people in the packed lobby seemed remotely interested in Victoria's plight, no doubt having seen too many fellow tenants die already and not wanting to look too closely into another face contorted by the specter of death. A cheer went up. Jonathan's head snapped angrily around to see old men dancing as an excited radio announcer yelled, "It's out of there!"

The policeman carried his mother up to their room. Her arms flew wide apart as he laid her on the bed. "Who is there?"

"It's just me, ma'am, Officer Herlihy," answered the policeman. "Your son's here too."

"You okay, Mom?"

Victoria hugged Jonathan so tightly he could barely breathe. But he said nothing; it was all his fault.

The policeman stayed until Dr. Oaks showed up. His mother's young, baby-faced physician quickly checked her vital signs, then patted her wrist. "You'll be fine, Mrs. Lusk. You just need to eat, drink far more water, and get more rest. Have you been taking the pills I gave you?"

"I threw them away," she answered smugly. "As I said, I am not a pill-taker."

The doctor removed a jar from his bag and set it on the nightstand beside the bed. "Well, do me a favor, will you? I'm leaving you more. Take one each night for the next five days, don't take more than one, and wash it down with a full glass of water. Okay?"

She mulled it over.

"If you don't," prodded Dr. Oaks, "you'll soon be back in the hospital. Would you like that?"

Victoria reluctantly shook her head.

"Then do the things I've asked you to do." The doctor gave her a shot. "This will help you sleep," he said before leaving.

Within minutes, Victoria lay motionless, her mouth open, snoring loudly. Jonathan sat beside her, holding her hand, keeping her covered, and wiping the sweat off her forehead. Even when the sun set and the room grew dark, he stayed with his mother.

"Jonathan!" his mother shouted, sitting up as if startled out of a bad dream.

"It's okay, Mom," he offered. "I'm right here."

His mother cried at first, saying she had feared he had been kidnapped. Then she yelled at him for making her go outside where everyone could laugh at her. Then her mood shifted yet again and she cried even harder, begging him to forgive her for being angry.

"I only wanted to look around for a second, to see what it looked like outside," he said, blinking back the tears. "I won't ever do it again. I promise."

"You are all I have left, Jonathan." She kissed him on the head, then sniffed his dirty ash-blond hair. "Have you been washing your hair?" she asked, an edge back in her voice.

"I forgot last time but I'll do it tonight," he promised, getting another kiss.

For the first time in weeks, he took an actual bath without even being told. And he washed his hair, not once but twice. As he ambled out of the bathroom, he saw his mother back in her chair and settling in, as she did each night before going to sleep. He snatched up the bottle of pills from the nightstand and ran to her side. "Here's your pills, Mom," he said, putting the jar in her lap. "I'll get a glass of water."

"Doctors cannot help me," she said, throwing the jar across the room. It bounced off the wall and landed unbroken on the rug. "Do I look like I have been helped? Do I look better?"

"You look beautiful, Mom," he offered, "the most beautiful mom in the whole wide world."

"Thank you, sweetheart," she said sadly. "I only wish it were true."

Over the next couple of weeks, no matter how much he prodded, she refused to do anything the doctor had asked – didn't sleep, seldom ate or drank anything, didn't even bathe anymore.

"I can hear you," she yelled, as Jonathan opened the door to get their dinner one night. She hadn't spoken to him in three days. "You want to leave me like everyone else did. Do not deny it, you little liar! You cannot stand to look at me, can you?"

"I'm not leaving, Mom. I'm just...."

"Go ahead, get out!"

"No, Mom. I'm not going anywhere. I'm just hungry."

"I said get out!"

Even though his stomach was rumbling, he sat beside his mother and lightly tickled her arm with his fingertips; *spider steps* she called it when she had done the same to make him feel better.

Each day, her face grew paler, more sickly looking. Before the explosion, she used to pay him a nickel for every gray hair he could find and pluck out. Now, the gray had overtaken the blonde ones. Worst of all, she had started to stink like the homeless men he had passed on the street.

A loud pounding on the other side of the wall awakened him one night. "Will you shut up in there, lady!" came a gruff male voice from the next room. "Some of us would like to get some sleep."

"Yusuf," Victoria shouted in the semi-darkened room.

"Shut the hell up!"

Jonathan rubbed the sleep from his eyes. He turned on the light, then stumbled to his mother's chair. "Dr. Makram isn't here, Mom. Don't you remember? He went away."

Victoria yanked off her dark glasses and threw them onto the floor. She locked her bulging, cloudy eyes on him as if staring straight into his eyes. "Mom, stop it. You're scaring me!" he pleaded, staggering back.

"How could you do that to Daniel? He was your friend. And what about me? What did I do to deserve this?" she said, shaking her hands in front of her face.

"Mom, I didn't..." he started. But before he could finish, she backhanded him across the face.

"Liar!"

The boy ran to the far corner of the room and wedged himself between the bed and the wall. The salty metallic tang of blood filled his nostrils and spiced his tongue as he studied his mother through burning, wet eyes. Each day she was becoming more and more of a stranger. And it was all his fault. Had he not found Dr. Makram's briefcase or just left it alone, his father would still be with them and his mother still her old self.

"Are you awake, sweetheart," Victoria cooed the next morning. "Bring me the pills the doctor gave me, will you?"

Jonathan tried to sit up but banged his head on the box spring. It took him a second to remember that he had slept under the bed... and why.

"Please, sweetheart," his mother begged, "I have to get some rest. I did not sleep a wink last night."

He didn't budge.

"I said get my pills!" she screamed. "Do NOT make me say it again!"

She had turned from sweet to vicious so quickly it made him even more hesitant to get up. But he could still taste the blood from her last slap and didn't want another. "I'm coming," he said, his voice weak and quivering.

His right leg had gone to sleep and he sounded like the bellhop as he staggered unevenly toward where the jar of pills still lay on the floor in the corner of the room. He picked it up and struggled with the cap. "I can't open it, Mom," he apologized, afraid she would be angry with him. But she wasn't. She calmly took the jar, used some trick to get the lid off, and shook one of the red capsules into her palm.

"I'll need some water too, sweetheart," she said, sounding like his old mom.

Jonathan limped into the bathroom and returned with a glass of water, just in time to see his mother shake a second pill into her palm. "The doctor said you're only supposed to take one," he objected but she popped both into her mouth and held out her hand for the glass.

It wasn't long before she fell sound asleep. He had barely slept the night before himself and quickly joined her.

Laughter awakened him. He sat up, enthralled. His mother was giggling like a little girl as she danced around the room, lifting her arms and twirling like a ballerina. Her hip bumped the end table and knocked over the glass, spilling water down the front of her legs.

Jonathan ran into the bathroom and grabbed a towel. When he returned, she was back in her chair, panting and smiling tiredly. He plopped down on the rug to towel off her spindly legs, now little more than bones sheathed in skin. Beside him sat the empty pill bottle. As he dried his mother's legs, her head tilted slowly forward until her chin rested against her chest.

"Okay, Mom, all dry," he said, looking up. Her happy face made him chuckle. One second, dancing, the next, asleep sitting up.

The bellhop's cart creaked down the hallway and stopped just outside. Jonathan jumped up. It was Sunday – waffle day. As he ran to unlock the door, he heard a loud thud behind him. He turned to see his mother face down on the rug.

"Are you okay?" he asked. Getting no response, he nudged her shoulder. Her body was soft and moved easily. He patted her cheek. "Mom, wake up!"

3

─────

B lack clouds filled the sky so densely that not a single ray of sunlight could break through to add even a speck of brightness to the dark, dreary day. Beneath its smothering blanket, an ever-thickening layer of fog pushed in from off Broad Sound and slid up the rolling hillside. It and a thin melting layer of snow masked much of the cemetery's grassy expanse, leaving only a checkered mosaic of remembrances that ran the gamut from humble stones to massive family mausoleums dating back to the Revolutionary War.

Jonathan stood on the mushy snow and studied the white coffin. The minister had said that his mother was inside, awaiting her journey to heaven, where she would rejoin his father. But she wasn't very strong. He didn't understand how she would be able to get out of the box if it was under the ground. He wanted to tell them to leave it where it was.

Eli Lusk smiled down at his grandson, his eyes crinkling at the corners as he rubbed his back reassuringly. Jonathan leaned against his long legs, the way he used to his father's. He had loved his grandfather right from the start. He was like an older version of his father. Both were big and funny and kind. The main difference, other than the wrinkles in his grandfather's face and the purple spots on his hands and arms, was their hair. His grandfather's was silver, where his father's had been blond like his own. "My two golden boys," his mother used to call Jonathan and his dad. Where his father's eyes had been blue, Eli Lusk's were hazel eyes, the exact same color as his own. And his grandfather spoke with a deeper, more powerful and commanding voice, where his father's had been soft and soothing. But, other than those few things, he was just an older version of his dad.

On Jonathan's other side stood the Japanese woman his father had called his *new grandmother* when they had visited the year before. His mother had come up with another name for her, one his father told him never to repeat. But he apparently hadn't told his mother because she repeated it to his new grandmother at dinner that night. His grandfather and new grandmother had left the next morning, three days earlier than planned.

Unlike his grandfather, who towered over him, his new grandmother wasn't much taller than Jonathan. She had a tiny nose, barely a nose at all; a tight mouth she tended to cover often with her hand; and narrow, black eyes that were shaped like those of the Levy baby, who had something wrong with him. She never seemed to notice anyone or anything unless she was not happy with them. His mother had hated the fact that his new grandmother was always "dressed to the nines," whatever that meant, in the latest Paris fashions, and never had even one of her "obviously dyed" black hairs out of place. And nothing had changed.

Her name was Hiroko but he had been warned never to call her that. She seemed to have a lot of names she couldn't be called.

"You can call her Grandmother, or *Obachan*," his grandfather told him.

"Does she ever smile?" Jonathan had asked.

"She is a princess in her country and was raised to be very serious," Eli said, then leaned close and whispered into Jonathan's ear. "Don't tell her I told you this but she's really very sweet and nice, like a puppy dog. She just keeps it hidden deep inside, like it's a big secret."

Jonathan looked over at his new grandmother. She was obviously very good at keeping secrets. Before they had left their hotel that morning, she had talked to him about crying at the funeral — proper people, according to her, don't show their emotions in public. But as he stood there on the melting snow, with Mr. and Mrs. Lundy, the Martins, the Greens, the Nelsons, even grouchy old Mr. Lynn crying behind him, Jonathan couldn't help himself. His eyes misted and he wiped his nose on his sleeve. His new grandmother wiped the tears away with her handkerchief. "Please remember what we discussed," she said. "You are a Lusk and Lusks do not cry for all to see."

Jonathan tried to stifle it, but instead of stopping, a loud sucking sound escaped his throat, shaking his head and shoulders on its way out. It was so loud it caught even him by surprise. He felt his new grandmother's hand on his shoulder. He looked at her in apology as she pinched a fold of sensitive skin between her surprisingly powerful fingers.

The clouds opened and rain fell. "Goodbye, Mom," Jonathan whispered as two workmen cranked Victoria's coffin down into the wet hole. When it reached the bottom, he tossed the white flower his new grandmother had given him on top of the coffin. But it slid off and landed in the mud.

His grandfather picked him up and hugged him as they walked down the hill to their waiting limousine. Tomorrow they would fly to his new home in a place called Japan.

4

———

Jonathan gazed down from the open hatch of the silver DC-4 as four thin-eyed men, jabbering in some harsh sounding language, wrestled a portable ramp into place.

"You can go ahead, Ambassador," the stewardess said, when the men were done.

Eli nudged his grandson, who hopped out onto the ramp, then stopped, captivated by the sprawling, bombed-out city of Tokyo in the distance.

"Yes," said his grandfather, "it is quite a mess, isn't it?"

A big DeSoto sedan with small American flags flapping on its bumpers pulled up and stopped at the foot of the ramp. The car's plump round black body reminded Jonathan of a giant stink beetle. But inside, it very soft and plush, like his father's Lincoln had been.

Hundreds of thousands of homeless and starving Japanese poured into the city in search of food and work. A human tsunami flooded every street they tried, people carrying all of their worldly belongings on their backs or in the rickety carts they pushed ahead of them. Taro, the Lusks' driver, pounded the horn as the DeSoto inched its way through the seemingly endless mob of humanity. Jonathan jammed his fingers into his ears and took it all in from atop the fold-down armrest, mesmerized by the scene passing outside.

The people didn't look friendly. Their flatter faces, strange eyes, and brown skin made him uneasy. Some bowed as they passed, but more simply stared. A few gave them the finger or waved a fist. A short muscular man in a tattered military uniform charged their car, his arms punching the air. Jonathan recoiled away as the man slammed into their side door and pressed his contorted face against the glass. Eli glanced casually over just long enough to see others grab and restrain the man. Even restrained, though, the man never stopped kicking and fighting and yelling words Jonathan couldn't understand.

"What's he so mad about, Grandpa?" Jonathan asked.

"You will address your grandfather properly," his new grandmother chided. "We are not uneducated merchants."

"What's he so mad about, Grandfather?"

"I couldn't hear him," Eli said. "But I'd imagine it had something to do with us defeating them in the recent war. They are an intensely prideful people, the Japanese. Many of the old-timers, the traditionalists, found defeat, especially to *gaijin*, particularly distasteful."

"To what?"

"*Gaijin*. Anyone not Japanese. Here, honor is more important than life itself. Many would rather have died than surrender to us."

Jonathan didn't like this Japan or *Nippon* or whatever it was called. Even his grandparents didn't seem to know what to call the place, calling it something different almost every time. But it wasn't just the obvious hatred of some of the people that bothered him. Everything was different there, like in a weird dream. There were trees and birds and houses and stores, but they were all different from those back home. The houses were like cottages, smaller and made of bare wood and white paper, not like real houses. The streets were narrow and bumpy, not smooth and wide like the ones in Boston. Japan even smelled different.

Construction crews worked night and day, his grandfather told him, rebuilding the city, clearing away rubble and erecting new modern buildings in its place. Shirtless construction workers with tattoos of dragons and tigers and warriors covering their sweat-drenched chests, arms, and backs wrestled teetering stacks of bricks up rickety four and five-story bamboo ladders.

"Why do they have pictures on their bodies?" Jonathan asked.

"They are *yakuza*," hissed Hiroko. "The scum of Japan. Thieves, murderers, drug dealers, thugs. They mark their bodies as proof of their low..."

A dump truck raced out from a construction-site forcing Taro to slam on the brakes. He waited several seconds for it to move, but it didn't seem to be going anywhere. So he honked. A brick flew from a group of construction workers standing beside the road, hitting the DeSoto's windshield and cracking it. The workers hoisted sledge hammers and picks and strode towards the car. Taro slammed the gearshift into reverse and floored it, horn blaring.

As they raced backwards, they spotted a policeman and stopped. Soon, police cars and motorcycles, sirens wailing, sped past and continued on. A minute later, four U.S. Army MPs, machine guns dangling from straps around their necks, roared up on motorcycles. They escorted the DeSoto past the construction site, where Jonathan saw the policemen battling the tattooed men with their clubs. Even with battered and bloody faces, the workers kept fighting.

Within a couple of blocks, their convoy stopped at the entrance to a broad, well-paved roadway, blocked by a bar gate. A sign said, "Official Vehicles Only." A soldier stepped out of the small guard shack, raised the gate, and saluted as the DeSoto continued on. Eli waved his thanks to their escort, who turned around and headed back towards town.

"Why did they hit our car with that rock?" asked Jonathan.

"It may have been merely venting anger at we Americans. Or we may have been targeted. The *yakuza* are unhappy that we have imprisoned and will very likely hang several of their leaders, evil men who did horrible things. I am one of those appointed to sit in judgment of them."

The big DeSoto sped alongside a wide green moat. Across it sat a lush island with a beautiful ancient castle at its center.

"That's where Hiroko's uncle, the Emperor, lives," said Eli, pointing at the castle. "He ruled Japan before our army beat his army." Eli smiled over at his wife. "Think we should stop in and say hello to the old folks?" he asked but she returned only a sullen glare which made him chuckle.

The DeSoto left the city and passed a string of small family farms. Each was surrounded by a checkerboard of rice paddies and tended by an entire family who waded through the shin-deep water to harvest their crop. As the car sped past, everyone turned and bowed almost in unison. The paddies looked so green and beautiful that Jonathan leaned over his grandfather and rolled down the window. He quickly wrinkled his nose and rolled it back up. It smelled like someone had forgotten to flush the toilet.

"You'll get used to it." His grandfather winked.

They passed an old farmer peeing at the side of the road. Without interrupting his stream, he gave them a polite bow and toothless smile. Jonathan twisted around on the armrest and stared until he couldn't see the old man anymore. "Bet you haven't seen that in Boston, eh sport?" Eli said. Hiroko clicked her tongue in exasperation.

A couple of miles later, the DeSoto slowed, then angled onto a dirt road. "Are we almost there?" Jonathan asked. His fanny was sore. Counting the plane ride and the long wait at one of the airports for fog to clear, he had been sitting for over twenty-four hours.

"We're almost there," said his grandfather.

The car climbed a steep hill, its tires spinning on a couple of the steepest sections, before the road leveled off again and wound its way through a dense pine forest. His grandfather rolled down the window and he and his grandson savored the deep pine aroma.

"Smells a lot better than the rice paddies, doesn't it?" Eli joked, then snorted deeply and noisily, making such a ridiculous noise that Jonathan laughed. To outdo his grandfather, he opened his mouth and scoffed in a big lungful of air.

"This has been my family home for ten generations," Hiroko said proudly as she pointed towards a sprawling Japanese estate in the distance, putting an end to their fun. "I hope you will be happy here, Jonason Chan, as I was when but a girl."

The place looked impressive from far away. But the closer they got, the less grand it turned out to be. He had expected something two-storied and made of stone, like the estates in Boston. This was like the bare wood and white paper places he had seen along the way, only more spread out. It was really not much of a house.

A pair of wrinkled old men waited on either side of the graveled driveway as they drove up and stopped. At first, Jonathan thought they were naked. But on closer inspection, he saw that they both wore what looked like tan handkerchiefs across their "diddle-dos," as his mother used to call them. The two opened the car doors, bowing to their bony knees.

"This is Matsuyama San," said his new grandmother, introducing Jonathan to the first of the old men. "He maintains our gardens. Are they not beautiful?"

"Yeah, real nice," Jonathan agreed. His grandfather chuckled.

"He doesn't speak English," added his grandfather, "nor does Kitaura San over there, our carpenter. He keeps everything shipshape."

A somber group of house staff, all as old as his grandparents, waited in a stiff row on the wooden landing.

"*Ohayo gozaimasu*, Lusk *Sama*," said the old woman who stood at the head of the group. Her eyes were little more than slits in a badly wrinkled face. Like the others, she was dressed in a plain gray *kimono* and a pair of split-toed white socks.

"This is Ayako *San*, Jonathan," Eli said. "She is head of our household staff." The woman gave the boy a low bow. Jonathan slouched forward and nodded his head in return.

"We take our shoes off here before going into a house. So you always have to make sure you don't have holes in your socks," his grandfather said with a wink.

Jonathan thought he was joking. His mother had never allowed him to take his shoes off, insisting it made him look like white trash, whatever that was. When Hiroko and his grandfather slipped off their shoes, he happily kicked off his too. Maybe Japan wasn't so bad after all.

Inside, the house was even smaller than it had looked from the outside. The entire house seemed to be made of plain unpainted boards and smelled like his mother's cedar chest. The odor was so strong it almost burned his nose. There were no curtains, carpets, or rugs – only hard straw mats covering the floors in every room. And there was hardly any furniture. It looked as if they weren't done building the place yet.

Jonathan's new bedroom wasn't much bigger than his old bathroom. And, it had no bed. "Where am I supposed to sleep?" he asked Fumiko, one of the wizened old housemaids.

"Bed here," she said, sliding open a small panel in the wall and sliding out two thick patchwork blankets. She set them on the floor. Reaching back inside, she removed a beanbag. "This pillow."

She pulled his pajamas from his suitcase and helped him out of his clothes. When he got to his underwear, he balked. "Panties off, most please," said Fumiko. He shook his head. No matter what she said, he wouldn't budge. Dumbfounded, she left to seek help. When she and Ayako San, the head maid, rushed back into the room, he had his pajamas on. Fumiko bowed apologetically to Ayako San, who clicked her tongue and left.

Fumiko laid one of the thick patchwork blankets on the floor. "Sleep here," she said. He looked puzzled. "Other on top for warm."

His eyes nervously scanned the room. "What about the bathroom?" he asked. "Where did you hide that?"

"We call toilet *otearai*. I will take you to the...?" She looked expectantly at him. "Can you say?"

"Oh... tear-in-my-eye," Jonathan said tentatively.

"Come." She took his hand and led him into the hallway.

"Does everybody go outside?" he said, thinking she was taking him to the backyard.

The question puzzled Fumiko. "Of course no. We have *otearai*."

They soon arrived at a *shoji* at the end of the long hallway. When she slid it open, Jonathan looked inside the tiny room. There was nothing but a round hole in the floor. "Where's the toilet? The oh...tear thing?"

She pointed at the hole. "That *otearai*. Pee pee there or squat down to do other, *neh*?" She turned and faced away. He shrugged, as if it were a game. Then, keeping his back to the woman, he peed into the hole.

Back in his bedroom, Fumiko helped him down onto the thick blanket and covered him with the second blanket. Lastly, she slid the beanbag under his head. It was hard as a rock. The maid bowed and left, sliding the *shoji* behind her.

Jonathan tried to find a way to make his so-called pillow comfortable but it was impossible. So he stuffed his jacket under his head.

A pillow that's really just a hard old beanbag, he told himself. *A bed that's really just a blanket. A house that's just wood and paper.* The faces, the smells, the names, the way they talked – like they were spitting or clearing their throats. He just wanted to go to sleep and wake up with everything back as it was supposed to be.

The next morning, his grandfather was standing at the foot of his blanket-bed when he opened his eyes. It was barely light outside. "Do you swim, Jonny Boy?" Eli asked.

"A little."

"Great! Let's go."

"Right now?"

Eli yanked off the top blanket, exposing his grandson to the cold morning air. He playfully tossed Jonathan his clothes, hitting him softly in the face. It was so cold that the boy scrambled into his pants and shirt.

"Come my trusted cohort and strong right hand!" Eli commanded in a grand, dramatic voice. "Into the woods we go!"

Reluctantly, Jonathan followed his grandfather out into the even colder predawn air and along a damp trail. The sun rose as they walked, brightening the sky and shooting brilliant shafts of sunlight through the hundred-foot pine trees that enveloped them.

Eli glanced back and smiled. "Isn't this fun?"

Jonathan's teeth chattered so badly he couldn't answer but, though miserable, nodded in agreement.

After walking for what seemed like an hour, they came to a narrow, meandering stream. "Are we swimming here?" Jonathan asked. It looked only deep enough to wade.

"No but we're almost there," Eli said. He led his grandson along the damp river bank until they reached a widening, where a natural dam had been created by a jumble of rocks and broken tree limbs.

Jonathan hugged himself as his grandfather stripped off his clothes and waded naked into the water, waving for his grandson to join him. But Jonathan didn't budge. "Come on, you big chicken," Eli yelled.

"I don't have my swimsuit."

"You got your birthday suit under there, right? Unless you forgot that too." Jonathan still didn't move. "Just wear your skivvies. It's okay. No pain in the ass women are here, right? We can do whatever the hell we want."

Stripping down to his briefs, Jonathan tiptoed into the cold water, his body rigid, his arms pulled tight against his chest. Eli splashed him. It was freezing but he splashed his grandfather back. Soon, the two were splashing and laughing.

With goose bumps pickling his skin, Jonathan ran shivering onto the bank. As he dried himself, his grandfather swam laps, back and forth across the river. Jonathan had no idea how many he swam but it was a lot.

"Well that was invigorating, don't you think?" Eli asked, joining his grandson on the bank.

"Y...ye...s," the boy answered, teeth chattering.

Eli wrapped his towel around Jonathan, then helped him back into his clothes. "Did you know your father was a champion swimmer?"

Jonathan had found a box of medals and trophies in his father's office closet once. But his dad had never talked about it.

"During his senior year at Stanford, he was voted Athlete of the Year." Eli grabbed his grandson in a playful headlock and mussed up his hair. "If you like, I'll teach you to swim like I did your dad. Maybe you can become a champion swimmer one of these days too. Would you like that?"

Jonathan nodded.

"Then, we'll make this our regular routine." He grabbed his pants and started to slip into them but stopped. "You ready to head back or you want to get in another couple of laps?"

"Back," Jonathan said quickly.

"Just in time for breakfast!" his new grandmother said as Jonathan and Eli slipped off their muddy shoes at the rear door.

Jonathan ran to his place at the low black lacquered table. He was starving after the swim and long walk and eagerly watched as Fumiko carried their breakfast in on a tray. But instead of regular breakfast foods – like cereal, eggs and pancakes – the tray was filled with dishes of pickled vegetables, squares of a reddish, slimy-looking meat, and bowls of sticky rice.

"Fumiko, get Jonathan a fork, would you?" his grandfather asked.

Jonathan hadn't noticed that there wasn't any silverware.

"You can use a fork for two weeks," his grandfather said, looking quickly to make sure his new grandmother was in agreement. "After that, you will have to use chopsticks or *hashi* as everyone else does, okay?"

Jonathan nodded, but had no idea what his grandfather was talking about. "What's this stuff?" he asked, poking the reddish blob with his finger. It was so cold and slick he jerked his finger away.

"*Sashimi*. It is good. Very fresh," Hiroko explained.

Jonathan picked it up with his fork and sniffed it. His nose curled. "Fish!"

"It is the very best tuna. Please eat it." Even though Hiroko had phrased it like a request, her tone made it sound more like an order.

His mother used to make him tuna sandwiches with Miracle Whip and sweet pickles to make it taste better than it smelled. This had nothing on it and looked like it would taste far worse than it smelled. And his mother would never have given him even a good tuna sandwich for breakfast.

"It doesn't look like they cooked it," he said.

"Just try it, sport, okay?" said his grandfather.

Jonathan took a couple of quick breaths to gather his courage, then stuffed the blob into his mouth. It was worse than he had feared. Even though he chewed as fast as he could, the more he chewed, the bigger it seemed to get. When he tried to launch it down his throat, he gagged.

"Do not spit that out," warned Hiroko... too late. The half-chewed piece of fish flew out of his mouth and landed on his plate.

"I'm sorry, I couldn't help it."

Hiroko snatched up the *sashimi* with her chopsticks and reached over to stuff it back into his mouth. Eli touched her arm. "He just arrived. I think he needs time to adjust, don't you?" Her arm softened and she put the *sashimi* back onto his plate.

"Fumiko, please get Jonathan something else to eat, would you?" Eli asked.

The maid soon returned with a bowl of beef teriyaki over rice, which Jonathan quickly consumed. As good as it was, though, it was still the strangest breakfast food he had ever heard of.

Throughout the rest of the week, he and his grandfather swam every morning. But on Sunday, Eli had to attend a meeting in Tokyo so Jonathan was allowed to sleep in. When he arrived for breakfast that morning, a cross-eyed, buck-toothed girl sat beside Hiroko in his usual place.

"Jonasan *Chan*, this is my niece, Nanami *Chan*," said Hiroko, her voice uncharacteristically sweet. "She is staying with us for a few days so you will have a little friend to play with."

Jonathan looked the girl over. She made the Levy sisters look like Miss America. Dwayne Ackerman in a black wig would have been prettier.

"Do not be rude," scolded Hiroko. "Have you never seen a girl before? Or never seen one so beautiful?" she said, stroking the girl's black pageboy hair. Nanami smiled lovingly up at her aunt.

At least she looks nice, Jonathan thought as Fumiko scurried in, her feet quick and light like a mouse's, a bowl of teriyaki and rice in her hand.

"Why is he eating dinner food for breakfast?" asked Nanami, her voice loud and grating. "Are all *gaijin* so very strange?"

"In his country, they have different customs," Hiroko answered. "He is endeavoring to learn our ways. In America, they eat sweets for breakfast."

Nanami made a face. "Mother says sweets are unhealthy and must be avoided or I will get fat and my face grow sores and my teeth rot."

"Well, your mother is a most wise woman."

The girl watched as Jonathan ate, a disgusted expression on her face. "How come he doesn't use *hashi* like normal people?"

"Americans use European utensils. It is their custom."

Throughout the meal, the girl questioned everything he did. Why was he dressed as he was? How come his eyes were green? "Is that not a strange color for eyes?" Eventually, even Hiroko seemed to tire of it.

"Jonason, why don't you show Nanami *Chan* your room?" she suggested when their breakfast was done.

"No, thank you," Jonathan said getting up and leaving.

He went to his room, opened his shoe box, and took out a fistful of tiny plastic soldiers. As he laid them out in battle formation, his *shoji* slid open.

"Auntie said I must play with you. She has business to attend to." The girl watched as he adjusted his deployment. "What are you doing?"

"Playing soldiers. It's only for boys."

"We had many real soldiers assigned to protect just us during the Great War, an entire company. Do you know how many that is?"

He didn't know and didn't care.

"Eighty. That is a lot. They lived on our lawn in tents. One time they brought a big gun with many barrels to defend us from *gaijin* bombers. But grandfather told my father that if we had such a gun, the *gaijin* would surely bomb us, so he made them take it away."

To escape her incessant talking, Jonathan excused himself to go to the restroom. But she wouldn't let him out of her sight, jabbering all the way down the hallway. When she tried to follow him into the bathroom, he slammed the door shut behind him.

"My brother, Kiyoshi, lets me accompany him," she yelled through the paper door. "How come you will not?"

Morning, noon, and night, she never gave him a minute of peace during her three-day stay. He was never so happy to see anyone leave in his life.

His joy, however, was short-lived. Within a few days, another unwelcome guest arrived, Mr. Kawamura, or Kawamura *San*, as he kept reminding Jonathan. He was to be his teacher. But for someone so careful about his own name, he always got Jonathan's wrong, as did everyone else except for his grandfather. So Jonathan decided it only fair to pay him back in kind and called him Cow Manure *San*. His teacher never seemed to notice, which made the joke even funnier. Only his grandfather ever caught it and laughed every time he said it.

"Ah, Jonny Boy, you remind me so much of your father when he was your age," his grandfather said, his eyes misting.

Cow Manure *San* tutored Jonathan in math, science, history, and Japanese language. Eight hours a day, seven days per week. Back home in Boston, he had only gone to school five days a week and for only six hours. "Aren't the teachers as good here?" he asked Cow Manure *San*.

"Most boys and girls in Japan attend school only six days," he answered in a huff. "Our schools are vastly superior to those in your country. That is why you must study extra hard so you may begin school here without embarrassing your family."

"If ours are worse, then how come my country beat yours?" Jonathan asked innocently. Cow Manure *San's* face reddened.

Japan was not a happy place. Jonathan had hardly been there a month and already hated it. There was no one but his grandfather to play with.

He had to study all the time. Sleeping on the floor had been fun for the first couple of weeks, like camping out, but he had grown tired of it, as he also had sitting on the floor all the time. He wanted to go home, where things were done the way they were supposed to be done.

The more he thought about it, the more he realized that there was no reason to stay. He hadn't seen his grandfather in a week – he was busy with some trial. His new grandmother couldn't care less about him. In fact, she would likely be glad if he were not there.

Even though he didn't have any of the details worked out, Jonathan decided he was going back to Boston. The next morning, he set out on foot.

A blond boy walking down a Japanese highway caught the immediate attention of the first person who drove past. The local police soon picked him up and returned him to his grandparents' house, where he was restricted to his room for three days, until his grandfather returned. Mr. Cow Manure decided Jonathan wasn't a serious enough student and quit. So in the end, it wasn't all bad.

When Fumiko slid his *shoji* open and said, "Hiroko *Sama* requests you join her," Jonathan wondered what he had done this time.

"There is someone I want you to meet," Hiroko said as he entered the main room.

Jonathan expected to find another old man or woman, hired to replace Cow Manure *San*. But, instead, he saw only a girl. For a split second, he feared Nanami had returned. She wore a pink kimono like the one Nanami had worn and also had shiny black hair. But she was clearly bigger and older, a teenager by his guess.

"This is Reiko, Jonason *Chan*," said Hiroko. "She will be living with us."

The girl bowed and kept her head and eyes glued to her feet.

"Why?" he asked, not crazy about the idea of having another girl in the house; they already had him and his grandfather badly outnumbered.

"Many reasons. To help care for you, teach you, be your friend."

Jonathan liked the last part. "Does she know how to speak English?" he asked pointedly.

"Yes, very well and will help you learn to speak Japanese. Why don't you show Reiko to her room? Fumiko has moved to the back bedroom so she may be next to you."

The girl shuffled down the narrow hallway, staying a few feet behind Jonathan, forcing him to turn his head to speak to her. "Do you really speak English?"

"*Hai,*" she said, her eyes never lifting from her feet.

"Then say something."

"I am most honored to meet you, Jonason *Chan.*"

"Jon-a-than not Jon-a-son," he corrected. "How come everybody calls me Jonason?"

She blushed. "I am most sorry for my bad manners. Your TH sound is impossible for Japanese tongues to pronounce."

He passed his own room and opened the next *shoji.* "I guess this is your bedroom now."

When she saw the room, her face lit up. She quickly bowed, scurried inside, and politely slid the *shoji* closed.

The next evening, while making Jonathan's bed and straightening up his room, Reiko came across a Lone Ranger comic book. She squealed with glee, then ran out of the room, leaving Jonathan mystified.

The teenager quickly returned with a Lone Ranger comic book in her hand, this one in Japanese and badly burned. "Lone Ranger *wa tomodachi desu ka?* Lone Ranger your friend?"

He nodded but she waited for him to say it. "*Hai.* Lone Ranger *tomodachi desu.*"

"He was my little brother's friend too," she said.

"How come he burned it?"

She started to answer but tears filled her almond-shaped eyes and slid down her cheeks faster than she could get her sleeve up to wipe them away. She tried to smile but her mouth and eyes refused and she cried harder. The young girl sat on the floor and pulled Jonathan into her lap. She hugged him tightly and buried her face against his as her body shuddered.

After a couple of minutes, she managed to gain a degree of tenuous control over her emotions. "I am most sorry," she said, dabbing at her eyes. "It is a very bad story. Perhaps I tell you some day." She delicately opened the comic book and pointed to a drawing of a lake. "*Mizu,*" she said, "water." She sniffed as she pointed to the blue sky above the lake. "*Sora,* sky, *wakarimasu ka?*" she asked. He nodded. "*Kore* wa," she said pointing to the white clouds in the drawing, "are called *kumo*, clouds."

Reiko's primary duties, besides teaching him Japanese, were keeping the boy quiet and out of Hiroko's hair. "Now, I will teach you something fun," she said after he had grown tired of the endless repetition of new words, "something we call *origami*. Can you say it?"

"*Origami*."

"Perfect! Would you prefer to learn how to fold a piece of paper into a beautiful swan, *hakuchou*? Or, would you prefer a frog, *kaeru*?"

"Kaeru!"

She reacted in exaggerated surprise. "Everyone always prefers swans!" she said, then smiled and kissed his hand. "Only Ryo, my little brother, preferred frogs."

Patiently, she taught the boy how to fold a piece of green paper into something resembling a frog. Over the next few days, she taught him how to fold other birds and animals – a dog, crane, turtle, dove, snake, lilly, and cat. When she had exhausted her knowledge of *origami*, she taught him how to paint birds on reeds and *koi* in a pond with water colors.

But the thing that became his favorite was the Button and Spool game. It was one of the *geisha* games Reiko had learned from Cheko, who had been her friend and next door neighbor. He watched as she stuck pencils through the holes in two empty thread spools. Then she attached string to each spool, with buttons tied to the ends. The game was to see who could roll their strings up the fastest. In their first contest, Reiko's button was up almost before Jonathan got started. Then, she taught him the *geisha's* secret technique – holding the pencil loosely in his small fists and moving them in tight circles, as if throwing a series of short, rapid punches.

"On your mark," said Reiko, as she and Jonathan readied their spools. "Get set." The boy hunched over, his small fists poised to spring into action. Behind him, the *shoji* slid silently open. Reiko's eyes fixed on Eli Lusk, who stood in the doorway, his index finger pressed to his lips. "Go!" she said.

Jonathan's hands were a blur as his string coiled and the button sped upward, touching his spool before hers did. He dropped his spool and thrust his arms up in victory.

"That was spectacular!" exclaimed Eli.

The boy's head snapped around. He jumped up, ran over, and clutched his grandfather's long legs.

"I really missed you, Sport," Eli said, picking his grandson up and hugging the boy tightly.

"You were gone a long time!" Jonathan said.

"I know. It couldn't be helped. I'm only home now because the man we were trying for murder decided to... well, execute himself for his crimes."

"*Seppuku?*" Reiko asked.

Eli nodded.

"What's that?" the boy asked.

"It's not something for little guys like yourself. Hey," Eli said, changing the subject, "what do you think of this?" He pulled his arm out from behind his back.

"A football!" Jonathan yelled, seeing the leather ball in his grandfather's hand.

"You wouldn't believe how hard it was to find one of these. They love baseball here but nobody plays football. I had to bribe a general to get it." Eli nodded towards the door. "Come on, let's give her a test drive."

Reiko tagged along as the two strolled outside.

When they reached the back lawn, Eli held up the football. "You ready?" The boy nodded and his grandfather tossed the football softly to him. Surprisingly, Jonathan caught it. "Nice catch! Your dad must have played football with you."

"Just with a foam one. This one kind of hurt a little," Jonathan said, rubbing his arm.

Eli gestured for him to throw it back. "Watch my arms as I catch it." As it arrived, he allowed it to softly land in his arms. "Don't try to stop it. Let your arms go with it, like you were catching an egg."

Jonathan held out his arms and Eli underhanded it easily to him. The boy did as he was instructed and allowed the oblong ball to fall softly into his yielding hands and arms. Reiko squealed and clapped. "Hey, that didn't hurt!" he exclaimed happily.

Hiroko strode onto the back landing and gave the girl a silencing look. But soon even she got carried away by the boy's skill as he caught throw after throw. "*Yatta!*" she yelled when he dove for the ball and landed on his chest on the lawn, the ball still clutched in his arms.

Drawn by the odd noise, the staff peeked out to see what was going on. Before long, everyone but sour Ayako San, head of the household staff, were cheering too, yelling "*yatta!*" whenever their mistress did.

"Go long," Eli yelled, waving his grandson deep. Jonathan ran hard, then turned and back-pedaled. His grandfather hurled a long, arcing spiral. As Jonathan jockeyed into position, he stepped into the *koi* pond. The ball sailed just over his hands and landed in the water. When he bent over to pick it up, he spotted a giant orange *koi*. He grabbed the large fish, hoisted it into the air, and drew his arm back as if to throw it. "Here's the football, Grandfather."

Eli let out a huge belly laugh as the women shrieked in horror.

"Your dad was a pretty fair football player," Eli told his grandson as he brought the ball back. "But you're far better than he was at your age. Maybe you'll be the one."

"The one what?"

"Don't get me wrong," Eli said, "I obviously like swimming. It's great exercise and gets you clean. But I loved football. I played quarterback at Stanford. Did you know that?"

Jonathan shook his head.

"Your dad could have been a greater quarterback than I ever was but it wasn't for him. I was thrilled to sit in the bleachers at the Stanford tank and watch him at swim meets. But my secret dream was to watch him quarterback Stanford to another Rose Bowl. Maybe you'll be the one to do it. You think?"

Jonathan shrugged. "Sure."

The next morning, Jonathan ran into the dining room, dressed in his swimming suit and towel in hand. His face dropped when he saw his grandfather in formal diplomatic attire – tailed tuxedo and top hat. He was reading a file.

"You're going swimming like that?" he asked.

"Sorry, Sport. The docket opened up and I have to render our decision on a general who did horrible things to our soldiers. He's a very, very bad man." Eli mussed his grandson's blond hair and kissed him on the head. "Why don't you get Reiko to take you swimming? I'm sure she'd enjoy it too."

His grandfather's hazel eyes, his eyes, hardened as he took on his trial face and strode away. He turned at the door, gave Jonathan a wink, then was gone. Jonathan heard the car door shut, the motor start, the tires spin in the loose gravel. He didn't know why but he felt alone, as he had the night his father died.

5

———

The War Crime Trials were held inside the former Imperial Army Headquarters in Tokyo's Ichigaya district. Eleven somber men, dressed in either formal top hat and tails or the uniform of a high-ranking military officer, sat on a raised *dais* on one side of the cavernous assembly hall. Writers, historians, photographers, cinematographers, journalists, and official observers filled each of the theater-style seats on the other. In the pit between the two sat the accused, their feet shackled and chained to steel rings anchored into the concrete floor. Fear was evident in the eyes of a couple but the rest glared scornfully at the panel of judges, their lips curled in the same defiant sneers.

Major General Myron Cramer, Judge Advocate General of the U.S. Army, struck his gavel. "I must ask that everyone clear the room for a special classified session. I will also be turning over the gavel to Former Ambassador Lusk for the conclusion of tonight's business."

As the massive military police presence quickly herded out everyone but the judges and stenographer, Eli strode onto the *dais*, bowed to the panel of judges, and sat down in the general's vacated chair. "Bring in the prisoner," he commanded.

Four burly MPs wrestled a short, wiry Japanese general through the prisoner's entrance. Even with his feet shackled and his hands cuffed behind his back, the general fought his captors every step of the way, twisting and jerking his body like an angry cat as he spewed an endless stream of obscenities in Japanese. The MPs shoved him down into the heavy metal defendant's chair and padlocked his shackles to the floor rings.

A sheepish Japanese man in wire rim glasses and threadbare blue suit slid up a chair and sat beside the accused. But even his interpreter didn't seem eager to get too close.

Eli banged his gavel. "This court is now in session!"

The general hawked up phlegm from deep inside his throat, leaned his head back, and spit at the judges' bench.

"You are a uniquely horrific man, General Murakami," Eli began. "And I use the word *man* in its most generic of senses. Of the thousands charged with war crimes, yours are easily the most horrendous, demonstrating clearly that you have no place in any civilized society."

He waited as General Murakami's interpreter translated what he had said. The general glared at Eli, his dark eyes cold as a snake's. He said something angrily in Japanese, spittle flying as he spoke. The interpreter blanched. He struggled to find the right words to explain what the general had said, obviously taken aback by it.

"The general wants me to convey his belief that trying men whom most Japanese consider patriots could possibly have serious repercussions," offered the interpreter.

"I am quite fluent in Japanese," Eli said harshly to the interpreter. "That is not what the general stated. If you would like to retain your position, I would suggest you be more accurate in our future exchanges."

The interpreter bowed. Then Eli turned his wrath on the general. "You threaten this court again, SIR, and you will be muzzled like a dog!"

The general jutted his chin out in defiance.

"The charges against you are heinous. Among them are cannibalism and conducting a contest with your second in command to determine who was the most murderous, the least human, to be the first to behead one hundred bound, defenseless prisoners."

Murakami scoffed.

"It is the unanimous decision of this court that at sunrise, you, General Shinji Murakami, will be hanged by the neck until dead."

Murakami sprang to his feet. He tried to rush the bench but the shackles held and he fell flat on his face. He looked up, glaring, blood flowing from his nostrils and split lip. "Only Emperor may judge me!" he screamed in broken English.

"We will see about that!" Eli said, slamming his gavel down so hard that it broke. He pointed the headless handle at an MP officer. "Captain! Please ensure that the general meets his date with the gallows as ordered. He is not to be allowed visitors or to communicate with anyone. He is also not to be allowed anything that might possibly forestall his appointment with his maker, nor is he allowed to perform what he might perceive as a more honorable early exit. His despicable actions deserve no such option. He will hang like the common criminal he is."

"Gladly, sir!" shouted the Captain, snapping his heels together with a loud *click*.

The general cursed and fought with every ounce of his being — biting, scratching, hissing, and twisting violently to break free — as the MPs carried him out of the room.

"Because of the unusual number of threats made against this panel in this case," Eli announced to everyone still in the room, "please consider these proceedings to be classified Top Secret. I and this court thank you for your service."

Eli and the other jurists gathered up their things and ambled towards the exit. "Disgusting bugger," said the Australian judge as they walked. "Back home, we would have simply shot him as we would a mad dingo."

"Yes," said Eli. "I feel like I need a bath."

As they passed the long row of press telephones that lined the main lobby, an MP was talking on one of them. "Please get off the phone," Eli told the man, taking the receiver from his hand and hanging it up. He glanced around until he spotted an MP officer. "No one is to be making calls," he told the lieutenant, who dressed the man down.

Outside, an MP opened the DeSoto's rear door and saluted as Eli climbed into the back.

"Home, Taro *San*" Eli told the driver, who waved at the two heavily armed MPs sitting astride their motorcycles at the curb. They kick started their bikes and roared off, with the DeSoto on their rear tires. The MPs led them almost at full speed through the late-night Tokyo streets, hitting their sirens to move slower cars and trucks out of the way, blocking intersections so the DeSoto wouldn't have to stop.

Eli laid his head back against the soft headrest and glanced out the side window, his face drawn, his eyes dull and lifeless. Taro glanced into his rearview mirror. "You appear to have had a most difficult day, Eli *Sama?*"

Eli slowly nodded.

"Would you like a song?"

"That would be nice, Taro *San.* I have another equally distasteful trial to face tomorrow."

The driver, in a beautiful tenor, began singing an old Japanese folk song. "*Sakura. Sakura. Noyama mo sato mo. Mi-watasu kagiri. Kasumi ka kumo ka. Nioi zo izuru. Izaya. Izaya. Mini yukan. Sakura. Sakura. Yayoi no sora wa. Mi-watasu kagiri. Kasumi ka kumo ka. Nioi zo izuru. Izaya. Izaya. Mini yukan.*

"*Kirei des ne,* Taro *San,*" sighed Eli when the song was done. "*Domo.*"

Headlights lit up the right side of Eli's face. A massive, blunt-nosed diesel grill smashed into the outriding MP, driving him and his motorcycle into the side of the car, crushing the man and knocking the DeSoto sideways. Eli had recoiled reflexively away just before the truck's impact and wasn't badly hurt. But Taro *San's* head lay motionless against the cracked side window, blood flowing from a cut in his neck.

"Call an ambulance!" Eli yelled to the other MP but the man wasn't listening. He had drawn his machine gun and was aiming at something. It was only then that Eli saw the tattooed construction workers pouring out of truck and the two sedans parked beside it. The MP opened fire. He dropped a few before the *yakuza* peppered him with bullets of their own.

Eli bolted out the side door and sprinted up a narrow side street, his regular workouts and athletic past serving him well. Much younger legs tried but were unable to catch him. He couldn't outrun their chase car, however. It sped past, then angled over and screeched to a halt, blocking his path and giving the *yakuza* on his tail time to catch up. Eli landed a couple of hard punches to the faces of his attackers before they poured over him. Even on the way down, he grabbed handfuls of hair and took a couple to the sidewalk with him. He didn't stop punching and kicking at everyone within reach until someone landed a boot heel to his chin, knocking him out. Even after he was clearly no longer a threat, the *yakuza* kept up their assault, kicking and stomping the downed American.

Thin silver wire cut into Eli Lusk's thick wrists and ankles where they had secured his arms and legs to a sturdy metal chair. His motionless body sagged forward, his battered face against his chest. Blood flowed from his broken nose, streaking the front of his white shirt.

Yakuza milled around the roofless top floor of a ten-story construction site, the place little more than the skeleton of a building – steel beams, construction elevator, and concrete flooring. Without walls, the place offered an unobstructed view of the city's lights, encircling them clear to the horizon.

A bare light bulb hung from an overhead girder. Beyond the circle of its yellow light, a suited man with long black hair sat in the semi-darkness at a chipped metal desk, talking to someone on the telephone.

One of the *yakuza* ambled over to the end of the floor and unzipped his fly.

"No. Here," said a *yakuza* lieutenant, pointing at a nearby bucket. After the man had relieved himself into the pail, the rest of the eight shirtless thugs took turns emptying their bladders into it as well.

The suited man hung up the receiver and stood. "Wake him up!" he said, buttoning his tailored suit coat, light sparkling off the diamond rings that lined his fingers.

The lieutenant hoisted the piss bucket and chucked its contents into Eli's face, jarring him back to consciousness. The former ambassador arms jerked upwards to wipe the stinging urine from his face, but only managed to dig the wire deeper into his skin. He squinted at the suited man in front of him, his eyes flaring briefly in recognition.

"Good, you know me," said the man in broken English. "That will make our negotiation simpler."

"I haven't the slightest idea who you are."

The man scoffed. "I am Kazio Zuma, as you well know."

"Kazio Zuma is dead."

"Many things in Japan are not as they appear, or as you might wish," said Zuma, blinking his bloodshot eyes as cigarette smoke curled into them. He tossed his cigarette onto the floor and rubbed it out with the sole of his shoe. "But time is short. I am here to trade you something I want for something you want."

"There is nothing you want that I have the power to give," Eli said.

"What about your life?"

"I am a representative of the United States government," shot Eli. "You kill me and they will hunt you to the very ends of the earth."

"What can we offer you to free General Murakami?" Zuma asked, in a calm, businesslike manner.

"There is nothing I can do, even if I wanted to. He has been convicted and will be executed in the morning."

"But as a senior judge and close friend of MacArthur's, you could surely find a way, a piece of missed evidence, something that could allow you to stay his execution long enough to discover a way to release him."

"In his case, we would need hundreds of bits of missed evidence."

Zuma strolled over and sat back down at the desk. After collecting his thoughts for a few seconds, he placed a call.

"U.S. Embassy," said the man on the other end, answering on the first ring.

"We are holding Eli Lusk," Zuma stated. "I would speak with someone who has the power to supply our demands for his release."

"I am prepared to discuss that subject with you, sir. May I ask who I have the honor of speaking with?"

Zuma was surprised. "So you are already aware he was taken?"

"Yes, sir. What can we do for you?"

"We have but one request, the release of General Shinji Murakami." He waited for an answer but didn't get one for several seconds.

"I will have to clear that with the Judge Advocate in Washington."

"Tell him that their fates are linked. What happens to the General will also occur to your judge."

"It is the middle of the night there, sir. It will take time to track everyone down who could approve such a request."

"I will call you again at sunrise. If the General has not been released by then, Eli Lusk will die."

"Please give me your number. I will call you immediately if I..."

Zuma hung up, rocked back in his chair, and lit a cigarette. His men squatted down on the floor and began a game of cards.

Eli's eyes were so puffy and swollen they were little more than red slits by the time one of the *yakuza* pointed towards the eastern horizon and the fuzzy glow of dawn. Zuma dropped his cigarette, where it laid smoking among a mass of lifeless butts. He reached for the phone. But before he could pick up the receiver, it rang, setting everyone on edge. He answered it and listened, then slammed the receiver down. His face contorted in anger, he snatched it up again and dialed.

"U.S. Embassy," said the voice on the other end. Zuma laid the receiver on the desk. "Please be patient, sir," said the voice on the other end, "we are still working on freeing the general."

"Liar!" screamed the yakuza leader, "You executed him five minutes ago." Zuma nodded to two of his men, who hoisted Eli's chair and carried it to the building's edge. On the roadway six floors below, the headlights of early morning traffic sped by.

"You might as well jump with me," yelled Eli. "You'll be dead almost as soon as I hit the ground."

"Please talk to me!" said the voice over the receiver.

Eli struggled to free himself, yanking his arms with all the strength he could muster. But the harder he jerked, the deeper the wire cut into his wrists, releasing more and more blood.

"How appropriate you now find yourself exactly where you put Murakami *Sama*, bound to a chair as your sentence is declared," Zuma taunted.

"But unlike him, I will not die a despicable criminal."

"He died silently, honorably. We will see how you die, *gaijin*, screaming like a little girl, I would wager."

"You will not have that satisfaction."

"We will see."

"If my death rids the world of *yakuza* scum like you, then I leave gladly."

"Get this piece of shit out of my sight," Zuma screamed.

"Please talk to me!" came the negotiator's desperate voice over the phone.

The men swung the chair back and let it glide forward.

"*Ichi*," one of the men said.

"Please, we can work something out!" pleaded the negotiator.

The men swung it back again, gathering momentum.

"*Ni.*"

The chair swung forward, then back once more.

"*SAN!*" yelled the *yakuza*.

As the chair came forward, they pitched it into space.

"No!" cried the negotiator.

In an exaggerated fashion, Zuma cocked his head, cupped his ear, and listened. But the only sound reaching those on the tenth floor was a faint cry just before the metal chair crashed into the aluminum roof of the guard's shack.

A loud wail startled Jonathan out of a sound sleep. He bolted upright. Hearing nothing more, he plopped back down onto his futon and closed his eyes. There were voices in the hallway. It sounded like an argument between Hiroko and Reiko. They were speaking in Japanese but he understood enough to get the gist of it.

"Please, Lusk *Sama*," came Reiko's girlish voice in a loud whisper. "Please! He has suffered enough."

"He has to be told," answered Hiroko's deeper cigarette voice. "He will learn soon enough."

"At least give him this night, a last sleep in sweet dreams. I beg you!"

Jonathan slid open the *shoji*. The women froze, their wet cheeks glistening in the dim light.

"Why are you crying?" he asked.

"They murdered your grandfather!" said Hiroko, before crumbling down onto the floor.

Eli Lusk's battered, bloodless body had been shoved from a speeding car near Sugamo Prison, where those convicted of war crimes were hung. A woman walking her dog had seen the body dumped but didn't get a license number. She only knew that they were driving a big American car.

General MacArthur launched a massive, military-like operation to capture those responsible and prevent or discourage similar incidents in the future. Both *yakuza* and ultra-nationalists were rounded up and interrogated by the 11th Airborne Division, men with little patience left after years at war and experts at quickly extracting what they wanted to know. But as former Ambassador Lusk's funeral neared, no one had been tied to the murder. All MacArthur could do for his friend was fly in the military's best morticians, in hope of repairing enough of the horrific damage to make Eli Lusk's body presentable.

Jonathan hopped out of the embassy's Cadillac limousine and gazed back at the endless line of other limos queued up behind them. He was attempting to count them when the Ambassador shook his hand, kissed Hiroko on the cheek, then led them across the front portico and into the lobby.

His father's coffin had been closed and he had had to take his nurse's word for it that he was inside. When he got back to the hospital, he tried to ask his mother but she wouldn't stop crying. Part of him still expected his father to walk in, as he often did after a business trip, with a new toy or a box of Cracker Jacks, teasing him about keeping the surprise himself.

The upper half of his mother's coffin had been left open, kind of like their Dutch Doors back home. She hadn't looked dead, just asleep. But when he kissed her cheek, he knew for sure. Her skin was cold and stiff.

As they entered what the Ambassador called the rotunda, light flooded in through its glass roof and Jonathan found himself engulfed in a sweet cloud. Four red-jacketed marines stood as rigid as robots at the corners of a mound of flowers that stood taller than he was.

They rounded the silver coffin and Jonathan saw its lid was down. "Is my grandfather in there?" he asked, but Hiroko didn't reply. "You are a Lusk and Lusks do not cry for all to see," she had told him at his mother's funeral. He looked into her eyes. She looked about to cry but no tears fell. Instead, she laid her cheek on the closed lid and whispered something soft and mournful in Japanese.

General MacArthur strode into the room. He saluted the coffin slowly and thoughtfully, shook Jonathan's hand, and kissed Hiroko on both cheeks. Then he escorted them to their seats. His grandmother hadn't said a word all day. She had just stared as if looking at something far away. And that didn't change. Her dark eyes never blinked nor strayed from the closed lid of his grandfather's casket, even when he forgot and wiped his runny nose on his sleeve.

People in uniform saluted as they filed past the coffin. Others touched or patted it. Several mumbled something, as if he could still hear them. One very dignified woman even leaned over and kissed his box. "Goodbye, my old friend," she murmured.

Except for the minister being dressed in an Army general's uniform, the service was a replay of Jonathan's two previous ones, down to the same Bible passage that started, "Let not your hearts be troubled."

When the eulogy was over, General MacArthur presented Hiroko with the flag that had been draped over his grandfather's coffin, folded into a neat triangle like one of Reiko's *origami*. Then, a long line of important people came to shake his hand and give Hiroko a kiss or hug. The general announced who each was but the names meant nothing to Jonathan. Only two were Japanese. The first was the new prime minister. The second was a man who couldn't stop bowing, reminding Jonathan of the plastic bird he had seen in the window in Boston.

When everyone were gone, except for the marines, he and his grandmother sat by themselves, her eyes still locked on the coffin as Jonathan wondered what would happen to him now.

6

———

Hiroko's mood for the next few weeks was as if the funeral had been relocated to their house. She never cried as far as Jonathan ever saw. But she seldom spoke and her eyes were always moist and red. So it was surprising when she opened the door to his bedroom one day with a smile on her face and two garment bags in her hands.

"One is for Jonason *Chan* and the other for you," she said to Reiko, offering the bags to the teenager. "You are to wear them tonight." The old Hiroko resurfaced as she pointed a stiff finger at him. "And you will eat whatever is put in front of you, do you understand?" He nodded, knowing better than to refuse.

As soon as the *shoji* slid closed, Reiko eagerly opened her bag. She squealed in glee as she pulled out a new green and blue *kimono* and clutched it to her chest. Jonathan was far less enthusiastic. His looked like a black silk bathrobe, like something a woman would wear.

"Put on your *kinono* so we can see how you look," Reiko said. He didn't move.

"I'm not wearing a dress."

"It is not a dress. Men and boys here wear black *kimono*, even samurai warriors."

He shook his head.

"I bet I can defeat you in speed dressing," she teased.

She peeled off her outer *kimono*. Jonathan unbuckled his belt and dropped his pants. His shirt was off in a few seconds and flung onto the floor. As Reiko pretended to struggle with her under-*kimono*, the boy slid his arms into the sleeves of his *kimono*, tied the *obi* into a clumsy knot, and held up his arms in victory. "Done!"

She straightened his collar, then stood back and looked him over. "You look so handsome. How do I look?"

"You look... nice."

"Merely nice?" she said, pretending to be hurt.

"You look very, very, very, very nice."

She kissed him on the cheek.

Reiko gave the boy's belt a final adjustment, then slid open the *shoji*. As they waited to be invited into the main room, Jonathan stared at the odd expression on Hiroko's face. Her huge grin was throwing him off.

She knelt at the black lacquered dining table, her legs folded tightly beneath her, her silver-and-blue *kimono* shimmering in the flickering candlelight. A short but muscular middle-aged man with close cropped hair, a bent nose, and twinkling eyes knelt comfortably across from her. His dark flat face made Jonathan giggle. He reminded him of Chimpie, the stuffed toy he had slept with until it lost most of its stuffing and his mother threw it away. The man looked as out of place in his ill-fitting suit as Jonathan felt in his dress.

The man leaned forward and said something to Hiroko. She covered her mouth as she tittered, like Reiko did whenever she laughed. Their guest seemed to notice Jonathan and Reiko for the first time. "I am sorry I did not dress properly," he said, bowing to Hiroko. "Your husband never appeared in anything but Western attire. I thought it might be your style of dress when home."

"My husband thought Westerners who dressed Japanese fashion looked foolish," she said. "But he thought it perfectly normal for Japanese to dress in Western attire. He would have been most honored you dressed as you have." Hiroko turned her eyes on Jonathan. "Jonason *chan*, please come greet our honored guest, Kubo Shinishi *Kancho*."

Reiko nudged the boy and he marched forward a couple of steps, as instructed, then bowed deeply. "Remember to keep your head low until our guest lifts his," Reiko had told him just before opening the *shoji*.

"It's like a contest?"

"Yes, to see who is the most respectful. The last to end their bow is the winner."

Jonathan kept his head down as long as he could stand it. When he looked up, their guest's head was still down so he bowed even lower. Reiko coughed quietly. "Did I win?" he asked, a big grin on his face.

Their guest chuckled. "Yes. You are victor!" he said, as Hiroko blushed in embarrassment.

"Jonason chan, *Kancho* is a direct descendant of one of the most famous *samurai* families of all time," said Hiroko. "He is also one of the greatest martial artists in all of Japan. The Emperor himself declared him a Living Treasure."

Kubo bowed humbly and let out a huff of air through his nostrils.

"How come he breathes like that?" the boy asked, shocking the two women.

"That is a most rude question!" shot Hiroko, her smile gone.

"*Iie*," Kubo said. "It is a most observant question. I like your question," he said to Jonathan, letting out another huff of air through his bent nose. "I breathe like so because my nose has been broken many times in battle, before I learned to better protect it."

Hiroko, her face still flushed in embarrassment, patted the cushion beside her and Jonathan ran over and sat down. Reiko shuffled over and knelt behind him. Fumiko's tiny feet twittered across the tatami, their dinner balanced precariously on a large oval tray. Jonathan leaned in as she set it on the table, but saw nothing he liked. He refused the crab and pickled cucumber *sunomono* and picked at the small tasteless squares of white *tofu* floating in his *mizu* soup.

Eyes flared in anticipation as Fumiko carried in an ornate tray. She held it down so that everyone could see the raw white slivers of flesh arranged in the shape of a flying crane. "Jonason," whispered Reiko, excitedly. "This is *fugu*, a most rare and wonderful delicacy. Please, please, you must try."

After Kubo and Hiroko had taken their portions, Reiko snatched up a small mound with Jonathan's chopsticks. She offered it to him but, after a quick sniff, he curled his nose and clamped his hand over his mouth. Delicacy must be another word for stinky fish, he thought.

Reiko popped the mound into her mouth, then quickly checked to see if she had been seen. But Hiroko's attention was on their guest. Jonathan chuckled as the teenager savored the rare, potentially deadly fish, humming as if it was the most wonderful thing she had ever tasted.

She made it look so good that he decided to try some. Reiko gladly snatched up another small mound and set it on his plate. He picked up a tiny piece and put it into his mouth, only to instantly spit it back out. It tasted exactly as it smelled, fishy. Reiko wiped his mouth with her handkerchief, then quickly ate the remaining *fugu* from his plate.

When everyone had finished, Kubo pushed away from the table, rubbed his flat stomach, and belched loudly. Jonathan's head snapped around, expecting his grandmother to throw a fit. But she covered her mouth with her hand, smiled, and bowed her head as if it were a great compliment. "I am honored you enjoyed our most humble meal," she said in a strange, airy voice.

"It was a meal to make the Emperor himself belch, *neh?*" Kubo said.

"Would you care to see our meager garden?" Hiroko asked in that same odd voice. "Although it is most plain, the night breeze is surely refreshing."

As soon as the adults had left, Reiko rushed out of the room and quickly returned with a bowl of teriyaki steak and rice.

"Do you want to hear the story of the forty-seven *ronin?*" Reiko asked while he ate. He nodded. It was his favorite story.

"Forty-seven *samurai* were made *ronin*, masterless warriors, when Lord Asano, their master, was ordered by the *shogun* to commit *seppuku*…"

"That's the word grandfather used," said Jonathan, bits of rice flying from his mouth. "What's it mean?"

Reiko struggled for an explanation but ended up saying, "It is a very serious punishment. I am sure your grandmother will explain it one day, when the time is proper."

Jonathan nodded.

"Anyway, simply drawing his sword within the *shogun's* palace would have been enough to earn such a sentence," Reiko said, raising her eyebrows and wrinkling her smooth forehead. "But Lord Asano had done much more than that. He had also used his weapon, attacking and seriously wounding the corrupt Lord Kira, the *shogun's* chief of protocol. Do you remember why he attacked Lord Kira?"

"Yeah, because Lord Kira said bad things about him, making him look stupid, right?" he mumbled, his mouth full of sweet beef.

"That is correct. Lord Asano's brave retainers knew that everyone expected them to seek revenge. So for an entire year, they hid their true intentions behind a false face, spending their time in the company of wicked women, seemingly only interested in pleasure and drink. But there can be no pleasure for an honorable man when a wrong must be avenged."

"And they found him hiding like a coward and cut off his head."

"Yes, they avenged their lord's death and became…"

Reiko and Jonathan both cocked their heads and listened – muffled voices, footsteps thumping softly towards the front door. A minute later, a single pair of footsteps padded rapidly their way. Reiko snatched up Jonathan's plate and hid it behind her back just as the *shoji* slid open.

Hiroko almost floated into the room, beaming. "I have wonderful news, Jonason!" she said. "*Kancho* Kubo has agreed to accept you into his school! You will be the first non-Japanese ever accepted. Is that not wonderful?"

Jonathan nodded but the pained look on Reiko's face told him it might not be as great as his grandmother seemed to think.

7

———

Jonathan watched Reiko pack his small suitcase. None of it made sense. "Why do I have to take my clothes and toothbrush and stuff to school? I didn't have to back home."

"You will be staying with *Kancho* Kubo at the Dai Kan!" said Hiroko. "It is most beautiful there and we will visit you often."

"But I thought I'd be staying here," he said, tears filling his eyes.

"Boys all over the world go away to school. Your father did it. Your grandfather did it. And you will as well."

"I don't care about them. I want to stay here!"

"The matter is closed."

He stared at her.

"You must also never forget that you are a Lusk and carry with you a great responsibility. What you do there will not only affect you, it will also affect me, your grandfather's memory, and how they forever view Americans."

"Then I will be bad," he said, the words shooting out, "so bad they will make me leave!"

Her eyes narrowed. "If you fail, you will be sent to live with your Aunt Muriel in Texas."

"But..."

"Not another word," Hiroko said. "Your grandfather and I worked hard to gain your acceptance. You were only allowed entrance as a personal favor to us. Now please gather up your things, Yuso is waiting."

Reiko carried Jonathan's bag outside, where their new driver loaded it into the trunk of their new DeSoto. Hiroko kissed Jonathan on the cheek, then wiped his tears and her lipstick away with her handkerchief.

"Your grandmother is not being cruel," Reiko told him as they drove away. Jonathan stared out the back window, watching Hiroko walk back into the house. "She is correct. To study at the Dai Kan is the greatest of honors. Thousands apply but only a handful are accepted."

"Bet you wouldn't have been so happy if they had made your brother go there when he didn't want to," he said angrily.

"We would have been overjoyed! But it could never have been. The Dai Kan is only for the sons of our Imperial Family, our top army and navy officers, and our most respected families. We were just farmers."

By the time they reached the highway and headed north, the boy refused to even look at Reiko; he just stared sullenly out the side window.

"May I tell you the story of the founding of the Dai Kan?"

Jonathan ignored her.

"Please do not be angry with me, Jonason," she begged. "I hate seeing you leave too. But in life we must make sacrifices to make our lives better when we are grown."

He glanced over at her and nodded.

"Thank you," she said, then gathered her thoughts. "Unlike European knights and American soldiers, who slew whoever they found before them, our *samurai* fought only opponents of equal rank and skill. They fought and lived by a special warrior code, *Bushido.* But a group of murderous assassins..."

"*Ninja!*" said Jonathan. "You told me about them."

"Yes. They were most despicable. Some say they should not even be considered human beings because of their lack of honor. All a *ninja* cared about was money. They would lie, pretend injury, cut a man down from behind, even murder him in his sleep."

"You know what? This *ninja* dwarf even hid under the seat in this outdoor *otearai* and, when his enemy went to the bathroom, stabbed him in the butt!" Jonathan said, laughing.

"That is true. But what about the *Great Shogun*, Iyeyasu Tokugawa? What do you remember about him?"

"That he never stabbed anybody in the butt!"

"Be serious now," she chided. "This is important."

"Was he the one who made everybody stop fighting?"

"Yes. But do you know what else he did?"

The boy shook his head.

"He is also the person who created the Dai Kan, the school you are to attend. Now it is our most honored school for boys. But back then, it trained only warriors, the greatest warriors in the world, to defeat the *ninja*."

Jonathan yawned. Reiko laid his head in her lap.

"The Great Shogun secretly assembled the best *samurai* from all Japan at the Dai Kan, where they were taught by our greatest *budo* masters and grandmasters. The graduates soon captured over one hundred filthy *ninja* in the first three months."

"Are we almost there?"

"Do you know what they did with the *ninja* they captured?" she said, her voice mysterious.

"Cut off their heads."

"No. Much worse. They put them into big pots. Then, they lit fires underneath them and boiled the *ninja* alive!"

"Really?"

"Soon, they had caught and boiled so many filthy *ninja* that those who remained alive decided it better for their health to become a farmers or fisherman, leaving their dishonorable lives behind them. Iyeyasu Shogun's warriors became known as *Tamashi Kami*. Do you know what that means?" Getting no response, she glanced down to find Jonathan asleep. Her eyes misted as the DeSoto sped along the roadway.

"Wake up, Jonason," she said, shaking him gently. "We have arrived."

He sat up and looked out the window.

"We are outside the Dai Kan. I am so excited for you!"

He didn't see anything even vaguely resembling a school. But then, he couldn't see much. A tall rough-barked log fence surrounded the place, blocking from view everything on the other side except for the tops of hundred-foot pine trees and the golden roof of what looked to be a large temple.

"You will find a bell beside the entrance," said Reiko, pointing towards the immense log gate. "You must ring it. Someone will come when they hear the bell. Tell them in Japanese as I taught you that you want very much to be allowed to study at the Dai Kan. *Wakarimasu ka?*"

He nodded.

"No matter what he tells you, no matter how long you must wait — hours, even days — you must not leave. You must stay near the gate until you convince them that you are a serious person. This is most important. You must not leave."

"Why do I have to wait outside? He already said I could go to his school."

"You were only given permission to apply for admission. Whether you are accepted or not depends on how serious you prove yourself. But," she said smiling and gently pinching his freckled cheek, "I know you are a strong, serious boy and will wait outside even if it takes all summer, as the Lone Ranger would do, right?"

"I'm strong. I can wait," he said. "But..."

"I know you will make us most proud," she insisted, taking his small face in her hands and kissing him on the forehead. "Now go."

Reluctantly, he climbed out, took his suitcase from Yuso's hand, then shuffled towards the gate, his mind vacillating between doing what he was told and running back and begging Reiko to take him with her. But his grandmother had made it clear, he had no choice. He hated Aunt Muriel. He hated Hiroko. He hated his mother and father and grandfather for leaving him. Most of all, he hated God for taking them. If he loved us as much as the minister had told them over and over, he wouldn't have let his parents and grandfather be killed, leaving him with some evil witch.

A frayed rope with what looked to Jonathan like cowbells down most of its length hung from a wooden arm beside the gate. He gave the rope a good shake, making the bells clunk and clang, each in its own tone.

No one came.

He peeked through a crack in the gate but couldn't see anyone inside. He glanced back at the car and shrugged, wondering what he should do. Reiko stabbed her finger at the bells and he gave the rope another yank.

A few seconds later, the gate creaked open a foot or two, revealing an old person who looked more like a skeleton than a live man. His cellophane-thin skin was stretched tightly over his thin bones and his back so bent it looked broken. The old man's skull seemed fixed in place, as if his neck didn't work. He angled his rigid body sideways and moved through the narrow opening like a crab, scaring Jonathan, who took a couple of steps back.

But when the old man fixed his gaze on his face, his eyes were as soft and warm as a puppy's. Jonathan grabbed his suitcase and started towards the open gate. The old man shifted over to block him. "Why have you come to our gate?" the old man asked in a voice sweet and flowing.

Jonathan bowed as he had been told to do and said what he and Reiko had rehearsed. "I want very much to become a student here," he told the old man in Japanese.

"I am sorry but that is not possible. Our school is full," the old man replied, then bowed politely, shuffled back inside, and closed and barred the gate behind him.

Jonathan couldn't have been more relieved. He had done everything he had been told to do. If they wouldn't let him stay, he'd have to go back home. He started happily towards the car but the DeSoto's big V-8 roared and the car shot forward, its tires throwing dirt and rocks. Jonathan dropped his suitcase and broke into a dead run. By the time he reached the street, the car was far away and picking up speed. He stood in the middle of the empty roadway, watching the taillights grow smaller and fainter in the distance.

8

---

onathan huddled against the gate's rough timbers, hugging his knees and shivering. After the sun had set, a cold, stiff southerly wind had arisen, buffeting his small body and causing his teeth to chatter. The trees and bushes across the roadway had become things black and sinister. They creaked and whipped eerily around, their limbs appearing at times to reach out for him, keeping the boy on edge.

The gate moved and Jonathan sprang to his feet, poised to flee. The old caretaker stuck his head through the narrow opening. "Please, come in out of the cold," said the old man. The boy didn't need to be asked twice.

Caretaker led Jonathan to a tiny paper-and-wood hut just inside the gate. There, the old man fed him pickled vegetables, rice, and a grilled fish of some sort. He was so hungry and relieved that he wouldn't have to sit outside all night that he ate everything without complaint.

After their meal, the old man cleared the table, humming a fast Japanese tune as he did. Soon, he began spinning in circles to the song, dipping and weaving in some strange dance as he washed, dried, and then placed each dish and utensil back into its storage spot. Jonathan watched, not sure what to make of it all, prompting the old man to dance even more exotically. When he finally realized that the old man wasn't crazy, that he was just trying to be funny, Jonathan laughed and Caretaker ended his dance with a grand bow.

The old man led the boy to the cubbyhole where he was to sleep. The space was smaller than his bedding, forcing the old man to fold the bottom quilt in half. Jonathan sank down into the cushy mattress and pulled the second thick quilt up under his chin. In less than a minute, he was asleep.

A nearby bell gonged so loudly it vibrated the small house and startled Jonathon awake. Caretaker shuffled up the hallway, candle in hand. "Please get dressed, little one," he said. "It is time to eat."

"It black night outside," said the boy, having trouble getting his mind to think in Japanese.

"Yes, we rise most early as each day there is much to do. Come, you may not get another opportunity to eat for many hours."

Jonathan wasn't hungry – it was too early. He picked at the barley gruel and pickled cucumbers on his plate, eating only enough to quiet the old man.

When they left, he was not taken to the school as he expected – which he still envisioned as a tall brick building, like the ones in Boston. Instead, he was taken back to the gate.

"Thank you, little one, for sharing my meager dwelling with me," Caretaker said, then slipped back inside.

"Why I must leaving? I something make wrong?"

"No, you did nothing wrong," said the old man. "It is merely as I said when we first spoke, we cannot accept more students at this time. Goodbye."

Jonathan slumped down onto the soft earth. Obviously he couldn't stay there. They didn't want him. And he couldn't walk home – it was too far and he didn't know the way. His only hope was that Reiko and the big car would come back for him.

By the time the sun was a blazing ball overhead, however, not a single car had even driven past. To escape the heat, he had moved across the road midmorning to a spot under the cool feathered branches of a pine tree. There, his stomach growled as he waited, making him regret not finishing his breakfast, as bad as it had been.

"Ah, you are still here, little golden one," yelled Caretaker from the gate. "Would you do me the honor of joining me for lunch?"

"Lunch?" Jonathan said, leaping up. "Hai, very starving!"

Lunch was far better than their breakfast had been. There was brown rice, *mizu* soup, and a sour chopped vegetable of some kind. He ate everything put in front of him, including the mystery vegetable, and looked up for more.

The old man bowed. "I am most sorry," he said in slow, deliberate Japanese. "We are poor and must ourselves grow all the foods we eat. There is no more."

Jonathan was given a container of water and taken back to the front gate, feeling much better as he returned to his comfortable spot under the pine tree. The sun was warm, his stomach full, and he knew they wouldn't let him starve.

As he lounged in dirty but relative comfort, he was unaware that inside the compound two powerful men were discussing his fate. He had already met *Kancho* Shinichi Kubo, head of the Dai Kan and the even more elite Kami Kan. But the second man was yet to make his presence, power, and threat known, although that would soon change.

Shihan Iwaki Sugiyama, known as *The Bear*, had long mistakenly believed that his nickname arose from his barrel chest and powerful ursine size. As the former head of both Kans, no one had ever had the courage, or the stupidity, to tell him the truth — they called him *The Bear* because he was the hairiest Japanese anyone had ever encountered. Course gray-streaked black hair covered his cheeks and chin, neck, chest, back, shoulders, arms, knuckles, and even sprouted from his ears and nostrils, as if he were perpetually dressed in a fur coat.

Air huffed from *Kancho* Kubo's oft-broken nose as he watched Sugiyama drone on and on about unimportant matters, his bushy eyebrows bobbing like drunken caterpillars. *The Bear* had come for a reason but was taking the long, circuitous route well known to all Japanese, even those who hated the practice. Their convoluted, hypersensitive social etiquette had arisen out of necessity. *Samurai* honor demanded that the slightest insult, even the perception of one, be redressed immediately, resulting in many deaths. As a result, intricate rules of behavior evolved over hundreds of years to lessen the chances of a confrontation. And since Japan had been run by *samurai* throughout most of its history, *samurai* etiquette was Japanese etiquette.

"Please forgive me for interrupting, Sugiyama San," said Kubo as politely as he could but stopping *The Bear* in mid-sentence. The older man stared at him in stunned silence. "One of the few qualities I admire in Americans is their ability to keep discussions brief and focused, allowing busy men like ourselves more time in which to accomplish our duties."

"Then you must greatly admire the despicable MacArthur," spat Sugiyama, offended by the interruption. "He was rude to everyone, even the Heavenly Sovereign!"

"And to think, MacArthur held you in such high esteem," Kubo said, sarcastically.

Sugiyama bristled. "Thirty-two years I served as head of the Dai and Kami Kan. Thirty-two! I had earned respect, even from a *gaijin*. 'Bear Shit,' he called me! 'Get out of my sight, you steaming pile of bear shit!' If I had been armed, I would have taken his head!"

Kubo scoffed. "You should be thankful he allowed you to leave with yours."

The Bear's eyes smoldered. "Since we are dispensing with all manners, let me be equally blunt. Is it true a *gaijin* has applied for admission and waits this very moment outside our gates?"

"You seem to have forgotten that you allowed entrance to two *yakuza*. Even a *gaijin* is superior to gangsters."

Sugiyama's puffy face contorted, giving it the appearance of a hairy frog. "Nothing is lower than a *gaijin*! Nothing!"

"Apparently His Majesty does not agree as he instructed me to consider the boy. It was not my place, or that of any loyal Japanese," he added, staring directly into Sugiyama's eyes, "to refuse an Imperial order."

A loud growl roared from Sugiyama as he sprang to his feet, upending the table. Kubo stood to face him.

"The order was written by the *gaijin* general, not the Emperor! As such, I was obligated to refuse it!" He hunched threateningly forward, like a grizzly about to charge. "Of course, a traitorous *gaijin* ass-licker, as some have described you, could not possibly comprehend true *gimu chu*!"

"Is that why the Emperor dispatched his own brother to demand you step down or be hung like a common criminal?"

"MacArthur gave that order too! And what of you? Insubordination during wartime. You should have been shot!"

"Japan is its people, not old men drunk on power like you," Kubo fired back, not giving an inch. "Had they ordered me to kill *gaijin*, our sworn enemy, I would have killed until I was out of bullets, my sword broken, and my body too battered to kick or punch. But I was told to torture our own citizens on mere hunches. And," he said, stabbing his finger at his predecessor, "that is why I am now Master General, with the Emperor's blessing, and you are not!"

The two men stood nose to nose, glaring at each other with such hatred in their eyes that it seemed certain a fight would erupt. Then, Sugiyama softened, just slightly at first. But soon his eyes angled onto the floor. "Please excuse my rudeness, my old *kohai* and now my *sempai*," he murmured. "I allowed my passion to interfere with my duty as advisor."

Kubo softened too. "We should not be fighting among ourselves, especially over something that will likely never be. The young *gaijin* possesses all the weaknesses that mark their society. He is soft in body and softer in spirit, devoid of *giri* or any sense of duty to anyone or anything beyond himself. If I allow him entrance, he will endure a life of pain and insult. It would be a kindness to refuse him, to send him back to his family where he could lead an easy *gaijin* life."

"*Oos*," said Sugiyama in agreement.

Jonathan heard the dull rumble of an approaching car. They were coming for him! He sprinted across the street and snatched up his suitcase. But the car that pulled up and stopped was a tiny black Datsun, not a luxurious DeSoto.

A buzz-cut man in a baggy Japanese officer's uniform crawled out. Jonathan was noting how short he was, not much taller than himself, when the man's head snapped around. What he saw sent Jonathan back a step. A red scar angled across his disfigured face. The cut had left one eye as white and cloudy as a poached egg. Jonathan felt like he was back in one of his recurring nightmares.

"Leave this place!" the stranger barked in broken English. "You not welcome here!"

Jonathan froze, not knowing what to do. "Go!" the man screamed. But where would he go? When he didn't move, the man came at him so fast and with such hatred that Jonathan angled his body to run for the gate. But the man shifted over and cut him off.

The stranger grabbed his suitcase and hurled it far out into the street. "Leave! Now!" he ordered.

The gate creaked open. Caretaker appeared with a gardening hoe in his hands. "One of you bring *Kancho*, *isogi*!" he yelled to someone inside the compound. The old man scurried out and positioned himself between the boy and the stranger, hoisting the hoe as if it were a weapon. "Why have you come, Kengoshi San?" he demanded.

"Get out of my way, old man," the Japanese said, shoving Caretaker in the chest, knocking him to the ground. The way now clear, he closed on Jonathan, pinning him against the rough pine log wall. Jonathan searched frantically for an avenue of escape. The partially open gate looked the most promising but Kengoshi launched a punch at his face. At the last instant, the fist veered over, smacked the log just beside Jonathan's head, and stayed there, cutting off any hope of reaching the gate. The man leaned in, his breath hot and foul. "You will take suitcase and..." he hissed.

"Move away from the boy or I will bury this into your skull!" Caretaker said, the hoe raised above his head, ready to strike.

The man swung his good eye around and fixed it on the frail old man.

"Take the boy inside," *Kancho* Kubo said, stepping through the gate.

Kengoshi snapped to attention, obviously surprised by the sudden appearance of the Master General.

"I thought you were imprisoned by the *gaijin?*" Kubo said, his voice civil but without warmth.

"They released me. My sentence was served."

"To what do we owe the honor of your visit?"

"I merely came to pay my respects to the new Master General," Kengoshi said, bowing.

"Thank you," Kubo said, nodding his head in the barest rudiments of a bow. "I spoke earlier with your mentor. I was afraid you too had come to challenge my authority."

"I was merely asking the *gaijin* if he was lost. Why else would a *gaijin* be at the Dai Kan gate?"

"In the future, it would be best if you refrained from approaching any student or potential student at this school without my personal permission."

"Are you saying that a *gaijin* is being considered for admission?"

"I am saying nothing. I am merely suggesting a course of action that will retain the harmony of this school and enable you and me to avoid a future confrontation."

Despite all the bowing and honeyed talk, Kubo kept his eyes trained on Kengoshi as he crawled back into his Datsun and drove off.

Although Jonathan was told he could remain inside the compound and begin his studies, Caretaker quickly added that his stay might not be permanent. It depended on how hard and serious a worker he proved to be.

The boy's first day began before sunrise, when Caretaker woke him up, prodded him into relieving himself into a bucket, and rushed him into his clothes, repeatedly saying, "You will be late!" Against Jonathan's protestations, Caretaker almost dragged him out the door without even giving him anything to eat. "You will be late!" the old man repeated as they hurried up a winding path to the *zendo*.

"The what?"

"It is where one practices *Zen*."

Jonathan shook his head, not understanding what he was talking about. *Zen*, the old man explained, was a form of mental training that warriors had practiced for hundreds of years.

The ancient, open-floored *zendo* had been fashioned out of logs stripped of its bark. Its ornate arched roof was constructed of gold-leafed wood and teal-blue tile. As Caretaker had warned, they were the last to arrive. He hastily ushered Jonathan up the steps and inside, where students sat in neat, motionless rows on the ubiquitous *tatami* mats. It was the first morning session of *seiza*, or seated meditation, and the air was chilly and damp. But none of the boys seemed to notice.

The old man bowed to the *jikijitsu*, a senior monk who oversaw the session. Then he led Jonathan to a vacant spot at the end of the back row of meditators. He shoved Jonathan down onto his knees, pushed in his lower back, and straightened his neck and chin. "Do not move," he whispered, "or you will be struck with the *keisaku*, the warning stick."

The monk roamed the *zendo*, checking each of the boys as he glided past. Jonathan kept his eyes closed and remained motionless as he had been instructed, holding his breathe when he heard the *jikijitsu* stop behind him. The flat of the warning stick smacked the boy lightly on his right shoulder. Jonathan's eyes sprang open. "I wasn't moving!"

His outburst earned another smack, this one harder. The *jikijitsu* bowed and moved on. Caretaker crawled quickly up. "Do not hold your breath," he told him. "Breathe deeply and naturally to calm your mind. In through your nose, out through your mouth, as you would when attempting to enter sleep."

And so Jonathan did as he was told, breathing in through his nose until his lungs were full, then relaxing and letting the air leak all the way back out through his mouth. Soon, he was in the rhythm... too much, in fact. His head began to tilt forward, just a little at first but sank lower and lower until his chin finally rested against his chest. A hard smack jolted him awake. *Stay awake, stay awake*, he repeated to himself.

The warbly, deep throated sound of snoring filled the room. One of the boys snickered. Then others joined in. Before the *jikijitsu* could weave his way across the room and bring his *kaiseku* down on Jonathan's shoulder, everyone was laughing so uncontrollably that even stern warnings and hard smacks couldn't stop them. For the first time in the history of the Dai Kan, *seiza* was cancelled early.

Caretaker was unusually quiet as they walked back to the house. Jonathan knew he had done something wrong but wasn't exactly sure what it was. He would have to work harder and be more careful, he told himself, or they would kick him out and he would end up at Aunt Muriel's in Texas.

After a simple breakfast, Jonathan was assigned chores that varied from day to day. The first day, he helped Caretaker tend the grounds – hoeing weeds, raking leaves, pouring excrement from the outdoor toilets onto the vegetable and fruit plants. The second, he helped Caretaker restock almost depleted wood stores for cooking. The third, he gathered bamboo to fix the inner fences. He did everything that was asked of him and did it as perfectly as he could, never complaining, except about the blisters on his hands. He even managed to keep himself awake in the *zendo* and was only struck five times all week for letting his mind wander. Another boy had earned six. By the weekend, he ached all over, from his chin to the muscles in his feet.

"*Iie*, Caretaker," Jonathan insisted as the old man shook him awake. "No today work. You saying yesterday."

"Today is not for work," said the old man. "You are to meet *Kancho*. It is most important, so dress quickly. We must not keep him waiting."

Kubo knelt straight-backed and as settled as a stone on the slightly elevated platform at the rear of a large tatami-covered room. He was dressed in formal *kimono* and *jinbaori*, or winged *samurai* over garment, with a small silver crest of the *Kancho* of the Dai Kan embroidered over his heart. He did not look happy.

To Kubo's left, five senior Dai Kan instructors sat motionlessly in a row, each man's face devoid of emotion, revealing nothing about their vote on the question that had been posed to them.

Following Caretaker's lead, Jonathan stopped just inside the large double *shoji*, placed his hands on his thighs, and bowed. Unlike at his grandparent's house, where he and the grandmaster had competed to see who was the most polite, *Kancho* Kubo barely nodded in return. Caretaker nudged the boy and he strolled confidently to the middle of the floor, knelt, and bowed again.

"How do you like life here?" asked Kubo, when the boy had straightened back up.

"It much hard work," Jonathan said, as if talking to one of his friends. The others sucked air in amazement.

"Life is hard," agreed Kubo, his tone making sure the young American understood that he was not now the family friend. He was the *Kancho*, the Master General. "We must be hardened if we are to survive. Do you think you are strong enough?"

"I want very much study," the boy offered, although it wasn't even close to the truth. If he really had his wish, he would be back with Reiko, eating teriyaki, and sleeping as long as he wanted. But she hadn't come back, hadn't even checked on him. And his grandmother apparently cared even less. So he had no choice.

"I am not so sure," said Kubo.

"I will work harder and try to learn to do things more better," he said, his eyelids fluttering away a tear.

Kubo didn't say anything for several seconds.

"I and this school are greatly indebted to your grandparents. It was through your grandfather's direct intervention alone that the Dai Kan was allowed to continue as it has for over four hundred years. It was his wish that you become the first non-Japanese to study here, believing you could do much to build a better understanding between our two nations. It is a noble quest. But I do not know if you are the right person to fulfill it. There is much doubt among the board about your ability to perform what will be asked of you."

Kubo's body sagged under the weight of the decision he had to make. He huffed noisily through his bent nose as he thought.

"But in Japan indebtedness creates an obligation," he continued at last. "It is for that reason alone that you will be allowed entrance into the Dai Kan."

A smile spread across Jonathan's face.

"Do not rejoice," Kubo said, his face hardening. "Regardless of our debt to your grandfather and your grandmother's royal blood, your life here will be no easier than that of any other pupil. To them, you are but a *gaijin*. That alone would make your life unbearable at times. But most of your classmates also lost fathers, brothers, and uncles to American bullets and mothers, grandmothers, and sisters to American bombs. They will undoubtedly let this affect their treatment of you. If you choose to stay, you must find your own ways to deal with that. We cannot help you. Do you understand?"

Jonathan bowed, although he had understood little of what was said.

"You truly want to stay?" asked Kubo in English, wanting to make sure the boy knew what he was undertaking.

"*Hai.*"

"Then it will be. Caretaker, see that our newest pupil receives his student uniform and bunk assignment."

Jonathan and Caretaker bowed and backed out of the room.

"You will soon be assigned a *sempai*," Caretaker said as he led Jonathan towards his new dorm.

"What is a *sempai*?"

"He is a more senior student whose job it is to guide your progress as if he were your older brother."

Jonathan smiled. "So he's like a friend?"

"A friend?" repeated the old man, obviously not finding that an apt description.

9

Jonathan fastened the last of the five silver buttons on the front of his *gakuran*, the traditional uniform worn by students throughout Japan. He checked his reflection in the mirror, liking what he saw. A hand reached out and slapped him hard on the back of his head. Jonathan spun to see a skinny boy with a shaved head. "Hurry up!" he yelled. "Do you want to be late?"

While Jonathan rubbed his head and sized up his shorter and thinner attacker, a group of other students closed in around them.

"Why are you still standing there, *gaijin*? Get moving!" the boy screamed, his face red with anger.

When he slapped his head again, Jonathan launched a hooking fist at his face. But the boy ducked easily under it, then drove his own fist deep into Jonathan's soft belly. The blow doubled him over. He couldn't breathe. Panic overwhelmed Jonathan and he tried to run, afraid he was going to die, but the other boys shoved him back into the center, where his attacker waited to finish him off.

Yame!" yelled Caretaker, who had entered the room unnoticed. "Murakami San, please come here." The boy hesitated at first, his anger raging. "Did you hear me?" repeated the old man. Murakami reluctantly shuffled over. "This is not your dorm. What is your business here?"

"Sugiyama *Shihan* said I am to be the *gaijin's sempai*."

Caretaker's normally placid face flushed. It took him a second to regain his composure. "It is the duty of a *sempai* to assist his *kohai*, not assault him," scolded Caretaker. "If you are truly his *sempai*, then you must apologize for your bad manners."

Murakami's eyes narrowed to defiant slits. Someone at the back of the room exhaled noisily through his nostrils. Everyone turned to see *Kancho* Kubo standing in the doorway, arms folded across his chest.

"*Oos*," said Murakami, quickly bowing to Caretaker.

"Now, apologize to Lusk San," the old man said.

Murakami glared at the American, unable, it seemed, to decide whether to do as commanded or to attack him.

"I said apologize to Lusk San!"

Murakami bowed, his palms pressed hard against the sides of his thighs, his eyes on the floor. "I am truly sorry for my disrespectful behavior," he said. "Please forgive me. I will endeavor to do better in the future."

Jonathan had recaught his breath and his panic now replaced by anger. His fists balled up and he fought the urge to make another attempt at Murakami's pouty lips. But as he felt everyone in the room staring at him, he reluctantly offered his hand. Murakami gave it a quick, cursory shake.

"You're supposed to shake twice on a deal," Jonathan said in English before catching himself. "Like this," he said, grabbing Murakami's hand and giving it a couple of exaggerated pumps. Murakami jerked his hand free, obviously thinking he was being mocked.

"I expect no more trouble here," said Kubo.

The boys bowed as the Master General and Caretaker headed towards the door. But as soon as the *shoji* slid closed behind them, everyone's eyes fixed on Jonathan. Murakami shoved him in the chest, knocking him backwards into the wall of boys who encircled them.

"He is your *sempai*," one of the larger boys said. "It is your duty to do as he asks."

"My *sempai* punched me in the face the first time we met and broke my nose," said another.

"Yeah," said a third, "all you got was a little slap." He shoved Jonathan forward into Murakami.

"If *Kancho* had not saved you," spat Murakami, "I would have bashed in your pink, cow-eyed *gaijin* face! He has been begging for an excuse to expel me ever since he arrived. But if I were you," he said, tapping Jonathan hard on the chest with his finger, "I would not wager on him saving you again. Beating your ugly face in might just be worth expulsion."

"I should have anticipated that Sugiyama would assign Yukio as Jonason's *sempai*," said Kubo. "It is the ultimate insult."
"And to you as well."
Kubo nodded.
"May I humbly suggest you name someone more appropriate?"
"I have stripped Sugiyama of all but the most menial of duties. To countermand him on this would almost surely spark a reaction and make life even more difficult for the boy."
"And it may be unnecessary," Caretaker reflected. "I would not be surprised if the boy soon quit or failed to measure up to our standards."
Kubo nodded. "I too have never held much hope for him. It would be best for everyone if he did fail or quit, and did it quickly. Then our obligation of *giri* would be lifted and life here could return to normal."

Although he was now surrounded almost every minute of every day by a dorm full of boys his age, Jonathan felt more alone than when he had been trapped in the hotel room with his mother. Everyone was either openly hostile or treated him as if he didn't exist.

It was no different in the classroom. His teachers sat him either on the front row, and called on him often so they could ridicule his answers or his still weak Japanese, or in the back of the room so they could completely ignore him. To escape, Jonathan spent much of his free time exploring the forests at the back of the Dai Kan's sprawling grounds. On one of his trips, he came across a white-water stream deep inside a pine forest carpeted with lime-green clover and feathery emerald ferns. It reminded him of the place where he and his grandfather used to swim and quickly became his retreat.

One day, as he forged a trail downstream, he discovered a spectacular twenty-foot waterfall. While admiring the way the water hit the rocks below and sprayed upwards like a giant white flower, he heard a faint rhythmic thumping sound.

He followed the sound to an odd circular enclosure that had been hewn out of a stand of tall bamboo. It was filled with neat rows of tapered boards that stuck straight up from the ground. Each was an inch or two taller than Jonathan and had hemp rope wound tightly around their tapered ends.

A man stood at the back of the enclosure. He was dressed in white pajamas with a belt around his waist that was so frayed Jonathan couldn't tell if it was a white belt with stringy black thread or vice versa. The man sank into a deep stance as he drove his fist into the roped end of the board, bowing it backwards. With each punch, he seemed intent on pounding it back even further.

In the distance, the bell gonged and Jonathan ran back towards the main compound to eat lunch before they stopped serving. As he crossed the campus, he passed a stream of students heading towards the gym, all dressed in the same white pajamas, only their belts were green or brown. They filed into what was mysteriously called the "new" gym. Like his new grandmother, it wasn't new at all, just not as old as everything else.

After the last students were inside, he sneaked over and peeked in through the side window. Caretaker shuffled silently up behind him. "I have been searching for you," he said, making Jonathan jump. "Do you know what they are doing?" he asked. The boy shook his head. "They are learning *karate*. It is a barehanded martial art that was introduced here by an Okinawan school teacher just twenty-eight years ago, although practiced in the *Ryukyus* for centuries."

"I saw the instructor beating his hand against a board in the forest," he told the old man, still fascinated by it.

"They train to toughen themselves to withstand abuse and turn their bodies into weapons – their fingertips into spears, fists into clubs and such. But you will soon see. *Kancho* wants you to begin your training after next bell. I left your *karate gi* on your foot locker."

Jonathan's face lit up. He turned and ran off as fast as his legs would carry him.

The dorm bay where he lived was open and bare except for the ubiquitous *tatami* and the precise rows of shipping trunks along both side walls, each with a rolled and bound pair of *futon* on top. Jonathan's dormmates stopped what they were doing and watched as he hurried across the floor and snatched up the clear plastic bag Caretaker had left him. Removing the white *karate* pants, he pulled them on over his school pants, making the other boys laugh.

"Take off your pants first, idiot," yelled one of the boys.

Jonathan stripped down to his underwear and pulled on his *gi* pants. But they wouldn't stay up. He tugged on one of the two long draw-strings. The other end came out and his pants wouldn't stay up. He looked to the others. But even if they would have helped, they were busy getting into their own *karate gis*. As the other boys chuckled, Jonathan tied the two ends together in a clumsy knot.

Fortunately the top was easy to figure out. He simply wrapped the belt around his waist and tied it in front, as if tying his shoes. But where his belt hung clear to the floor and his knot big and with multiple loose loops, everyone else's were neatly tied and only hung down a foot and a half at most. To correct it, he tied the loose ends of his belt into a double knot, then a triple. In the end, it looked nothing like the other boys' but at least it wasn't dragging anymore.

As he waited for the bell, he noticed that his *karate* uniform wasn't actually white. It was really the color of wheat, as was his belt, and smelled like the gunny sacks his mother used to buy potatoes in. Except for the smell, he liked it. It was loose and comfortable, the opposite of his student uniform.

"What is this?" demanded Murakami, stopping in front of his *kohai* and staring with disgust at Jonathan's belt. He muttered angrily as he untied it, then noticed the drawstring. "Are all *gaijin* so stupid they cannot even dress themselves?" He tried but couldn't fix the string and ended up just tying it tighter. Then he showed Jonathan the knot on his own blue belt. "This is properly tied. Tie yours exactly like it!" Jonathan tried but couldn't improve beyond his first attempt. Murakami slapped his hands aside and disgustedly tied it in a neat square knot.

"Get outside!" he ordered. Jonathan ambled across the floor. "Run!" screamed Murakami, kicking him in the butt. Jonathan ran and didn't stop until he reached the *dojo*, where the instructor stood blocking the door.

"You are early," said the *karate sensei*, scowling at Murakami. He was the same man Jonathan had seen earlier in the bamboo enclosure.

"The *gaijin* is always late, *sensei*," Murakami responded, bowing low. "I did not want to get into trouble because of him again." The *sensei* merely grunted.

The bell sounded. Students poured out of the dorm and headed their way. Murakami shoved Jonathan inside, then grabbed his lapel and dragged him across the bare wooden floor to the back corner of the room.

"Don't embarrass me further," Murakami ordered, poking Jonathan hard in the chest before heading to the opposite side of the floor, where those of his rank were warming up.

The *dojo* was constructed of bare wood and rice-paper *shoji*, as all buildings seemed to be in Japan. But this one contained an assortment of fascinating pieces of training equipment. Heavy body bags hung from ceiling beams. Kicking pads and paddles lined the back wall. Oval metal rings, large enough for Jonathan to walk through, leaned against the side wall. In the corner were stones with wooden handles, rows of clay jars, U-shaped iron dumbbells, and traditional Japanese *geta* sandals but made of iron.

"*Shugo!*" commanded the *karate sensei*.

Everyone ran into place.

"*Seiza!*" yelled the most senior student from the far end of the line. The boys knelt in meditation position.

"*Mokuso!*"

The instructor and students closed their eyes and breathed deeply and slowly, clearing their minds of all thoughts but their *karate* training.

"*Mokuso, yame!*" yelled the senior after several seconds, bringing meditation to a close.

"*Shomen ni rei!*"

Placing their fingertips on the floor, everyone bowed low towards the small shrine mounted on the front wall, where the *dojo kami* resided. The instructor turned and faced them.

"*Sensei ni rei!*"

The students bowed to their teacher.

"*Otagai ni rei!*"

Instructor and students bowed to each other.

"*Tatte!*" yelled the instructor and everyone rose to their feet in unison.

After warm-ups and the seemingly endless repetition of *karate kihon*, or fundamentals, the *sensei* instructed everyone to pair off. Murakami rushed down the line and stopped in front of Jonathan.

"*Iie*, Murakami!" yelled the instructor. "Find a partner your own rank, unless you would like to be a white belt again."

Murakami stomped angrily up the line and paired up with another blue belt.

"Hiroshi," commanded the *sensei*, "partner with the *gaijin*."

The skinny white belt shifted over. He was a bit shorter than Jonathan but had the same cocky smile as had his *sempai*.

The *sensei* called out one of his senior students and the two bowed to each other. Then the student drew his leg back. On the instructor's command, the student threw a powerful front kick and stepped in. While the kick was en route, the *sensei* stepped back, blocked the kick with his front arm, then caught the kicker in the stomach with a well-controlled reverse punch.

"*Ippon kumite!*" yelled the *sensei*. "*Mae keri!*"

Jonathan readied himself as his partner took his leg back.

The instructor gave a crisp *kiai*.

Hiroshi kicked. Jonathan stepped back... but not quickly enough. The boy's foot sank into Jonathan's soft belly, doubling him over.

"Ha!" laughed Hiroshi, then thrust both fists into the air. "Winner!"

Everyone laughed as Jonathan went down onto one knee and struggled to catch his breath. His partner leaned in close. "You should wear a dress, soft *gaijin* girl!"

Jonathan charged, grabbing Hiroshi around the waist and driving him hard into the wall.

"*Yame!*" yelled the *sensei*. "Stop!"

Jonathan straightened up. "He kicked me on purpose."

"This is *karate*, not ballet. If you do not want to be kicked, do not allow it. Thirty push-ups."

It wasn't right, Jonathan told himself, thrusting out his chest in angry indignation. But he dropped down nonetheless and did a set of what were more butt-ups than push-ups, so pathetic that even the instructor laughed.

"Murakami! He is your *kohai*, is he not?"

"Yes, *sensei*!" Murakami admitted, bowing low and trying to hide his apprehension. "Sorry, *sensei*."

"Pair off with him."

A sadistic smile swept across Murakami's face as he eagerly ran into place. But before they could continue the drill, *Kancho* Kubo paid the group a rare visit. "Prepare them for *kata*," he told the instructor.

"*Kata*! Line up!" screamed the *sensei*, his voice breaking. Instantly, the class assembled into neat rows by rank. "*Pinan Shodan*," said *Kancho*. Everyone, except for Jonathan and the other beginners, knew the form by heart and moved easily through its twenty-one moves. He followed as best he could, mimicking the more advanced students.

There were twenty-six *kata*, he soon learned, each created by a legendary grandmaster and composed of a unique series of self-defense techniques strung together as in a choreographed fight. Even more important than memorizing the series of moves seemed to be perfecting the *kihon*, the basic strikes, kicks, stances, and blocks from which everything in *karate* was constructed.

While Kubo led the others through the next two *kata*, *Pinan Nidan* and *Pinan Sandan*, one of the senior students showed Jonathan and the other white belts how to correctly perform the first, *Pinan Shodan*.

By the time class was over, Jonathan had memorized all twenty-one moves. Hiroshi, the boy who had kicked him, could only get through the first nine. No matter how frustrated their teacher got with him and he with himself, no matter how angry the rest of the students got when they saw him falling behind the *gaijin*, Hiroshi kept turning the wrong way, sending a loud collective moan through the room.

"I would like to thank you, *Kancho*," said Caretaker, bowing to his bony knees as Kubo walked out of the *dojo*. Purely by accident, of course, the old man had discovered that the juniper bush beneath the *dojo's* side *shoji* was badly in need of trimming. As he pruned its branches, he had seen, also purely by accident, what had occurred inside.

"For what?"

"Preventing the boy from being injured."

"What I did, I did for myself. If he does not want to be kicked, he must learn to block properly or move more quickly. Pain is one of our greatest teachers. I would be remiss if I denied him its message. I stopped the drill because I did not relish explaining to Princess Lusk Sama how her grandson had become badly injured while under our care."

"*Oos*," said Caretaker, bowing in understanding.

All in all, Jonathan's first *karate* class had gone far better than his first class in meditation. Although the *karate sensei* never paired him off again with his *sempai*, he became increasingly more hostile with each class, singling Jonathan out for criticism even when others were making the exact same mistakes. "The other leg, Lusk!" he would yell. "You call that a punch, Lusk? It looks as strong as an *udon* noodle." Nothing he did was ever good enough.

Bedtime had never been a happy time for Jonathan, even before he came to Japan. After his mother or father had switched off the lights and he was alone, the usual childhood fears crept out of the darkness. But after his parents' deaths, the images that visited him at night changed from goblins under the bed or in the closet to bodies being blown apart, people without eyes, and thoughts of his own death.

Jonathan lay on his *futon* in the dark dorm, tears filling his eyes and sliding down his freckled cheeks. He didn't know why he was crying. Nothing unusual had happened that day, making it any worse than previous ones. Embarrassed, he quickly wiped the tears away and dried his face on his blanket.

Even in the darkness, he always felt people were watching him. It was not just the eyes of the other boys or his teachers, who seemed to scrutinize and criticize his every move; there were also the constant watchers who could read his thoughts and see what no one else saw, making quick judgment on everything he did or thought or should have done or should have thought. It was as if his father, mother, grandfather, and grandmother were always there, whispering in his ear. More and more he found himself trying to do what they expected of him.

If asked, he would have been hard-pressed to pick the worst time of the day. Nighttime. Meals. Classes. *Karate.* They were all bad. But the top of his list would have likely been mail call.

The first couple of weeks, he sprinted out of his last morning class and ran all the way across campus to the central fountain, where Caretaker handed out mail each weekday. There, he would wait expectantly as a mob of boys slowly gathered behind him. Soon, however, the other students noticed his desperation and did everything they could to thwart him, racing *en masse*, then pressing so closely together that he was forced to stand at the back.

But when they discovered that no mail ever came for him, not a single letter in weeks, the boys changed their tactics. They would step aside and give him easy access to the front of the group, where his disappointment could be savored by everyone. Eventually, Jonathan stopped going to mail call.

The only reason he had gone to mail call that day was to ask Caretaker about the meaning of a Japanese phrase one of his teachers had used in class. He was afraid it might be included in next period's geography test. As he waited, Jonathan sat on the grass and read his textbook, paying no attention as the old man worked his way through the long list of names of those receiving mail that day.

"Jonason Lusk!"

His head snapped up to see Murakami shaking a letter at him. Jonathan jumped to his feet, his eyes glued on the envelope.

"I just wanted to tell you," his *sempai* said, "that I got another letter today. My second. How many did you get?"

The other boys laughed.

"Actually," said Caretaker, holding up an envelope, "a letter did come for Lusk San. You boys are so rude I had planned to give it to him privately."

Jonathan ran over and snatched the letter from the old man's hand. Murakami and the others pressed in, their eyes riveted onto the front of the envelope to see who had written it. But Jonathan stuffed it quickly into his coat pocket and headed off for his next class.

As the sweet floral aroma of perfume wafted up from the envelope, he stifled a grin. It was the scent Hiroko had given Reiko for her birthday. He wanted to run and leap and yell but any sign of happiness would earn him reprisals from the others. So he walked stoically to his geography class, sat down, and took the test. Then he casually walked back to his dorm, never once pulling the letter out of his pocket, although he did reach in and touch it a time or two.

When he was sure he was alone, he sat on his foot locker and carefully opened the thin, rice-paper envelope, easing out a small photograph and two sheets of delicate parchment. He first studied the portrait of Reiko in her pink kimono. She was so serious it made him chuckle. Then he unfolded and began reading her letter.

"Dear Jonathan *Chan*, Matsuyama *San*, Kitaura *San*, Fumiko *San*, and, of course, your grandmother most of all, send their greatest love."

"What do you have here?" Murakami said, snatching the photo out of his hand.

"That's mine!" he cried as he tried to grab it back. But Murakami turned away, keeping the photo out of reach.

The other boys filed back into the dorm, saw what was going on and quickly encircled Jonathan and Murakami, keyed up by the possibility of a fight.

"What is a *gaijin* doing with a picture of a human girl?" asked Murakami, shoving Jonathan away. "I expected some pale, pig-nosed, cow-eyed *gaijin* girl."

"It's Reiko. She took care of me when I was little," he said.

"She must be a *gaijin joro*," said Murakami, grinning at the other boys, who all laughed and nodded in agreement.

"She's not *gaijin*. She's Japanese," Jonathan said in her defense, not knowing what *joro* meant. But everyone only laughed harder.

"No, she is not *gaijin*," said Murakami. "She is the only thing lower than a *gaijin*. She is a *joro* for *gaijin* – one who allows them to stick their filthy dicks between her legs, if they pay her enough *yen*." Murakami curled his thumb and index finger into a loose fist and slid his middle finger rapidly in and out of the hole.

A primal scream erupted from low in Jonathan's throat. He lunged at Murakami, catching him off guard with a hard punch to the face. The other boys scattered. Murakami stumbled backwards, tripped over one of the boy's feet, and fell onto his back. His face scrunched up in anger as he rolled onto his hands and knees to get up. But Jonathan kicked him in the head, as if it were the football in his grandfather's back yard. The blow snapped

Murakami's head back and stunned him. The American jumped onto his dazed *sempai* and didn't stop punching him in the back of the neck and head until several spectators pulled him off. Four of them restrained him while two others helped Murakami out of the dorm, trailing a red line of blood across the *tatami*.

Jonathan sat on his foot locker, clutching his letter and photo as he waited for *Kancho* or Caretaker or whoever would be coming to punish him. And within minutes, Mighty Mouse, one of *Kancho's* aides, arrived. Jonathan had given him that name because of his short, muscular, v-shaped body. As the aide entered the dorm, Jonathan had stood up, resigned to his fate. But Mighty Mouse ignored him, speaking first with each of his dormmates, one at a time, obviously collecting evidence against him. He couldn't hear what was being asked or said, they were too far away. But he noticed that Mighty Mouse stared hard into each boy's eyes as they spoke, his body firm, his hands on his hips. The boys, on the other hand, were all limp and subservient, their heads bobbing in an endless succession of quick bows. When the aide was done, he turned and left.

Instead of making him feel better, the man's silent departure left Jonathan feeling worse. The waiting was pure torture. Every time someone entered the dorm, Jonathan's eyes snapped around and his gut clinched into a tight fist. When he encountered Caretaker on the path, he would bow his head in guilty apology. The old man always smiled and continued on.

There's no way Kancho Kubo doesn't know, Jonathan told himself as he walked to class. His aide had spoken to his dormmates and surely to Murakami too. There was zero chance his name hadn't come up. Every person Mighty Mouse had talked to would surely have blamed the entire incident on him.

He had barely gotten that thought out of his mind when he spotted *Kancho* heading straight towards him. The master's face was set and he was moving at a brisk, no nonsense clip. *This is it*, he told himself.

"Good morning, Lusk *San*," *Kancho* said and kept going.

As he watched the Master General stride up the walkway, it dawned on Jonathan what was likely happening and it sent another shiver through him. They were going to expel him and needed time to contact his grandmother and arrange for him to be picked up.

In the end, however, nothing was ever said or done, not even so much as an acknowledgement that they knew about the fight. But some good did come of it all. He didn't know if Murakami had been ordered to stay away or if the beating had made him afraid to come around, but he didn't see him for a couple of weeks and life was significantly better, except for the weather.

It had turned incredibly hot, reminding Jonathan of summers in Boston, where the temperature didn't drop even when the sun went down. His dorm's side *shoji* were left wide open at night to catch any breeze that might blow their way.

It had been a long draining day. Jonathan had fallen asleep almost the instant his head hit his beanbag. He lay flat on his back with his mouth open, snoring so loudly that it woke up some of the other boys.

"Are we being attacked by a *gaijin kami?*" muttered one of them.

The boy on the next futon gave Jonathan a shove and he rolled onto his side, stopping the noise. Everyone went quickly back to sleep, except for one boy who slipped quietly out the door. In a few minutes, he returned and crawled back into bed.

An hour later, a small black-cloaked figure, carrying a bucket in his hand, silently weaved his way through the maze of sleeping bodies to Jonathan's futon. After his dark eyes had swept the room to make sure he hadn't been detected, the figure hoisted the bucket, filled to the brim with a mushy mixture of urine and excrement drawn from the fifty-gallon barrel of night-soil used to fertilize the gardens, over the sleeping American. Carefully, he tilted the bucket until a slow stream of the putrid mess oozed down over the lip, then traced an outline of Jonathan's body, from his feet to his neck. When he reached the boy's head, he shook the last bit of slime loose and let it fall near Jonathan's freckled nose. His job done, the intruder tiptoed back across the room and out the doorway.

Jonathan was awakened by a foul burning odor in his nostrils. His eyes sprang open and he sniffed the air, trying to identify its source. When he placed his hands on his futon to push himself up, a cold, syrupy fluid oozed through his fingers. The fetid smell and repulsive feel of it sent him scrambling to his feet.

"Who did it?" he yelled, turning on the lights and scrutinizing each of the sleepy, confused faces. None looked guilty. Being careful not to spill any of the mess onto the *tatami*, he gathered up his blanket and rushed it outside, where he dropped it into one of the large laundry sinks used by students to hand-wash their clothes and bedding. But no matter how much he scrubbed, he couldn't get the smell out of it. Finally, he gave up and stuffed his blanket into the garbage can.

After that night, whenever he passed or came close to anyone, they would stick their noses into the air and sniff conspicuously as if they could still smell the foul odor on him. In class and the mess hall, the other students would scoot their chairs and desks as far away as they could get. Basically, nothing changed, except now everything they did, they did at a greater distance.

The good news was that *karate* class actually improved around this time. With their last belt exam, all of the students who had the ability to hurt him, and tried on regular occasions to do so, were promoted and moved into the intermediate class. None of those who remained were fans of his either, and would gladly hurt him if given the chance, but none were better than he was. And he had come to know how each of them fought. With that knowledge, he was able to deny them the ability to use their best techniques to any advantage.

His *karate sensei*, however, didn't go anywhere. He continued to oversee Jonathan's instruction Mondays through Saturdays and to find fault with everything he did. Had he understood that Jonathan considered it a blessing to remain in his class, he would likely have promoted him immediately. By holding him back for so long, the American became far stronger than his classmates in his *kihon* – his basic kicks, punches, blocks, and stances – and at applying them against a hostile partner.

The *sensei's* constant criticism also taught Jonathan a valuable lesson – those who disliked him would give him far more helpful information than friends. People who liked him would sugar-coat everything. Those who hated him would tell him every single mistake he made, no matter how small, allowing him to identify and correct them. With such a huge number of "helpers," he made great progress.

The instructor finally had no choice but promote Jonathan. He had gotten too good to be denied. His *sensei* wore an unaccustomed smile as he presented him with his new purple belt. Jonathan feared he knew the punch line to the unspoken joke and found his theory confirmed when he walked into his first intermediate class and saw Murakami waiting for him. Part of him wanted another shot at his *sempai*. He was all but positive he was the one who had fouled his bed. But he decided it best to avoid being paired with him until he had time to determine just how fast and skilled he had become.

Yamaoka *Sensei* was a little taller than Jonathan and almost as wide as he was tall. He was legendary throughout the Dai Kan for his fierce spirit. Jonathan didn't know if his reputation had arisen because of his notorious temper or his fearsome appearance, but either would have been sufficient.

After practicing their *kihon* and taking a short break, Yamaoka *Sensei* ordered everyone to form into opposing rows. Jonathan had a pretty good idea which drill was coming next, *ippon kumite*. Each student and their partners would perform or defend against whichever technique Yamaoka *Sensei* assigned them. Then the line would rotate so that everyone ended up performing the drill with everyone else in the room. But because there was an odd number of students that day, Jonathan knew that some would not be paired off. Quickly, he calculated where he had to start in order to avoid ending up opposite his *sempai*. But after the third rotation, he found Murakami standing across from him. Either he had miscalculated or his *sempai* had traded positions with someone.

The far side was instructed to attack with a high roundhouse kick, *jodan mawashi geri*. Jonathan's side was to respond with a high outward block, then follow up with a reverse punch to the head. On the instructor's command, Murakami's side lashed out with head-high kicks in military-like precision.

Jonathan's forearm intercepted his *sempai's* bony shin perfectly. Had he been a split second slower, the kick would have smashed into the side of his head. But he had paid a price. As he stopped the kick, he heard something crack and a sharp pain shot up his left arm. In spite of it, Jonathan still managed to get off a reverse punch that caught Murakami square in the mouth. As his *sempai* angrily wiped the blood off his lips with the back of his hand, Jonathan readied himself for the attack he knew would be coming.

"*Yame!*" commanded Yamaoka.

The two boys straightened, but never took their eyes off each other. Yamaoka slid up Jonathan's sleeve and inspected his elbow. The upper and lower bones were no longer aligned properly.

"You will move to the side of the workout area and remain there until class is over," *Sensei* ordered.

After the initial jolt, his elbow had gone numb. But as he sat on the sidelines, watching, the numbness was gradually replaced by a sharp, burning pain. Even with Murakami smiling at him every time he rotated to a new partner, Jonathan soon couldn't ignore it any longer or fight back the tears.

"Poor little baby," said one of the green belts. "Maybe your mommy will come to wipe away your tears."

Jonathan sprang to his feet. "Don't talk about my mother!" he screamed, his voice breaking. "She's dead!"

"As is mine," the boy responded, now equally hot. "She was killed by one of your bombs!"

"I don't have any bombs! I never had any. I'm just a kid. Where would I get bombs?" he yelled, tears pouring down his cheeks against his will. Yamaoka wrapped his thick arm around his shoulder and shuttled him outside.

Kancho Kubo soon arrived. As he started to inspect the boy's arm, a group of students started to gather around them. So he led Jonathan away, down a long trail that wound through junipers, bright red azaleas, and pink blossoming cherry trees. It ended at the edge of a sheer cliff overlooking a lush green valley.

"Allow me to examine your arm," Kubo said, holding out his thick, calloused hand.

"Can it be fixed?" Jonathan asked as Kubo inspected his elbow.

"Yes. It is not broken," the Master General said, speaking slowly to ensure the young American understood. "It is merely dislocated. Please close your eyes."

The boy did as he was told.

"I want you to imagine you are a hawk, flying high above us."

"It is hard, *Kancho*. My arm hurts so bad, I can only think of it."

"Do not think, only see and feel. The boy who stands here on the earth is not you. The pain you think you feel is not the hawk's pain. You are the hawk. You are in the warm air, among the clouds."

"Yes, *Kancho*."

"Look down at the boy below. Do you see him?"

"Yes."

"What is he doing?"

"Crying."

"He has hurt his arm. But you feel no pain, only happiness that you are a hawk and not the boy, that you can fly while his feet are stuck to the earth."

"Okay."

"Someone is going to pull on the boy's arm to straighten the bones and make it well. I want the hawk to watch his face, to watch it closely to see if the boy is strong or weak." Gently, Kubo lifted Jonathan's bony, golden arm and grasped it tightly at the biceps and wrist. "Does the boy feel anything?"

"My arm hurts!"

"You are a hawk! Hawks do not have arms!"

"Yes, *Kancho*. I am a hawk, not a boy."

"What is the boy doing?"

"He cries," he said, tears flowing down his freckled cheeks.

"Is the hawk crying?"

"No, *Kancho*. Only the boy."

"Good. Forget the boy. Turn your head towards the sun. You must beat your wings as powerfully as you can and climb higher towards the bright round sun. Feel the warmth flowing through your wings and body, moving from your curved, sharp beak to your thick brown tail-feathers. You are above the clouds! You are free and powerful, god of all you see."

A smile spread across the boy's round face, melting the tension. Then Kubo pulled and twisted the crooked arm, snapping the dislocated parts back into place. As he did, a shudder swept through the boy's body. But it just as quickly vanished.

"You are a very good and brave hawk," said Kubo. "What would the good brave smart hawk like to do now?"

"To dive into the forest and catch a plump rabbit for you to eat."

"Then dive my little hawk." As the boy's mind focused on what he had been asked to do, Kubo studied the young American as if he seeing him for the first time.

"Why does Murakami hate me so?" Jonathan asked as they headed back.

"There are many reasons why one hates another. But honor is perhaps the most powerful. We say duty to our family, master, and Emperor presses more heavily on us than a mountain while death less than a feather. Yukio has been living under a great dishonor."

"But it is me who was dishonored. He attacked me."

"You are wrong, my little hawk. Your fight with Yukio began many years before you even met. It began when the Americans hung his father at war's end."

"His father was hanged?"

Kubo nodded.

"Why?"

"The details have never been fully released but from what I have heard, the Allies charged him with many so-called war crimes, mainly executing unarmed prisoners."

"Were they bad men?"

"On August 16, 1945, a day no Japanese will ever forget, the Emperor made his unprecedented broadcast. He called upon our people to do the unthinkable, to surrender to the Allies. It is impossible for one not Japanese to understand what that meant. General Murakami could not accept what he had been asked to do and ordered the over two hundred American and British prisoners in his possession to be taken to an open field outside the city of Yokohama. There, he and his aide executed each of them with their swords."

"Then he should have been punished, *neh?*" said Jonathan, half as a question. His eyes darted to Kubo's face to make sure he agreed. But the master's flat expression told him nothing.

"Although I suspect otherwise, as did your grandfather, many Japanese believe General Murakami was a good warrior, a filial retainer, dedicated to the Emperor and his country. He argued that the *Gunkan*, the military document that outlines the proper behavior of a man of *giri*, states clearly that a battle once started must be won. So if the surrender was illegal, then the Americans were still his enemy and so he had the right to execute his prisoners for their crimes against innocent Japanese civilians. Most of his prisoners were captured airmen, who he claimed had killed tens of thousands of Japanese during their fire-bombings. To this day, his supporters believe the Americans punished him simply for doing what any good warrior would have done, and many are still committed to avenging his death."

"Like the forty-seven *ronin*?"

"Yes," Kubo said, apparently surprised the boy knew the story. "There is a saying that a true son will not live in the same village as he who wrongs his brother, in the same country as he who wrongs his mother, or under the same sky as he who wrongs his father. With you, it is simple. But with Murakami, his task is an impossible one."

"What is simple for me?"

"To avenge the deaths of your father and mother, you have but one man to destroy. For Yukio, it would require killing millions to make his name pure once more." Kubo's narrow eyes searched the young American's puzzled face. "How do you feel about the man who killed your parents?"

"He was a nice man. His son, Saied, was my best friend."

"He brought the bomb that killed your father. Was that nice?"

"I don't think he meant to hurt him. I think he was just mad at Dr. Levy and his friends."

"But who died because he was mad at Dr. Levy? And who should have been more careful if he truly cared about your father?"

They walked in silence for a while.

"Sometimes I wish I had died too," said Jonathan, sharing with the Master General something he had often thought but never told anyone.

Kubo stared at the boy for several seconds, then put his arm around him. "But you did not. Everything has a reason. Can you think of any reasons to explain why you were spared?"

"To punish me?"

"Why would you be punished? You have done nothing."

"Neither did my father but he died. And it was my fault. I told him of the...*kaban*, the suitcase," he said, not knowing the Japanese word for briefcase. "If I had not said anything, he would still be alive."

"But you and your mother would have died in the explosion."

"I don't care."

"If your father was anything like his father," continued Kubo, his voice uncharacteristically soft, "I am sure he would be glad he died so that you and your mother might live."

Tears filled the boy's eyes and he had to look away. They walked a bit in silence as Jonathan struggled to regain control.

"It is normal for a son to feel guilt over a father's death. One's parents are the trunk of his family's tree. The sons and daughters, its branches. What cuts the trunk, cuts all. *Giri*, duty to one's parents, does not call for you to feel personal guilt for their deaths, only to feel the need for *kataki-uchi*, the avenging of their deaths."

"But it was me who...."

"Did you know, or did you have any reason to believe, that there was a bomb in the suitcase?"

Jonathan shook his head.

"Of course not. How could you?"

"But my mother's death was my fault too. If I had not gone outside, she wouldn't have followed me and the doctor would never have given her the pills that killed her."

"Where would both your parents be if the man had not walked in that night with his evil intent? It is he who is solely to blame."

"So it's not just my fault for getting my parents killed but also for not trying to kill Dr. Makram?"

Kubo chuckled. "Of course not. None of it is your fault. When Murakami fouled your bed...."

Jonathan's head snapped around. "You know?"

"Nothing here escapes my knowledge."

"I thought it was him but I could not prove it." He shuddered as if he could still feel the stinky goo on his skin.

"The only proof that is important is that within your heart. What does your heart tell you?" The answer was clear on the boy's face. "Do you not feel the pull to seek revenge? Does your blood not boil at the thought that Yukio smiles and tells everyone that you are a coward? Do you think he believes your father to have been a brave, good man? Or does he believe him a coward as he believes you to be?"

"Is that what he thinks?"

"And what he tells your classmates."

They walked again in silence. Then Kubo said, "If you one day met a man who told you he had poured excrement, urine, and vomit on your father and your father had done nothing about it, how would you feel about your father? Would you feel proud to be the son of such a man? Or would you feel shame? Well, that is how your son could one day feel."

Jonathan said nothing but his anger was rising, flushing his face.

"Now you know how it feels to be Japanese," Kubo said before stopping the boy and looking him square in the face. "But one must never make the mistake of being foolish in his quest for honor. A brave but stupid man is perhaps better than a smart coward. But he is far inferior to one who is brave, smart, and victorious."

That night, Jonathan couldn't sleep. His elbow burned as if on fire. But there were also the images in his mind of the filthy bucket and the sound of laughter as the putrid, slimy mixture streamed down around his body. Soon, he couldn't stand it any longer. He snatched up his sandals and tiptoed outside.

A three-quarter moon floated overhead, illuminating the grounds below, forcing him to keep to the shadows as he made his way across the inner compound to Murakami's dorm. There, he crept up the stairs towards the second floor sleeping-bay, shifting his weight slowly onto each new step to keep the old wood from creaking.

The darkened stairwell opened into a large, open room, partially lit by moonlight flowing in through the open side *shoji*. He held his breath and listened. Hearing nothing but deep breathing, he started towards Murakami's bed. A mysterious whistling sound froze him in place, then something struck him softly in the back of the neck. He tried to turn, to see what had struck him, but the room went black and the floor seemed to melt beneath him.

10

When Jonathan opened his eyes, he found himself in an exquisite little room. He had recently begun studying *cha-no-yu*, the tea ceremony, in class so he knew from the room's emptiness, the delicacy and fragrance of its cedar supports and beams, and the familiar utensils and earthen cups atop an ancient cabinet that it was a tea house. But whose?

He tiptoed to the doorless entrance and peeked out at the *Zen* garden surrounding the tiny house. There was no one there and no clue as to where he was or to whom it belonged. Except for a five-foot high enclosing wall, which he could easily vault over if he chose, there was nothing to prevent him from leaving. So he sat down and waited.

It had baffled him why a military school would require its students to learn how to drink tea. Back home, tea had only been for girls. Now and then, his mother invited her lady friends over for it and once bought a plastic tea set as a birthday present for one of the Levy sisters. But he had not known any men who drank tea.

"Good! You are awake," said Kubo, stepping through the doorway.

Jonathan sprang to his feet and bowed. "How did I get here?"

"I brought you. You were preparing to commit an unwise act."

"I did as you told me."

"No. That is not what I said."

"But you said...."

"I told you an honorable man always seeks to punish those who have wronged him or his family. You failed to heed the part about cowardice being only slightly better than failure due to poor planning. You cannot win every battle through *tamashii*, through fighting spirit. Often your opponent will be bigger, stronger, or more skilled. You can only hope to defeat enemies such as these through your ability to control the fighting environment. Unless you are attacked, a battle must only occur at a time and place that best guarantees your success."

Jonathan started to speak but *Kancho* stopped him.

"If you are to gain true revenge," he continued, "you must not do it as your enemy did. If he is a coward, attacking while you slept, you must defeat him like a man, where all can see. Study your enemy. Learn his habits, his strengths, his weaknesses. And only then, when your skills have been honed equal to the task, should you enact a plan that cannot fail."

"That could take a long time."

"Then you must begin your journey immediately, before anything can rob you of this opportunity. Defeat him with your mind in the classroom. Defeat him with your mind and body on the *dojo* floor for all to see – not in the dark, behind his back like a cowardly *yakuza*. Go. Rest. Begin tomorrow with a new resolve and let nothing stand in your way."

Long before the first bell sounded, Murakami quickly dressed and headed outside, as he did each morning. The sky was black and the air damp. The aroma of pine permeated the dark forest as he headed up the sodden trail.

Thrup. Thrup.

The sharp, repetitive sound stopped him in his tracks. He cocked his head and listened, then broke into a run.

The double-row of *makiwara* rose from the earth like black fingers in the twilight. Rhythmically punching an end board was the dark silhouette of another boy. A twig snapped underfoot and the silhouette turned. It was Jonathan.

"Mother-fornicating *gaijin*," Murakami said loudly, not caring who heard him. He took up a quick stance, gritted his teeth, and drove his fist deep into the layer of hemp rope that thinly padded the stiff tapered end of the punching board. The blow reddened his knuckles but he hit it again, even harder.

Jonathan drove his fist into his *makiwara*, bowing it well back and creating a solid *cracking* sound. He had been coming to the *makiwara* forest for weeks, after learning of Murakami's regular morning workouts there. If his *sempai* was trying to harden his knuckles in order to more seriously hurt him one day, he had to surpass him. Until that morning, he had kept his daily training sessions secret. Having plateaued, however, he thought the side by side competition with his *sempai* would stimulate him to greater heights. And he was right.

Thrup, *thud*, *thrup*, *thud*, the two boys punched their boards, their blows falling louder and louder as each tried to drown out the sound of the other's strikes.

Murakami's morning *makiwara* workouts were not the only thing Jonathan had discovered about his *sempai* when he followed *Kancho* Kubo's advice. He had also learned that Yukio Murakami had been the second of his family to attend the Dai Kan. His father, the infamous war criminal General Shinji Murakami, had been the first. Others had applied before them, their pathetic applications still on file in which most offered thinly masked bribes or threats, but all had been rejected. No reason had ever been given, or likely needed. To be even a distant member of the Imperial Family was the highest of honors. To be descended from *samurai*, as were most at the Dai Kan, was only slightly less prestigious. But except for the last few years when comic books and contemporary fashion lent it a romantic quality it never possessed during its actual existence, no one was openly proud of having descended from *ninja* – except the Murakamis. A straight familial line could be drawn directly from Yukio to Sandayu Momochi, one of the most infamous *ninja* in Japanese history.

Although no investigation had ever been undertaken, from what Jonathan could find, there was little question in anyone's mind as to why the Dai Kan had finally relented and allowed one Murakami and then his son to enter. A substantial bribe had been paid to Sugiyama, Master General at the time.

Out of the corner of his eye, Jonathan could see that Murakami, after every couple of punches, glanced over to stare daggers at him. While his focus was misdirected, his punch hit at a bad angle and peeled the skin off his middle knuckle. "*Che!*" he cursed. Jonathan stifled a smile but kept his rhythm constant. *Thrup, thrup.*

The forest was silent the next morning as Murakami jogged towards the *makiwara* stand, his hand bandaged. His face soured when he saw Jonathan preparing to begin his hand conditioning work. "Mother fornicating *gaijin!*" yelled the young Japanese.

"Get used to it!" he yelled back, wanting to antagonize him. He launched his first punch. *Thrup.*

Murakami jerked his left foot back and drove his undamaged left fist hard into the punching board. "*Che!*" he cursed.

Jonathan smiled.

Besides his predawn *makiwara* workouts, Jonathan also secretly stepped up his *karate* training in other areas as well. After finishing his homework, he spent most of his free time performing hundreds of pushups and sit-ups each day, along with an even greater number of reps of *kihon* and *kata*.

He found the repetition of kata to be especially soothing, almost therapeutic. When performing one, he could focus so completely on each move and the position of every part of his body – the angle of each joint, the amount of tension in each muscle, the direction of his gaze, the rhythm of his breathing, his *chakugan*, the power and focus within each block, strike, and kick – that everything else – his *sempai*, the cruelty of other boys and teachers, worries about coming exams – found no room to exist in his consciousness. It gave him a respite from his troubles like a psychological island.

Over time, most – although certainly not all – of his instructors gradually eased up on him. A couple even complimented him on occasion. But while they had gradually climbed off his back, he had climbed on. Nothing he did was ever good enough. At times, his body seemed outright traitorous, perpetually too weak or uncoordinated to do all he asked of it, often flooding him with muscle-singeing fatigue in an effort to persuade him to quit. His mind could learn things – like *karate* techniques and *kata* – far faster than his body could perform them to his standard. As his mind grew stronger, his body seemed to lag further and further behind.

But as unhappy as he was with himself, his skill had vastly improved as a result of his obsessive training regimen. His punches flattened out and penetrated deeper into the *makiwara* or the heavy body bag, no longer slapping upwards or sideways at the end. Force equals mass times acceleration, he had learned in science. The more of his body he could put into his techniques and the faster he could accelerate it, the more force or power he generated. So he always put everything he had into everything he did. "Practice every technique as if your life depended on it," Gichin Funakoshi, the father of Japanese *karate* had said, "and should your life ever be put at risk, your techniques will be up to the task."

A new boy had been accepted into the Dai Kan without fanfare or explanation. He just walked into Jonathan's math class one day. Normally, boys didn't enter the Dai Kan in the middle of a term.

The only open seat was at the very back of the room, next to Jonathan. The teacher bowed repeatedly to the new boy, calling him "Yoritomo *Sama*," and asked one of those up front to surrender their chair. But the new boy refused to displace anyone and happily took the chair next to Jonathan.

Kiyoshi Yoritomo was handsome enough to be in the movies. He had long black hair, unlike the crew cuts worn by everyone else. A year older, he was stockier and a head taller than Jonathan and most of the other boys in the class. His irreverent attitude permeated everything he did, even his style of dress. His uniform was never quite up to code. The top button of his jacket was often left undone. Or he may not have seen fit to button any of them. Smudges or smears of food or dirt or whatever he had done or consumed last were always in evidence somewhere – on his sleeve or collar or the knees or seat of his pants.

Jonathan found him unusually carefree for a Japanese. While most others covered their mouths with their hands when they laughed, Yoritomo would tilt his head back and laugh without reservation, his mouth so wide Jonathan could see his tonsils fluttering.

Although he could easily poke fun at himself or accept it in return from someone he had teased, he would not tolerate it from anyone mean spirited. The first time one of the meaner boys made him the butt of an unkind joke, the sparkle left Yoritomo's eyes and he stared so intensely into the eyes of the other boy that he quickly bowed in apology. And, Jonathan noted, the boy didn't give him a regular bow, the one between equals; he gave Yoritomo a full formal bow, as if to someone more senior. The other boys stayed well away from him. Jonathan naturally assumed it was because he was not only bigger but a brown belt in *karate*, far ahead of everyone else.

When Yoritomo first strolled to the back of the classroom and plopped down on the seat beside him, Jonathan had avoided talking to him or even acknowledging his presence, afraid he was being set up. But Yoritomo never seemed to notice he was a *gaijin*. In his eyes, he apparently wasn't any different from anyone else. In fact, he actually seemed to prefer him to the other boys. As a result, Jonathan found it impossible not to like him. He was friendly and funny and couldn't care less what anyone else thought of him, as long as they weren't rude or disrespectful.

Jonathan and Yoritomo had two classes together, math and science. A couple of weeks after that first day, Yoritomo didn't show up for math. As everyone opened their textbooks to that day's section, an aide leaned into the room and whispered something to the teacher, who looked right at Jonathan, sending a chill of fear through the boy. "Lusk, you are wanted in *Kancho's* office."

"*Sayonara, Gaijin San*! No offense, but may it be our final farewell," said one of the boys, as Jonathan gathered up his things and hurried out.

The voice that greeted him when he knocked on the Master General's *shoji* was clearly not *Kancho's*. It sounded familiar, although he couldn't place where he had heard it before. To his surprise it was Yoritomo who greeted him. Even more surprising, Hiroko was there too, with a beautiful young girl sitting next to her on the *tatami*. Jonathan wanted to run to Hiroko and hug her, but she had never been much of a hugger, so he awkwardly stood in the doorway, waiting to be told what to do.

Hiroko waved him over and he ran to her, where she gave him an uncharacteristically warm hug. She patted the mat beside him and he sat down opposite the girl, who wore a *kimono* exactly like Hiroko's, her jet black hair done in exactly the same style. His grandmother gestured towards Yoritomo. "Jonason Chan, this is my nephew, Kiyoshi Yoritomo, who is a student here too. And you, of course, remember our Nanami Chan. They are my brother's wonderful children."

The two boys waved a hello to each other. Then Jonathan looked at Nanami, who was pressed hard against Hiroko's side. He was amazed that this was the same homely chatterbox he had met at their house years earlier. Now, she was shy and beautiful, so beautiful that when she finally raised her eyes to his, he had to look away.

"While her mother recovers from surgery, my little Nanami *Chan* has been keeping me such wonderful company," Hiroko said, giving the girl a hug. "You should be most honored. She would not stop pestering me until I brought her to see you." The girl's face flushed red. She whispered rapidly into Hiroko's ear. "And see her brother too, of course."

Yoritomo laughed. "Nana is such a copycat. She copies everything Auntie does. Auntie buys a new *kimono*, Nana has to have one exactly like it. Auntie gets a new hairdo, she has to have hers done the same. Auntie married an American..."

Nanami's eyes flared and her hand shot out and slapped Yoritomo on the arm. "That is not true! You are so cruel."

Yoritomo grabbed his arm and pulled it to his chest as if it were broken. Nanami scooted over and kissed his arm. "I am sorry," she said, then glanced up to see a big grin on her brother's face.

"You cannot hurt me. I am made of steel," Yoritimo declared, flexing his muscles like a bodybuilder. His sister slapped his arm again but he ignored the blow, mouthing, "It is true" to Jonathan, which earned him another slap.

"Kiyoshi Chan tells me you are in some of the same classes," said Hiroko.

"We have science and math together," Jonathan offered.

"My two best subjects," said Yoritomo.

Jonathan's eyes flicked to Yoritomo in surprise, then saw his big grin and the two boys laughed.

"I am told Jonason's grades are among the top of his class," said Hiroko, matter of factly, as if it were only natural. "Perhaps the two of you can study together."

"Sure," Jonathan said, a bit too eagerly. "If you want?"

"Okay," said Yoritomo, "I guess I can help you with your science and math."

Hiroko found no amusement in it, but Jonathan couldn't help but chuckle.

"Could you help me with my *karate?*" Jonathan asked.

"Always happy to have someone to beat up," a smiling Yoritomo responded.

"I intend to formally adopt Jonason," Hiroko announced, out of the blue. "So you will soon be cousins."

Jonathan tried to stifle both his surprise and joy without much success.

Yoritomo smiled. "Welcome to our crazy family."

"It is a bit premature to celebrate," offered Hiroko. "Much has yet to be done legally."

Nanami whispered into Hiroko's ear. "I am sure he would not mind," said Hiroko, turning to Jonathan. "Nanami Chan would like a tour of the grounds."

A wave of panic swept through Jonathan. "Kiyoshi probably knows it better than I do."

"Sorry," said Yoritomo, grinning. "I have a meeting with a teacher."

Left without a choice, Jonathan escorted the girl outside and showed her around, much to his excitement and gut-wrenching fear.

"Do you still eat only teriyaki?" she asked as they walked.

He chuckled shyly. "No, I acquired a more proper taste in food. If I hadn't, I would have starved to death years ago."

Everywhere they went, students and faculty stared at them, many clearly disapproving of a princess walking with a *gaijin*, others simply love struck by her beauty.

"Is there a place we can go where everyone is not gawking at us?" she asked.

"I go to the river to be alone but it's back in the forest."

"Sounds perfect."

He led her along the little-used trail he knew by heart. The midday heat had prodded the towering pines to release their fragrant oils. With their wonderful aroma filling the air, a warm blue sky above, and Nanami beside him, the day was magical.

As they walked, the old Nanami began to resurface. She asked endless questions about their daily routine, the time they arose each morning, when they went to bed, the subjects he studied, what he liked best and least. She asked about the other students – if they were nice to him, if they accepted him as a *gaijin*.

When she abruptly fell silent, he was afraid he had said something wrong. His pronunciation of Japanese had vastly improved but wasn't perfect and had gotten him into trouble on more than one occasion. He nervously glanced over at her.

"Do you have a girlfriend?" she asked with less confidence in her voice than before. "Auntie said she did not know."

Jonathan blushed. "There are no girls here, only boys. So... no girls to have as girlfriends."

"Would you like one?"

"Sure, I guess," he said, thinking it a hypothetical question.

"I would be your girlfriend, if you find me acceptable?"

He searched her face to see if she was joking. "You must have millions of boys who would fight to be your boyfriend."

"Very few have the courage to even speak to me. And those who do are arrogant and unappealing." Her small chin dipped down and her eyes angled sweetly up to his. "Are you afraid to be my boyfriend?"

"I'm not afraid," he said, definitely afraid. "I just... don't think it would be a good idea. Your parents would not approve."

"Then we will keep it our secret. Give me your hand."

"Why?" he asked, jerking his hand behind his back.

"Because that is what girlfriends and boyfriends do, they hold hands. Do you mind?"

"I guess not."

When she took hold of his hand, it was as if he had suddenly connected to some wonderful force that filled his body like helium, making every inch of him light and tingly. He chuckled in joy.

"What is wrong?" she asked.

"Nothing. I am just happy that I get to miss math class," he lied.

It was the most perfect day of his life. He didn't yet know that it would become even more memorable, etching itself so deeply into his memory that for the remainder of his life it would make him smile whenever he thought of it.

When they reached Uemezu Falls she asked, "How deep is the water?"

"Over our heads."

"Good! Do you know how to swim?"

"Sure."

"Then we will swim!"

He watched, paralyzed with shock as she stripped off her clothes, tossed them over a bush, and strolled naked into the water. Turning, she waved for him to join her. He had never seen a naked girl before and his eyes refused to stay where he commanded them.

"Auntie told me your people are ashamed of our human bodies," she said, strolling back onto the bank and helping him out of his student jacket. "Here, everyone bathes together. I have seen many, many boys before. So you need not be shy." She undid his belt and pulled down his pants. He stood motionless in his briefs. When she reached for them, he jumped back – but not fast enough. She slid his shorts down, then stood back and studied him, a puzzled look on her face. "Your penis is much larger than those of the other boys I have seen. Are all *gaijins* thusly?"

He shrugged. Nanami was so nonchalant about it all, as if it were an everyday affair, that he began to relax a bit, though he kept his body sideways as much as he could. She waded back into the stream. When he didn't follow, she turned and splashed him. Soon, they were both laughing and playing.

Too soon, the temple bell bonged in the distance.

"We had better get back," he said. The two dressed, then strolled back towards the main campus, hand in hand. As they ambled past the dorms, a teacher confronted them.

"Please come with me," he said, his face red with anger.

"Don't tell them about us swimming," Jonathan whispered in Nanami's ear as the teacher led them to *Kancho* Kubo's office. The teacher motioned for Jonathan to wait outside, while he escorted Nanami inside. Soon, Hiroko emerged and sat down on the step beside Jonathan. He couldn't bring himself to even look at her.

"You were gone so long that everyone was worried," she said, her voice consoling. But he could tell she was holding something back. "Our uncle is not just the ruler of Japan," Hiroko finally began. "He is considered by many to be a god. In the old days, to even look upon him could cost a person his life. The teacher thought it unacceptable for a *gaijin* to hold hands with an Imperial Princess. He will be seeking employment elsewhere."

Jonathan stared at his muddy shoes.

"Do not worry, Nanami explained that you are cousins, or soon will be, and she merely held your hand as she does with her other cousins."

He could breathe again. Looking up at his grandmother, he smiled with relief.

"But," she began, her face growing serious, sending a wave of fear back through him, "I know her very well and understand what may have occurred." Hiroko's gaze drifted off into the distance, her brown eyes misting. "I understand it as well as any person can."

She lightly stroked Jonathan's cheek. "Hearts know no borders, religion, nationality, or class distinction, as your grandfather and I proved. I also know well the cost of such a choice. Even in America, we were never completely accepted, and I a member of the Imperial Family. Here, it was tolerated because of his lofty international position. But Nanami's parents will surely not welcome this."

"Will she get in trouble?"

"Do not worry about Nana Chan. She tends to want what she cannot or is not supposed to have, as I also did. So it must be your responsibility to be strong and ensure you two remain just cousins, at least until you are older and know the full weight of such a decision. Can you do that?"

He nodded.

"Good."

The tension drained from his face and shoulders. He had learned several lessons that day. One of them was how a small and seemingly insignificant word like "but" could so quickly wipe away all the joy he had experienced only seconds earlier.

"But one of the students followed you and saw you and Nanami swimming unclothed. Are you two prepared to explain that to her father?"

11

Yoritomo was telling a joke about a wise old farmer caught by the Imperial Guard fishing in the Imperial moat as he and Jonathan walked to class the next day. "Your sister shows her naked body to *gaijin*," someone yelled from the middle of a group of boys. A wave of fear shot through Jonathan. But it took Yoritomo a few seconds to realize what the boy had said.

"Who said that?" he demanded as he shoved his way to the center of the group. No one volunteered anything. Under Yoritomo's scrutiny, however, all eyes drifted onto Murakami. "So the shit carrying *yakuza* scum thinks himself good enough to spy on a royal princess," spat Yoritomo, his mouth curling in disgust.

Murakami bristled, his eyes burning into Yoritomo's face.

"Common *benjo* trash like you," Yoritomo continued, "are not good enough to even look her way. But I guess we should not have expected anything more from one of your despicable lineage."

"Your sister is a *gaijin joro*…" started Murakami.

Yoritomo's fist smashed into his mouth before he could finish. The blow snapped Murakami's head back, bloodying his nose, splitting his lip, and knocking him back a couple of feet. The boy spit out a tooth, then covered his mouth and ran off, crying.

"I expect silence will reveal who among you descended from *samurai* and people of honor," Yoritomo said to the remaining boys. "A *yakuza* insulted an Imperial Princess. Until recently, he would have been killed on the spot." The boys bowed in agreement.

When later asked by Dai Kan staff about the incident, no one remembered seeing what had happened. And no one pressed them on it.

Jonathan hadn't mentioned anything about the swimming incident to Yoritomo. He was too ashamed and assumed he knew about it but hadn't said anything because he didn't approve. After the confrontation with Murakami, however, he learned that Yoritomo hadn't mentioned it because he considered it merely the Japanese way.

"Does your father know?" Jonathan asked.

Yoritomo threw back his head and laughed. "You are still alive, are you not? You will know when he knows."

12

During the eight years since her and Nanami's surprise visit to the Dai Kan, Hiroko's battle with lung cancer, the cost for a lifetime of cigarettes, was nearing its end. She had never been one to allow anyone or anything to dictate what she did or didn't do. And she told Jonathan she wasn't about to allow doctors or the cancer eating her lungs away to cheat her of attending the year-end Dai Kan awards ceremony, where he was to be honored.

Bone-thin and ghostly pale, Hiroko sat in a wheelchair directly in front of a raised platform that had been erected at the edge of the exercise field. A tiny plastic hose transported oxygen from a green cylinder attached to her wheelchair to her nostrils. In spite of her frail condition, her back and neck were still as rigid and straight as steel bars.

Nanami, now an elegant and even more beautiful young woman, perched on the edge of a chair beside her aunt, clasping Hiroko's spotted hand in both of hers, as Reiko hovered behind them. She too had grown into a mature woman. But her farmer's lineage had given her a stockier build and rougher features.

Hiroko's sunken eyes sparkled as Jonathan strode formally up the steps and bowed to *Kancho* Kubo. "The last award," announced the Master General, "is for the student who scored the highest on the National

Exams – Jonason Lusk – who, I am proud to say, scored a perfect 900, one of only three in all of Japan to do so."

Jonathan formally accepted the scroll with both hands, then bowed and touched it to his forehead. A few of the students and parents applauded; most did nothing. But their silence was drowned out by the wild hoots and clapping of Yoritomo and the more restrained applause of Nanami, Reiko, and even Hiroko.

Jonathan bounded down the steps, eager to show his award to his newly adopted mother. As he hit the ground, a taller but still skinny Murakami intentionally bumped into him, knocking him sideways. He tripped over a chair and fell, tearing the certificate he had just received.

"You! Rude boy!" Hiroko called, stabbing a bony finger at him.

Murakami pointed at himself.

"Yes, you. Come here!" she commanded.

Murakami dismissed her with a wave of his hand and started away. Kubo grabbed him by the collar and butt of his pants and lifted him onto his tiptoes. He half-shoved, half-carried him over to where Hiroko sat.

"What is your name?" demanded Hiroko.

"Why?"

Kubo slapped the back of his head.

"Murakami Yukio."

Hiroko's eyes narrowed. "Murakami? What was your father's name?"

"Shinji. He was a general and a great hero."

Hiroko blanched. "What is your relationship to my son?"

"I am his *sempai*. I…"

"Leave us!" Hiroko said, waving him away. She turned her fierce eyes onto Kubo, who hung his head. "Jonason Chan, please leave us for a few minutes."

Reiko, Yoritomo, Nanami, and Jonathan ambled towards the back of the seating area, where students had congregated and those who had received awards chatted with their parents. Nanami stopped to dig something out of her purse, forcing Jonathan to double back.

"Do you see that man watching us from near the stage?" she whispered.

A suited man stared at them through dark glasses.

"He is here at my father's insistence to ensure we do nothing inappropriate."

"Then we must make sure we don't," he said, getting her drift.

"I am sorry I have not written for the last couple of months," she said as they continued on. "My father discovered your letters and demanded I stop. He even has staff watching me. But I will soon be attending the university and lose my censors. Then, I will be able to write again, if you still want me to?"

"Of course, I do," he gushed as they caught up with the other two.

A group of fifty or so students milled around at the back of the field, all eyes riveted onto the two young women. One boy shoved another out into the open space between the two groups but he frantically raced back and wiggled his way inside the protective anonymity of the herd.

Mitsuru stood apart from the group as he always had. He had once greeted Jonathan as they passed on the walkway and been attacked so harshly by the others that he had never done it again. As his classmates watched in amazement, Mitsuru boldly crossed no-man's-land, bowed to Jonathan and offered a word of praise for the honor he had brought to the Dai Kan. Jonathan thanked him, then introduced him to Nanami and Reiko.

With Mitsuru's success, boys rushed across the open ground and enveloped the four. People who had avoided or ignored or insulted Jonathan since his arrival at the Kan, now praised him – and not just for that day's award. They praised him for things he never even thought anyone knew about, like getting an Outstanding on his paper about the Battle of Sekigahara or a successful *ippon* against the student who was now praising him.

"Why was such a horrible person assigned to my son?" Hiroko pressed Kubo.

"The former..."

"Surely you are aware that his father was a *yakuza* high boss?"

"Of course. Even though it was before my..."

"Are you also aware that informed sources believe his father's henchmen murdered my husband?"

Clearly Kubo did not know that.

"He has lost everyone," she continued. "Soon I will be gone as well and he will have no one but..." Her eyes burned into Kubo. "I cannot tell you how disappointed I am in you and this school."

Kubo's body sagged under the sting of her assault.

"Please allow me to spend time with my son," she said, waving him away.

As the Master General bowed and backed meekly off, Jonathan caught the pale, drained look on Hiroko's face and hurried over. "You should not have come, Mother," he said, using the term she had asked him to use. "You are not well enough."

"I am most proud of you, Jonason *Chan*. I could not possibly have missed it."

"Thank you, Mother. I have requested permission to be with you for your surgery."

She shook her head. "I would prefer you remain here. The operation is but a futile attempt by the doctors. I am at peace and prepared for my end. The only thing that concerns me is your future. But I believe I have put everything in order to ensure you will be well cared for."

Jonathan's eyes misted. "You should not worry about me."

She reached out and gently touched his face. "I could not have asked for a better son nor come to love you more had I given you birth myself. Your letters and calls gave me strength in the darkest of times." She pulled him to her and hugged him with surprising strength. Tears ran down both their cheeks as Nanami came up behind Jonathan. She was crying too.

Hiroko took Jonathan's and Nanami's hands and kissed them, then pressed them together as she looked into their eyes. "You two remind me so much of Eli and I when we were young. I would die a very happy woman if I knew you would also enjoy the wonderful life we had together. I still miss him more than words can say."

Nanami's chaperon strode towards them. "How dare you presume to approach me while I am speaking privately with my son and niece!" spat Hiroko. The man stopped, bowed, and backed hastily away.

After saying their goodbyes, Jonathan watched Reiko and Nanami push Hiroko up the path, knowing it would likely be the last time he saw her alive.

A few weeks later, the letter arrived from Reiko.

"Dear Little Brother, I write some bad news. The cancer within your mother's lungs finally overtook her. She died today, joining your grandfather. I am most sorry. I hope to see you at the funeral. Love, Reiko."

Jonathan pulled a stack of letters, held together by a rubber band, from his footlocker and added Reiko's to it. Then, he returned the stack, silently donned his *karate gi*, and trudged up the path to the *makiwara* grove, oblivious to the cold rain soaking his hair and *gi*. Squaring his stance, he drew his fist back, and began pounding the punching board over and over with all his might, wanting to either break the *makiwara* or his hand to relieve the pain and anger roiling up inside him.

The sprawling Meiji shrine in Tokyo had been built on the site of an ancient iris garden, where Emperor Meiji and Empress Shoken had reportedly spent much of their free time. Jonathan and Yoritomo, dressed in their Dai Kan uniforms, strode through the shrine's *torii* gate and up the gravel path towards its central sanctuary.

At the entrance to the inner courtyard, Jonathan hesitated, not eager to enter the place where the last of his family would be cremated. Yoritomo put his arm around his friend and they continued.

Hiroko's frail body lay on a raised viewing platform made of flawless fragrant cedar. Behind her loomed the Imperial Shrine, her family's shrine, reportedly containing the ashes of Emperor Meiji and his wife. Jonathan gazed at his adopted mother's face. She was smiling, the cords of pain no longer contorting her face. He was thankful she was at peace.

The Emperor, Hiroko's uncle, and his wife sat nearby in the ornate gold leaf and maroon velvet Meiji thrones moved to the site for the funeral. Thirty or forty plush chairs were arrayed in rows behind them, all filled except for several at the rear.

Jonathan could feel the royal couple's eyes on him as he leaned over and kissed Hiroko's forehead. Keeping his head bowed to hide the tears Hiroko would have hated, he hurried towards the back row of seats. The Empress whispered something to Yoritomo, who jogged over and quickly returned with Jonathan in tow. She clasped his hand in both of hers as she and the Emperor spoke in their low sing-song voices about their beloved Hiroko *Sama* and happy memories from when she was a little girl.

When Yoritomo touched Jonathan's shoulder, letting him know they should move on, he bowed apologetically, then scurried away, intending to find a seat in the back row. Yoritomo grabbed his sleeve. His friend's eyes scanned the front row of family seats, searching for two empty chairs. There was only one, Yoritomo's.

"It's okay," Jonathan said. "She told them I wouldn't be here." Hiroko had actually left instructions that he not attend her funeral. He had buried enough family already, she had said, and his time would be better served by staying focused on his studies. But Yoritomo wouldn't allow it.

A wizened old man, standing inconspicuously against the back wall, snapped his bony fingers and immediately a chair was rushed over. As the two sat down, the audience of mostly members of the royal family clearly had differing opinions about the presence of the young American. Some looked at him with sad, sympathetic eyes, others glared coldly. Yoritomo turned in his seat and stared the hateful ones in the eye. Some looked away, but others met him glare with glare.

"Let it go. I'm used to it," Jonathan told his friend.

"Well, I am not!"

What did bother Jonathan was Reiko's absence. Nanami was there. He had caught a glimpse of her beside her father. But he had not seen Reiko.

Following the short Shinto ceremony, Hiroko was cremated. As often happened, her body was not completely reduced to ash. Bits of bone remained. It was Jonathan's job, as her closest family member, to remove each unburned piece with a pair of chopsticks and place it into her urn. It was not a task he would have chosen voluntarily. But it was his duty and he did it diligently as her memory deserved.

A massive white tent billowed in the gentle breeze. From the music and chatter inside, Jonathan could hear that the reception was well in progress by the time he finished. He also knew there was no chance he would be allowed to speak with Nanami. Her father would never allow it. But Reiko had said she would be there and he had been looking forward to spending time with her.

Two household staff members drew back the tent flaps as he approached, revealing an angry Nanami, who shuffled towards him as rapidly as her stilted *geta* sandals and form-fitting *kimono* would allow. He froze, afraid he had done something wrong. Then he saw her father on her heels. Prince Yoritomo grabbed his daughter by the arm but she yanked free and continued.

With tears flowing down her cheeks, the princess stopped in front of Jonathan and bowed formally. "I am very sorry for your loss," she said, her voice breaking. "She was a most wonderful woman."

Jonathan bowed formally to her and then her father, who stood awkwardly beside his daughter. "I am very sorry for the loss of your sister, sir," he said to the Prince, then turned to Nanami. "She always loved you as if you were her own child. She could not have loved anyone more."

Nanami bowed. Prince Yoritomo nodded grudgingly, then took his daughter's arm and led her back to their table. A tent full of eyes stayed glued on Jonathan as he searched for Reiko. She wasn't there.

Long ago, he had gotten used to the cold or hateful stares – he had even come to expect them. But with the loss of Hiroko, Reiko's absence, and Nanami and Yoritomo forbidden from being near him, he felt so alone that he left the tent, wanting only to return to the Kan.

Maybe this was the real reason Hiroko hadn't wanted him to attend her funeral, he thought as he trudged across the yard.

"Jonason!"

A woman's voice echoed around the courtyard. He glanced back, thinking it might be Nanami but no one was there. "Jonason!" he heard again and spotted Reiko waving from the back of an alcove.

He ran over and gave her a hug. "I'm so glad you came," he said. "Are you hungry?"

"Am I never not?" she asked, and they both laughed.

"Then come on."

The Household Staff drew aside the tent entrance. Reiko took one look inside and balked. "I cannot go in there."

"Why not?"

"It is not my place."

"It's not mine either but I went in."

Nanami shuffled over, to her father's obvious chagrin. Reiko bowed to her knees but Nanami raised her up and hugged her like a sister. Arm in arm, she led her to the elegant serving tables, lavishly covered with food and drink. The former maid's eyes flared at the opulence.

Prince Yoritomo got to his feet and angrily waved his daughter back. "I had better return," said Nanami, "before he has another heart attack." She glanced quickly into Jonathan's eyes. Even though nothing was said, her beautiful almond eyes were so open to him that he felt he could read her thoughts and see deep into her heart. Within that split second, more was said than could have been revealed during a day, a week, a month, a year of conversation.

Jonathan handed a plate to Reiko and pointed toward a dish. "Look. *Fugu*." The server bowed and placed mounds on their plates. "What else?" Jonathan asked.

"For me, nothing. I am the world's most happy woman. *Fugu* and my brother. My heart is overflowing with joy!"

Jonathan filled his plate with other exotic Japanese dishes, mainly things he thought she would enjoy and gestured towards an open table at the back. But Reiko shook her head and rushed outside, where she led him to a bench on the far side of the courtyard.

When she took her first bite of *fugu*, she closed her eyes and hummed.

"What will you do now?" he asked.

"I am going to Kyushu to work for a family in Kumamoto," she said, pulling a sheet of paper out of her pocket. "This is the address."

"Kyushu is a long ways away. Couldn't you find something closer?"

"Unfortunately, no. Jobs are difficult to find and many are without work."

"As soon as the estate is settled, I will have money to reopen the house. Then you can come home."

She kissed him on the cheek. "Home," she said. "What a wonderful word."

"Did she ever say anything about my grandfather's death?" he asked.

"Only *yakuza*."

"Which group?"

"She said she feared more information would put you in danger."

"From who?"

Reiko shrugged, then eyed his untouched plate. He handed it to her and she went to work on his *fugu*.

13

———

Yoritomo ran up the Dai Kan's central pathway, weaving his way around the mass of students heading in the opposite direction for their noon meal. He plopped down on the grass beside Jonathan, who had already started eating his *bento* lunch.

"My sister sent this for you," said Yoritomo, handing Jonathan a letter. He sniffed his hand and curled up his nose as he wiped his palm on the grass. "She must have dunked it in perfume."

Jonathan slid his finger along the edge to open it.

"No, not now!" Yoritomo pleaded. "I just remembered I have a Bio test in…" he said, glancing at his wristwatch "…thirty-five minutes."

Jonathan tucked the envelope into his pocket and picked up his biology book. "What are you having trouble with?" he asked, but Yoritomo was no longer looking at him; he was watching students scoot off the walkway and bow low to someone.

A man strode past. He was dressed like an old warriors, *hakama* pants, woven top, a winged *samurai* over vest, and stilted *geta* sandals.

"It is Aoshima *San*. He is a Kami," Yoritomo said.

"You think so?"

"I know so. The Kami used to guard our family, before Sugiyama messed things up." Yoritomo waved. "Aoshima *San*!"

The man stopped and glanced over.

"It is me, Kiyoshi Yoritomo!"

The man bowed formally, then continued on.

"I am going to take the Kami Kan test," Yoritomo announced to Jonathan.

"You never told me."

"I just decided."

"I thought you had to have top grades?"

"If my father makes a request, they will not say no. You should apply too."

"I'm a *gaijin*."

"But if you could, would you?"

"Who wouldn't?"

Hirokazu Aoshima waited at attention. In addition to his style of dress, he also had the classic build of many of the best *samurai* of antiquity – thin, wiry, and quick. His face, like his body, was thin and sculpted, his skin concave at the temples and the narrow, distinct line between his cheekbones and jaw. He also had the solemn demeanor of a *samurai*, perhaps more from his early schooling as a *kabuki* actor than his years at the Dai and Kami Kan.

Kancho motioned for Aoshima to sit. Rather than take one of the nearby chairs, the Dai Kami knelt rigidly on the floor.

"What did you find?" asked the Master General.

"There is no prohibition," Aoshima said, his voice pitched high and crackly. His father had been a famous *kabuki* actor and wanted his son to follow in his footsteps. But the senior Aoshima had eventually given up on his adventurous son and asked a rich patron to gain entrance for him at the Dai Kan, where he had excelled. But by that time, his years of the highly stylized *kabuki* voice training had become a part of him.

Kubo made a face. "Unfortunate. I was hoping for an easy solution to this dilemma."

Aoshima nodded in agreement.

"And what of the traitors?"

The senior Kami pulled a scroll from his sleeve and handed it to *Kancho*. "These are the names I was able to verify thus far. There will surely be more. But the disloyalty of these is assured."

Kubo read the list, his shoulders and back sagging under this new burden placed upon them. "Much is to be added but much destroyed. I pray I am not leading us down a destructive path."

"I am most thankful I am not *kancho*."

Kubo stood up. Aoshima popped to attention. "Are you available to serve as my *uke* this evening?"

"I live only to serve, sire."

After his classes and final meal were done, Jonathan slipped into his *gi*, as he did each evening. He jogged along the dark pathways, his sandals slapping rhythmically against his bare soles. At the *dojo* door, he kicked off his sandals, stepped inside the dark room, and froze. *Kancho* Kubo knelt on the worn wooden floor, his eyes closed in meditation. No one had ever been there at that hour.

Quietly, Jonathan turned to leave, but as he did, he caught a faint glimpse of a second man with a dagger in his hand. The shadow crept up behind Kubo so slowly and delicately his movements were almost imperceptible. Jonathan didn't know what to do. If they were practicing, he would interfere. But if they weren't… As the man eased into striking range, he jerked his knife up, then slashed down at the Master General's exposed neck. "*Kancho!*" Jonathan yelled.

In a blur, Kubo flattened himself and swung his leg around, sweeping his attacker's legs out from under him. In one continuous motion, he sprang onto his downed opponent, applied a wrist lock to his knife hand, and torqued it around until Aoshima dropped the knife and slapped the floor in submission.

"*Oos, Kancho,*" said the senior Kami. "I thought, with the distraction, I would win this time."

Blushing, Jonathan bowed and kept his head down. "I'm very sorry, *Kancho*. I wasn't sure you were merely practicing."

Kubo smiled. "No, I thank you. Your presence split my attention and forced me to more finely focus my awareness, making our practice even more valuable." He gestured towards Jonathan. "This is Jonason Lusk… the boy I told you about." The Dai Kami bowed. "Aoshima *San* is my senior aide at the Kami Kan. He too was once a student here." He nodded to Aoshima.

125

"I won't keep you from your duties any longer. It was refreshing to feel the honest sweat of a hard workout instead of plots and counterplots."

As Aoshima left, Kubo snatched up his towel and wiped his face. "I am sorry we interfered with your workout," he said to Jonathan.

"I was just going to practice my *kata*."

"Then I will leave you to your practice. You will need it soon."

Jonathan bowed as Kubo headed towards the doorway. "May I ask a question?"

"Of course."

"I learned recently that *yakuza* murdered my grandfather. But I don't know anything else. Do you know the details – how he died, where it happened, which *kumi* was responsible?"

It was obviously not a question Kubo wanted to be asked. "Because it was an American investigation," he said hesitatingly, "we were never informed of the final outcome." Clearly, he was dancing around the issue and Jonathan caught it. "What do you plan to do when you graduate?" asked the Master General, quickly changing the subject.

"Go to college. My father and grandfather both attended Stanford University in California. I will probably try to do the same and hopefully become a diplomat like my grandfather."

Kubo lingered a bit, running something over in his mind. "Before her death, I received a call from your mother," he said at last. "In fact, Aoshima *San's* visit was partially to discuss what she asked of me."

Jonathan stiffened, not sure he wanted to hear what *Kancho* was about to say.

"She requested I consider you for entrance into the Kami Kan."

"I'm a *gaijin*. I thought..."

"There is no rule that says an applicant must be Japanese. Would it be something that would interest you?"

"*Hai*," he blurted, then caught himself and bowed low.

"Then you shall be included among the applicants. For the time being, however, it is best you say nothing to anyone, not even that we discussed the topic."

Jonathan bowed again.

As soon as Kubo was out of the room, he bowed crisply, widened his stance into ready position, stepped quickly to the left and sank into a low forward stance. Once he had checked the placement of his feet, he lunged forward, his hand lashing out, making his *gi* sleeve snap. His face tightened as he stepped back and swung around, performing Heian Shodan *kata*, the first one he had ever learned.

"Dear Little Brother. Everyone within my new family continues to be most kind. They took me on a picnic to the beach yesterday. We played in the ocean and ate sushi! It was a most wonderful day! But as wonderful as it was, I await the day when we can both again live in our home. With much love, your sister, Reiko."

Yoritomo sat on Jonathan's *futon*, struggling with a set of geometry questions. Jonathan glanced down and checked his answers. "Number three and five are wrong." He opened his footlocker and searched for his stack of letters. It was not where he had left it. He rifled through his things. Nothing.

Yoritomo looked up from his paper. "What's wrong?"

"My letters. Someone stole them."

14

A scalding midday sun hovered above the old *batjutsu* field, the only place large enough to accommodate the Dai Kan's full contingency of staff and students. As recently as fifteen years earlier, it was where Dai and Kami Kan students practiced the old *samurai* arts of *kyudo*, Japanese archery, and *batjutsu*, archery on horseback. Dirt paths crisscrossed the grasslands, where over hundreds of years the pounding hooves of galloping war stallions had compressed the earth so thoroughly that nothing would ever grow there again.

Grouped by dorms, students were arrayed around the field like a checkerboard. Yoritomo's and Murakami's dorms were in the front row, as they would be graduating in a couple of months. Even though Jonathan's accelerated academic work had jumped him one grade level, his dormmates wouldn't graduate for another year, placing his dorm behind theirs. He sometimes smiled when he thought of what Cow-Manure San would think of him now.

"I assembled you all here for a couple of reasons," Kancho said from a raised platform especially constructed for the occasion. "First, I want to congratulate most of you for your hard work this past year and encourage those who have not done your best to dig inside yourself and find your *tamashii* for the final push."

"Oos!" shouted the students as they bowed in unison.

"Second, I would also like to announce that we have implemented a new application process this year for entrance into the Kami Kan. Rather than having to be selected, anyone who so desires, has sufficiently high grades, and is brown belt or higher in *karate* may apply. If you are graduating this year and would like to be considered, please see Yamaoka *Sensei*."

The instant they were dismissed, Murakami hurled himself towards the podium, pushing aside anyone who got between him and it. When others saw Murakami running, many ran too, worried he knew something they didn't. A noisy riot of boys soon converged on the platform.

"*Yame!*" commanded Yamaoka, stopping them in their tracks. "You," the senior *sensei* said, pointing at the mass of boys. "All of you, move back!" Some skittered away quickly, back to where they had started. But a few, including Murakami, were reluctant to give up their front positions. "If you remain where you are," Yamaoka spat, "your applications will all be rejected!"

Reluctantly, the group moved away as Yamaoka waved over the boys who had restrained themselves. When Murakami noticed Jonathan and Yoritomo ambling past him, he started for the *dais*. Yamaoka stabbed his finger at him. "Get back where you were or you are out!"

As he wrote his name on Yamaoka's clipboard, Yoritomo turned and smirked at Murakami. Then he made a show of handing the pen and board to Jonathan.

After the last of the group had registered, Yamaoka addressed the others. "If it were up to me, you would all be expelled for your rude manners. Not only do Kami not act thusly, neither should a Dai Kan student. If you walk here with proper decorum and dignity, in keeping with the organization you so desire to join, I will allow you to add your names to the list."

Murakami immediately started around the other boys. "Murakami!" Yamaoka commanded. "Get to the end of the line. You will be last!"

A gleaming black Cadillac, its paint and chrome polished to a mirrored sheen, sat near the Dai Kan's front gate. Smoke curled up from the foul-smelling cigarette in Kazio Zuma's hand as he leaned against the Caddy's side door, waiting. The *yakuza* underboss still dressed like a fashion model, that day in a black tailored sharkskin suit, giving him a youthful appearance… but only from a distance. Closer inspection revealed his truer age. His hair was still as black as the day he ordered his men to throw Eli Lusk to his death. But it now had that dull, flat glint of cheap dye. Booze, cigarettes, and drugs had clearly taken a serious toll on his face, turning it into a wrinkled, leathery roadmap of a hard-lived life.

Three dark-suited men – all big but one massively so – stood at a distance, vigilantly scanning the area for potential threats, clearly feeling in enemy territory.

Murakami, his face pinched in anger, stepped through the gate and strode towards his half-uncle. Zuma extended his upturned hand as he bent his knees and hunched forward, bowing in the *yakuza* fashion. Murakami glared at him.

"I expected a visit on my birthday," spat the teenager. "I received not so much as a card!"

"I submitted a formal request to visit on the day itself," Zuma said, his voice bitter, "but I was rejected. This was the first day they found… acceptable."

Murakami stared off into the distance, pouting.

"Do not be angry, at least not with us. We are here to honor you."

He snapped his fingers. Togo, a mountainous ex-*sumo* wrestler, lumbered over, bowed stiffly, and placed something small and shiny into Zuma's upturned palm. The thumb-sized ruby in the burnished gold ring caught the sunlight and glowed a brilliant red.

"This has been the symbol of our family's leaders since the days of Momochi Sandayu," said Zuma, his voice formal. "It belonged to your father and was on his finger when he died, having received it himself on his birthday from his father and he from his, back to the beginning of our time." He slipped the ring onto Murakami's finger. "And as you are now of age and the blood of old Sandayu, it is hereby rightfully passed to you."

Murakami admired the ring with obvious pride.

"My request to attend your graduation was also denied," said Zuma. "But I will have a driver standing by to take you home after the ceremony."

"No need," replied Murakami, excitedly. "I have an opportunity to join the Kami Kan! Even with father's connections, he was not allowed to even apply."

"You are now the *oyabun*. You cannot stay."

"I can and will. Even father would have approved of it."

"But..."

"I will not leave," snapped Murakami, "not until I have become *kami* and brought down this *gaijin* dog."

Jonathan packed the few personal possessions he had been allowed to keep – the Mickey Mouse watch his father had given him and photos of his parents and Reiko. He had never found his letters.

As he rolled up his bedding for the last time, his dormmates filed by to say their goodbyes. Many hadn't said a word to him in all the years he had been there. He was just the *gaijin*. Now, as *karma* would have it, he was a serious candidate for the Kami Kan, the only one most of them had ever met.

Jonathan was surprised how uneasy he felt about leaving. Though he had never felt welcome, he had lived in that room longer than he had lived anywhere. There, he at least knew what was expected of him, what was acceptable, how he stacked up against the others in his dorm. In the new place, he would be competing against the best and couldn't help but worry how he would measure up.

With his *karate gi*, student uniform, and couple of personal items – his entire world – stuffed into an athletic bag, Jonathan Lusk strode outside to whatever *karma* next had in store for him.

15

___

Jonathan, Murakami, and eighteen other boys waited with their gear just outside the main gate. It was the first time some had left the compound in years.

A thin, wiry Japanese, who introduced himself as Hiroyoshi Ishishima, strode through the gate and stopped in front of the group, his hands on his hips. "Line up!" he commanded. Everyone scrambled into place. "Follow me!" Hiroyoshi began running up the same dirt road that the old DeSoto had traveled after dropping Jonathan off so many years earlier.

Murakami immediately sprinted around the others and positioned himself on Hiroyoshi's heels. After going a few feet, he glanced over his shoulder to see where Jonathan was in the line. When he saw him bringing up the rear, he snickered.

Their leader set a quick pace but not one that any of the boys couldn't easily match. Besides, everyone thought they were merely moving their things from the Dai Kan to what was called the Upper Camp, so they expected the trip to be a short one, maybe only two or three kilometers.

Originally known as Hawk's Peak, the Upper Camp was built by Dai Kan creator *Shogun* Iyeasu Tokugawa in 1604 for the purpose of training his Tamashii Kami in mountain warfare and anti-siege techniques. It was located at the edge of a sheer mountain ridge that later became the north eastern demarcation of the more gently slopped Dai Kan grounds. Over time, the Upper Camp came to be used for a variety of special purposes – the housing of important guests, a facility in which to host high level retreats and workshops, and where Kami initiates lived during their examinations.

After an hour of running at the same steady pace, Jonathan realized they were likely going far longer than expected and paced himself accordingly.

When the road first angled upwards, it was at such a gentle incline that no one seemed worried by it. Everyone just dug in a little harder. But before long, the added effort began to take its toll. Murakami's proximity to Hiroyoshi began to erode more and more until he had lost contact by fifty, then seventy-five, then a hundred yards. As he dropped farther back, Murakami's rearward glances became more frequent, although needless. He was still well ahead of the *gaijin*, who was loping along easily at the back of the group.

As the hill steepened even more and the run seemed never to end, the applicants began dropping farther and farther back, except for Jonathan who had kept his pace constant, figuring it best to conserve his energy in case there was a sprint at the end and only the top finishers allowed entrance. But it had become clear that it was endurance, not a speed, contest. Gradually, his steady pace carried him past one man then another until he and Murakami were the only ones still in sight of their leader.

The road seemed to go on forever upwards. Murakami had slowed almost to a crawl, allowing Jonathan to rapidly close the gap. His *sempai* looked drained and wild-eyed as he pulled alongside him. The Japanese tried to fight him off, but as he pushed himself beyond his limits, his legs went rubbery and he fell face-first onto the dirt roadway.

"Come on," Jonathan said as he passed, "you can do it!"

Murakami pushed himself up and gathered his legs beneath him, but they lacked the strength to lift him. Jonathan doubled back and grabbed his wrist to help. The Japanese angrily yanked his hand free and fell onto his butt.

The sight of the *gaijin* loping up the hill, coupled with a minute of rest, got Murakami to his feet. Anger alone seemed to motivate his legs to run again and hatred kept them going.

Just when Jonathan was beginning to believe that Hiroyoshi's real purpose was to run until everyone dropped out, he rounded a turn and saw the Japanese leaning against a red *tori* gate, smoking a cigarette. Exhausted, Jonathan plopped onto the ground beside him. Hiroyoshi smiled, tossed his cigarette away, and jogged up the steep gravel path, forcing the American to follow him up yet another hill.

Thankfully, this one wasn't very long, soon ending at an ancient temple that sat perched at the top of a jagged peak. Without saying a word, Hiroyoshi motioned for him to stay put, then jogged off.

Cold water sloshed noisily down a network of thick, half-sections of hollowed bamboo that emptied into a small pool, chiseled out of solid rock. After drinking his fill, Jonathan pulled off his shoes, lay back on the moss-covered bank, and plunged his burning feet in the soothing water.

He didn't even look up when he heard someone shuffle up and fall nearby. He knew who it was and why he had made it. But a second set of footsteps crunching across the gravel, surprising him. He opened his eyes to see who else had survived the trip.

"Welcome."

Jonathan jerked his feet out of the water and jumped up. "Thank you, *Kancho*."

Sprawled on his haunches, too weak to stand, Murakami moaned, "*Oos*."

"Have you ever been to the Upper Camp before?" asked the Master General.

"No. We ran so far I assumed we were going somewhere else."

Kancho chuckled. "Did you think you had run all the way to your Heaven?"

"Well, it is beautiful enough."

"Hiroyoshi *San* was instructed to take a... more challenging route. Did you enjoy your trip?" he asked, a playful smile on his face.

"He was very successful. Are all the Kami so well conditioned?"

"He is our very best runner but not Kami. He won the bronze medal in the marathon at the Melbourne Olympics but failed the final test."

Jonathan shot a concerned glance back towards the path. "The others should be here soon. I didn't think we were that far ahead."

"The others are clearly not yet ready. They were picked up and returned to the lower camp. You alone saw the trip for what it was," he said to Jonathan.

"But I also felt like quitting, especially back a few kilometers, by the bridge."

"You did not quit, however. You considered the task and paced yourself from the start. That is why you are here and the rest are below."

"I made it too," Murakami snapped.

"But because of hatred, not intelligence," said Kubo. "It is no disrespect, just the truth. You will need to work far harder and more intelligently to complete the tasks required for admission."

"If a *gaijin* can do it, I can do it better!"

"We will soon see."

Jonathan and Murakami were but two of the five candidates to advance. Two of the other three had come from Japan National Defense Academy, a military high school founded by MacArthur after the war in hopes of replacing the Dai Kan as the primary training institution for Japan's military leadership. The fifth to advance was a previous candidate who had been forced to miss his exams because of an infection that put him in the hospital.

The first of the three-day academic exams focused on mathematics. The test began at seven o'clock in the morning and the examinees didn't receive a break until noon. Twenty minutes later, they were back at their low lacquered tables, pencils in hand, and didn't re-emerge until after six that evening.

The next day's tests weren't any easier, just different. The subject was language skills in Japanese, English, and French. By that evening, Jonathan had filled five Blue Books with his answers to the multitude of essay questions.

He lay that night on his futon, conscious of the fresh blisters between his index and middle fingers from all the writing. Just one more day, he told himself.

The last of the academic exams were supposed to measure general information, creativity, and basic logic. The creativity portion worried him most as he could be asked literally anything. But as it turned out, all they wanted was to determine whether or not he could take information learned in one subject, like history or science, and apply it in solving problems encountered in a different subject.

The basic logic portion turned out to be the most difficult as, ironically, there didn't seem to be any logical answer to many of the questions.

"You are given a direct order by your superior to kill the single mother of three small children, as he believes she is planning to assassinate a top government leader the next day," one of the questions asked. "But you learn from a source you consider very reliable that she is innocent. You relay this information to your superior but he insists she be killed. What would you do?"

As mentally drained as he was when the tests were over, Jonathan couldn't get to sleep that night. His mind kept going back over his answers. But no matter how many times he reviewed them, he still couldn't come up with a satisfactory answer to most. There was little doubt in his mind that he had failed at least the final portion of the test. The only question was how much weight would that one section carry?

He sat beside the pond the next morning, watching a small blue *koi* swim lazily in the placid water. The approaching sound of *zori* slapping softly against the soles of someone's feet echoed through the garden and tightened his gut. *I did the best I could*, he told himself. *We will see if my karma is to stay or go.*

"I am surprised to see you up so early," said *Kancho*. "You appeared most tired last night."

"I wake at the same time each morning. I can never remain in bed."

"As you become older that will change. It is a beautiful day, is it not?" *Kancho* gazed up at the sky, sniffing the early morning air, heavy with the perfume of pine and damp earth.

"*Hai*. Perfect."

"Please excuse me. I must be going about my duties," *Kancho* said, continuing on his way down the path towards the training camp.

"What about the test?"

"The test?"

"Did I pass?"

"Easily. But surely there could have been no doubt in your mind?" said Kubo, smiling knowingly. "Rest today. Tomorrow we begin preparation for your *dan* exam."

"What about Yukio?"

"Surprisingly, he passed as well. The former applicant was the only candidate eliminated."

Jonathan watched as the master strode up the winding trail. As soon as he was out of sight, he punched the air and let out a *kiai*, startling the small birds bathing at water's edge.

After his excitement had subsided, his mind locked onto something odd in Kubo's tone when he mentioned Murakami's results. It sounded as if he suspected something amiss, which had occurred to him as well. Yukio had never been a good student. It had amazed him that his former *sempai* had had sufficiently high grades to even reach applicant status. And he definitely never impressed him as being bright enough to pass the academic exams. Unless he had gotten smarter since they arrived at the Upper Camp, someone had to have either supplied him with the questions and answers beforehand or graded his answers incorrectly. If that were the case, the same people could make sure he failed. He would have to be even more careful.

Jonathan's *karate* workouts ramped up as soon as the academic tests were behind him, the very next morning in fact. Each of the applicants had been assigned their own *karate* mentor from among the senior staff. Murakami's was Sugiyama. Jonathan's was *Kancho* Kubo.

The Master General, himself a 9th *dan* in *karate*, one degree below the ultimate rank of 10th degree black belt, began by teaching the young American something he found shocking at first — how to alter the previously inviolate *kihon* to enable him to get far more speed, power, and extension from his strikes and kicks. Every one of his former *karate sensei* had taught the basic strikes, kicks, blocks, and stances as if they had been handed down from the gods. Not only did he change the *kihon* but *Kancho* also revealed little-known *tai* and *ashi sabaki* tricks that enabled Jonathan to abruptly shift or shuffle his body forwards and backwards, side to side, angle to angle, with double, even triple the speed he had been able to attain before.

Along the way, he discovered a common error most of his fellow *karateka* at the Kan had made – mistaking familiarity for mastery. If they could repeat something, they thought they knew it. But *Kancho* had opened his eyes to what it took to truly master a physical technique.

"It requires at least one hundred repetitions," he had told him, "just to execute a complex technique smoothly. After a thousand, you will be able to throw it with passable skill Genuine skill, however, and the ability to apply it without thought in a high-intensity situation, comes only after tens or hundreds of thousands of repetitions, perhaps as many as a million."

So Jonathan's goal had become to get in as many reps as he possibly could before the *dan* exam.

Kancho arranged for him to spar each day with some of the Kami black belts. Every one of them scored on him at will the first day. The second, *Kancho* turned up the heat. The black belts were instructed to attack with faster and more powerful techniques and encouraged them to make light contact with his face and body. Jonathan walked away with a mass of welts as painful reminders that he needed to be quicker, more mobile, more precise.

In the beginning, his focus was solely on preventing them from hurting him seriously. The thought of landing anything himself never entered his mind. They were too far beyond him in skill.

"Sun Tzu was the first to differentiate between Invincibility and Victory," Kubo told Jonathan as he reset his broken nose, a reminder from one of the black belts to better protect his face. "Invincibility merely means one is so proficient in his own protection that no one can land a crippling blow and defeat him. It says nothing of his ability to best his attacker. Invincibility must be your first goal. Perfect your control of distance, improve your defensive techniques and *tai* and *ashi sabaki* to a point where no blow can ever land. Only then should you concern yourself with developing the skills necessary to achieve victory. These require you to dominate your opponent and are far riskier."

"*Oos*. I will spend more time on my blocks," Jonathan said, making a mental note.

"No! Work on all of your defensive options. Blocks are a last resort, necessitated by a failure to properly control distance. Never forget, if your enemy cannot reach you, he cannot hurt you. That is a universal law of war."

One of Jonathan's persistent weaknesses had been his midsection. He knew it. *Kancho* knew it. And Murakami surely knew it. So in addition to his daily round of sit-ups, *Kancho* introduced some old-school stomach drills. Jonathan lay on the floor while he walked across his stomach. As soon as Jonathan could handle that, *Kancho* would stand on his stomach and bounce up and down.

The solar plexus – the soft, inverted "V" at the bottom of the breast-bone – is a place of natural weakness in all men because little muscle or bone protects the intricate network of nerves beneath it. When struck there, breathing can be temporarily stopped, making it difficult to fight. To guard against this, Kubo taught Jonathan to drop his ribcage, sliding his sternum down over the solar plexus, whenever he would *kiai* or needed to protect the area against a kick or punch.

Next, he had the young man stand in horse stance, with his hands tucked into his belt behind his back. *Kancho* then punched him in the gut, lightly at first but increasing in strength until he knocked him out of his stance, forcing him to take a step backwards to keep from falling.

Under *Kancho* Kubo's tutelage, Jonathan's defensive skills quickly improved, though that improvement was purchased through a significant expenditure of sweat and pain. He improved so much that the Master General began teaching him attack techniques, tactics, and strategies that enabled him on occasion to actually score against his Kami seniors.

Jonathan's bare arms were tanned and tightly corded as he strode across the old Dai Kan *dojo* floor, his former classmates giving him a wide birth. He paid them no mind as he slipped off his t-shirt and put on his *gi* top and frayed brown belt, keeping his mind focused solely on the task before him.

The test was held on a Sunday morning – at least it began in the morn-ing – and ended late in the afternoon. In addition to those testing for black belt, several Dai Kan students were testing for brown.

Shihan Sugiyama led the four senior instructors, who were to serve as judges, onto the floor. Kubo had not objected when he insisted he be allowed to oversee the examination. In fact, he had welcomed it. Jonathan was more than prepared. He was so good, Kubo told the teenager when Jonathan voiced his concerns about the selection, that even Sugiyama could not deny him promotion without publicly verifying his lack of honor. Although he didn't say anything, Jonathan didn't share his mentor's confidence.

They began with the brown belt candidates. As the panel plodded through the endless evaluation of their *kihon*, Jonathan knelt at the edge of the hardwood floor, his back ramrod straight, his body motionless. His mind, however, was anything but still. It drifted back and forth between what he would be called upon to do at the exam and what he would do if he failed. One thing was certain – he would not return to the Dai Kan. He would likely go to school somewhere else, probably Stanford. But, he told himself emphatically, I will not fail.

Jonathan assumed that how he conducted himself while waiting to test was as much a part of the test as the test itself. Whereas he and Kumagai, one of the Japan National Defense High School applicants, sat motionless in painful *seiza* throughout the *kyu* testing. By the time the brown belt testing was finally winding down, Murakami and Yamaguchi, the other outsider, had relaxed and allowed their backs to round and their chins to drop.

"*Yudansha* candidates, line up!" Yamaoka commanded in his powerful voice. Jonathan ran to his place in line, legs still rubbery and tingling from hours of kneeling.

The judges sat expressionless, jotting down notes on their clipboards, as Yamaoka led the four examinees through every technique they had ever learned. After a short water break, the test moved on to the first twelve *kata*. Everything seemed to go well until *Passai*.

"Who taught you this *kata*?" Sugiyama demanded.

"*Kancho*," Jonathan replied, without hesitation.

Sugiyama lumbered stiff-leggedly across the wooden floor to where Kubo sat on the *dais*. A thick silence fell over the room as the two high masters spoke briefly. Although no one could hear what was said, they could see the expressions on the two men's faces. Sugiyama's smirk faded as the Master General gave him a curt, dismissive response that clearly caught The Bear by surprise. His face flushed and his eyes flared, but only for an instant. To most Westerners, it would have likely been missed. But to the Japanese and Jonathan, honed through centuries of subtlety, it was glaring. Everyone's eyes followed Sugiyama as he strode to the door, bowed crisply, and left.

"*Shihan* Haraguchi" commanded *Kancho*. The barrel-shaped Japanese who had been sitting nearest to Sugiyama during the test thrust down hard with his legs and sprang to his feet in one quick motion. He was as wide as he was tall and walked so solidly that he moved like a tank, from which he had earned his nickname.

"*Hai?*" said Haraguchi, bowing stiffly towards the *dais*.

"Please continue."

"*Oos,*" he said before taking Sugiyama's place in the middle of the row.

"Takahashi *San,*" said Kubo. "Please join the board."

A small *karate sensei*, whom Jonathan had trained under for a time, leapt to his feet and ran to fill the vacant spot on the five-man panel.

"*Jiyu kumite, ippon shobu!*" declared Yamaoka. "First pair, Yamaguchi and Kumagai."

The two military high school teenagers took their starting marks. Jonathan looked both of them over carefully, noting their physical attributes, anything that they could use to their advantage against him and any he could use to his. He would face one of them in the second round.

Yamaguchi was built much like Murakami, small boned and thinly muscled, but for a Japanese his eyes were large and round, as though he might have had other blood in him as well. His build suggested quickness and mobility, more prone towards attack than counter-attack. Kumagai was almost Yamaguchi's exact opposite, stocky and powerfully built. His eyes were little more than slits, so thin they appeared closed. Jonathan wondered if his square, solid jaw meant that he could take a punch or did it make him more vulnerable? If he had to guess, he would say the former. With that build, Jonathan would expect him to fight *go-no-sen* – wait, block, and counter-punch.

"Traditional rules will apply," announced Yamaoka in his deep, gravelly voice. "The first to score *ippon*, a full point, will be declared the winner. To receive *ippon*, a technique must be deemed capable of rendering an opponent unable to continue had it landed. A technique that would have done serious damage but not necessarily ended an opponent's ability to continue fighting shall receive a score of half point, or *waza ari*. Two *waza ari* shall also constitute a win."

Yamaoka chopped his hand downward, starting the first match. The two fought hard, making frequent and heavy contact, as Jonathan had heard they had done when they met previously at the All Japan High School Karate Championships. Although Yamaguchi, as predicted, clearly wanted to attack, Kumagai never let him. Every time his opponent set himself to launch an attack, he either shifted off-line, forcing Yamaguchi to readjust, or he attacked himself, robbing the smaller Japanese of the opportunity. Not only did he attack, but he did so with surprising swiftness. Jonathan shook his head. He had been completely wrong about him. In the end, Kumagai prevailed, as he had the last time the two had met.

As he waited to be called, Jonathan reflected on the fact that the officials definitely hadn't applied *Kancho's* standard relative to control.

"Hitting is easy," Kubo had told him. "Anyone can hit. But to possess the skill to throw your techniques while moving at full speed against an opponent also moving at full speed and yet always stop just short of contact is the mark of a true master. It is what separates those who are martial artists from those who are merely fighters."

"Next pair!" Yamaoka growled.

Murakami sprinted to his starting mark, where he teetered on the balls of his feet, clearly eager for a shot at the American. Jonathan strolled to his mark, running over in his mind a final time the points he wanted to remember.

The two bowed. Yamaoka raised his hand, then chopped downward. "*Hajime!*"

Murakami flinched as if attacking. Jonathan jumped back.

"Coward," Murakami said, smiling coldly.

"You will not talk to your opponent," Yamaoka scolded as he lined the two back up. He stabbed his finger at Jonathan. "This is a sparring match, not a foot race!"

The instant he restarted the match, Murakami launched a powerful roundhouse kick, aimed at the side of Jonathan's head. The American jerked both arms up just in time to take the full force of the kick on his forearms. But the impact still knocked him sideways a step.

Without missing a beat, his former *sempai* thrust out his other foot, attempting to power through Jonathan's defenses and bury a front kick deep into his *solar plexus*. But his target sidestepped, grabbed his leg, and reverse punched towards Murakami's smirking face. The Japanese raised his arms and center in defense, just as Jonathan wanted him to do. This made it easy to sweep his supporting leg out from under him. In fact, he swept it so cleanly that Murakami's body rotated upside down in midair and he landed on the side of his head and shoulder. Jonathan hesitated. His former *sempai* had fallen from such a steep angle that he feared he had broken his neck.

"Follow up!" admonished the referee.

Too late, Jonathan looped out a half-hearted punch aimed at his downed opponent.

"Fail to follow up again and your test is over!" scolded Yamaoka.

Murakami climbed painfully to his feet, his neck stiff and his rage palpable. The instant Yamaoka signaled the restart, Murakami leapt forward with a powerful lunge punch. Jonathan shifted slightly to the side, snap kicked his *sempai* lightly in the groin with his front leg, then caught him with a well-controlled reverse punch to the face.

"*Yame*!" yelled Yamaoka, stopping the match. He lined the two back up, then called for scores. One of the four judges held up a red flag, Jonathan's color. The other three shook their flags, signaling "no point". Yamaoka swept his arm downward across his chest, signaling a half point for Jonathan.

Murakami bristled. "It was off target! Even they agree," he spat, pointing at the corner judges.

"Would you like to fight me?" demanded Yamaoka. Murakami shook his head. "Then keep your mouth shut! I have already warned you once."

When the match was restarted, the livid and now predictable Murakami attacked again, driving Jonathan out of bounds with a flurry of punches, none effective.

"*Yame*!" commanded Yamaoka, but Murakami refused to stop, continuing to press his attack, obviously not just trying to score on his American opponent but to hurt him. Jonathan's quick footwork, however, honed from his matches with the Kami black belts, allowed him to evade his former *sempai's* wild, desperate attacks. Yamaoka grabbed the back of Murakami's collar and kicked his legs out from under him, slamming him down onto his butt.

Dragging the Japanese backward across the floor to his starting mark, he jerked him onto his feet and aimed a finger at his face. "Warning! Fail to stop again and you will be disqualified!"

The whole incident had given Jonathan a few seconds to think... and to remember. "Opponents will always try to do what they do best," Kubo had told him that morning. "You must deny them that option. If they want to attack, you must attack. If they want to hold and counter, you must hold and force them to attack you." So far, he had only fought defensively. Perhaps it was time for a change.

Murakami's body was coiled like a snake, waiting to strike. When the referee's hand dropped, Jonathan lunged forward with a blindingly fast punch to the face that caught Murakami flush in the nose, snapping his head back. Three of the judges swung their red flags in small circles, signaling excessive contact – a penalty.

Yamaoka returned the two fighters to their starting marks, then stabbed his finger at Murakami, "*mubobi,*" he declared, "failure to take proper precautions for one's own safety." Yamaoka swept his arm diagonally upward in Jonathan's direction. "No *kachi*! Winner!"

Murakami blew up. "*Bakaya...*!" he screamed at Yamaoka, but his nose started bleeding more profusely, forcing him to pinch it closed. Yamaoka grabbed him by the front of his *gi*, dragged him to one of the mirrors that lined the side wall, and shoved his face toward it. "Does that look like the face of a winner?" he growled, slinging Murakami aside.

A hum of muffled chatter filled the room as the final two, Jonathan and Kumagai, took their starting positions.

Stone silence filled the room as Yamaoka raised his hand. The instant it slashed down, Kumagai lashed out with a lunging jab aimed at Jonathan's face. Jonathan shifted away from the attack but not fast enough.

"*Yame,*" yelled Yamaoka.

As they retook their starting marks, Jonathan cussed himself for his mental lapse, especially since he had already seen how quick Kumagai was. He nodded to his opponent in acknowledgement. When Yamaoka awarded the technique a half point, the room erupted with wild applause. Faint smiles glistened the eyes of two of the judges. *Had I not been moving backwards when the jab landed,* Jonathan told himself, *he would have received an ippon and won the match.* He would have to be far more careful with this opponent.

Since it had worked once, Kumagai tried the same technique again. But this time Jonathan was ready. He sank down onto one knee, under Kumagai's punch, drawing his attacker straight into a powerful reverse punch aimed at his liver. The blow landed so hard it briefly knocked the wind out of the Japanese. The judges who had smiled a few seconds earlier now shot their flags into the air and emphatically circled them, wanting Jonathan penalized for contact.

"On the street, you need but do two things to win," Kubo had once told Jonathan. "First, you must not allow your opponent to injure you and reduce your ability to defend yourself. And second, you must injure him and reduce his ability to defend himself. But in a sparring match, you must also do a third thing; prevent him from gaining points for excessive contact."

Jonathan's heart sank. He had just supplied exactly what the biased judges needed to rob him of any hope of victory.

Yamaoka called for scores. Two judges wanted a penalty assessed for contact. Two held their flags in front of their eyes, meaning they hadn't been sighted, hadn't been in a position to see if the technique was on target.

Jonathan bowed in apology to Kumagai as Yamaoka walked over to speak with the two judges who had called for a penalty. The solemn teenager gave Jonathan a thumbs-up.

When Yamaoka returned to his position and whistled for the judges to make their final calls, Kumagai looked disgustedly at the flags – two still circling and two still covering their eyes. He jogged across the ring and bowed to Jonathan. "Perfect *ippon*. Nice and clean," he said loudly enough for everyone to hear, then jogged back to his starting mark.

Yamaoka waved the judges' flags down. He stood motionless for several seconds, struggling with his decision. Then he swept his arm upwards for Jonathan. "*Aka, no kachi!*" Jonathan had won.

"Line up!" commanded Yamaoka.

The four black belt candidates ran into place. *Shihan* Haraguchi gathered up the clipboards from the other four examiners and delivered them to *Kancho*.

Sweat ran into Jonathan's eyes as he and the others waited for the Master General to render his decision. Although he tried to keep his gaze straight ahead, as if he didn't care, his eyes betrayed him and flicked onto *Kancho* when he heard him say something to Haraguchi in a low voice.

The chief examiner marched to the center of the floor. "Yamaguchi *San*!" he yelled. Yamaguchi stiffened to attention. "It is the board's decision that you are not yet ready for advancement to black belt."

Yamaguchi slumped under the rejection.

"Murakami *San*! You too will not be advancing."

Murakami's entire body went rigid, as if he had received an electric shock. He pounded the sides of his legs with his fists.

"Kumagai *San*," said Haraguchi. "Because of your martial skill, your warrior comportment throughout the test, and your strong and fearless spirit, you will be promoted to *shodan*."

Kumagai bowed. The teenager tried to remain stoic but couldn't restrain his joy. Briefly, the tiniest of smiles played at the corners of his thin lips. Jonathan turned and bowed his congratulations.

Everyone in the room stood in motionless silence, awaiting the *gaijin's* fate.

"Lusk *San*!" said Haraguchi. Jonathan bowed. He was unemotional on the outside but his heart was pounding so hard he feared everyone could hear it. "It is my... honor to announce that you have been advanced to the next level as well," said Haraguchi, but without any hint of joy. The two failing boys had visibly shuddered at the news.

"You who have advanced will undoubtedly find," continued Haraguchi, "that attaining a black belt is but the beginning, not the end, of your learning in the martial arts. The real work will now truly begin."

Jonathan congratulated Kumagai, then turned to say something in sympathy to the two who had been rejected. But all he caught was a quick glimpse of their backs as they stomped toward the door.

"Do not let them bother you," said *Kancho*. "They are merely hiding their shame behind false arrogance. You will leave many such people behind as you move through life."

"Did I make a mistake in *Passai*?"

"No, you were the only one who was correct."

"*Shihan* Sugiyama seemed to disagree." Like everyone else in the room, he had wanted to know why the old master had left. But it would be impolite, too *gaijin*-like, to be so blunt as to ask directly. Kubo would tell him what he wanted him to know.

"His interpretation of the *Passai kata* is not correct," Kubo explained, leading Jonathan outside. "I trained under the highest authorities in Okinawa, where this *kata* is said to have originated. Sugiyama San rejects anything not Japanese. As a result, his is a bastardized version and I reject it. Today was not merely a test of your *karate* ability, it was a test of his power and he lost."

Although *Kancho* was too short to see beyond the knot of boys who milled around just outside the *dojo* door, Jonathan, at a little over six feet, had a clear view of Sugiyama and the angry group of instructors heading their way. "*Shihan* Sugiyama is…"

Sugiyama parked himself directly in front of them, blocking their path. He spoke in such rapid Japanese and used crude phrases he wasn't familiar with that Jonathan had trouble following some of it. But he gathered that The Bear was demanding that he not be allowed to take the final exam. Sugiyama claimed that *Kancho* would surely manipulate the outcome of the final test, the arrow catch, as he believed he had the *dan* exam.

Kubo answered calmly and slowly, informing Sugiyama that the matter was closed.

"If that is your final decision, you leave me no alternative," said Sugiyama, his rage still very much apparent even though his speech had slowed.

"You have many choices," said Kubo, his tone harsh and uncompromising, "but only two of any true importance – you will perform your duties honorably or you will not. What will it be?"

"As an advisor, it is my duty to attempt to sway you from destroying the two Kans. Since you will not listen to my advice, I must register my disagreement as any man of honor must when his opinions are ignored by those he serves. I intend to commit *seppuku* tomorrow at sunset."

"If you were truly a man of honor," scoffed Kubo, "you would have already committed *seppuku* and let the action speak for itself."

Kubo pushed past Sugiyama and his followers and continued on. Jonathan tucked quickly in behind him and stayed close, ignoring the hard looks and hostile words directed at him as he passed. He would have to be even more careful. These men no longer wanted to drive him away, they wanted to kill him. And sometime soon they would likely make an attempt.

16

The sun floated atop the lower cusp of a blood-red sky. Silently, Kubo led Jonathan through the rock garden and down a path that had always been off limits to students. Soon, the trail opened to a verdant, steep-walled valley with a small lake at its center. Near the far bank, a tiny island protruded from the green water. Gnarled tree roots intertwined like a knot of snakes, creating a natural bridge that connected the island to the bank.

On the island, Sugiyama sat in *seiza* on a pair of *tatami* as white as his *hakama* and surcoat. Eight steel-eyed witnesses armed with *katana*, *wakizashi*, and *tanto* stood at somber attention behind him. *The Bear* peeled off his top, revealing the mass of wiry gray hair that smothered his chest, shoulders, and broad back.

He glanced down at the unsheathed *tanto* glistening on the mat in front of him. For several seconds, he considered it, as if a debate was still raging inside him. Then, his eyes hardened, he pressed his lips tightly together, and picked it up. As if trying to move as quickly as he could, before he lost his resolve, *The Bear* wrapped several sheets of white paper around all but the last couple of inches of the dagger's razor-sharp blade.

His *kaishaku*, or second, a bald, muscular Japanese with a long handlebar mustache, unsheathed his *katana* and dropped to one knee behind and slightly to the right of Sugiyama. Rays of the red, setting sun rippled down the long blade as the *kaishaku* slowly lifted his killing sword high overhead.

The Bear pressed the tip of his *tanto* lightly against his skin, just below his ribcage, releasing a trickle of blood that meandered downward. He turned his head and searched the opposite bank. At first, Jonathan thought it was to implore *Kancho* to change his mind and intervene. But as he fixed his chilling gaze onto Kubo's face and his mouth twisted into a cruel sneer, Jonathan realized Sugiyama was taunting him.

Abruptly, *The Bear* drove the tip deep into his stomach. Without shifting his eyes or changing his expression, he slid the blade to his center, opening a scarlet ribbon in its wake, then jerked the dagger upwards.

His task almost done, Sugiyama removed the dagger from the flowing wound. The once-white sheets of paper around its shaft were slick and dripping red. He laid the dagger on his thigh and bowed his head. His *kaishaku's* sword was a blur, cutting deep into the back of the old master's neck, slicing easily through muscle and bone, and stopping just short of exiting the other side. Sugiyama's head toppled forward and hung against his hairy chest, suspended only by a sliver of flesh. A second later, his body slumped forward onto the mat.

Jonathan turned his head away from the jerking corpse.

"*Iie,*" said Kubo. "As misguided as it was, you will not dishonor his act. If he was strong enough to perform it, you can be strong enough to witness it."

The *kaishaku* drew his *tanto* from his belt. Gently cradling Sugiyama's face in his palm, he cut the remaining flap of skin and set the head, its eyes staring fixedly into space, onto sheets of white tissue paper. The bald stranger calmly removed a thick needle and coil of horsehair from his satchel and sewed the old master's eyes closed.

"This is the *kubi-shozoku,*" said Kubo as the *kaishaku* washed the blood from Sugiyama's face with a damp cloth, "the preparation of the head for viewing by Sugiyama *San's* family. He will attempt to make him as presentable in death as he had been in life."

The head-dressing done, the *kaishaku* carefully eased Sugiyama's head down into an ornate cylindrical box.

"Sugiyama *San* would have prepared himself for death prior to his arrival here," continued Kubo. "After writing his death poem and leaving his gift of nail and hair clippings, he would have bathed, oiled and combed his hair, and drunk scented water so no foul odor would escape the cut."

As the witnesses placed Sugiyama's headless body into a wooden coffin and hoisted it onto their shoulders, the *kaishaku* strode across the root bridge to where Jonathan stood on the bank. The man stared so coldly into his eyes that Jonathan felt the urge to step back. Instead, he held his ground and narrowed his gaze, trying to appear as if his own hatred was as intense as the stranger's. Kubo stepped between them, blocking the man's line of sight. The stranger shifted his gaze onto the Master General, then bowed low, deferentially. In return, he received nothing, not even a nod.

When the coffin and box containing the head reached the stranger, he bowed again to *Kancho* and moved on with his cortege.

"Who is that man?" Jonathan asked once the group was beyond earshot.

"A man born without a heart," said the Master General, "Minne Kengoshi. He approached you at the gate many years ago, when you were seeking admission."

Jonathan's eyes fixed on the stranger as he strode arrogantly away. "I thought there was something familiar about him. But he was very skinny back then and had a bad eye."

"He was Sugiyama San's senior student and adopted son. Several years ago, his eye mortified and was replaced by one of glass. You must never forget that he will kill merely on a whim. As a *gaijin* and one of the two he surely holds responsible for his adopted father's death, it would give him the greatest joy to be provided an excuse to take your life."

17

———

"Did you say tomorrow?" Jonathan asked. *Kancho* had said it so nonchalantly that he wasn't sure if he had heard right.

"Yes. And you will be happy to learn that Kiyoshi Yoritomo decided to take the exam as well. As he had already met the other qualifications, his application was accepted."

Jonathan snickered to himself. Apparently Yoritomo's grades had been judged good enough, as he said they would be. He wondered who had called, Prince Yoritomo or were they so bad the Emperor had to call himself? "So there will be three of us?"

"Five. The Admissions Board also deemed that while the *dan* test results are being reviewed..."

Jonathan stopped in his tracks. "You mean I could be disqualified?"

Kubo shook his head. "No. Your results were beyond question. Some, however, felt Sugiyama *San's seppuku* warranted his protest at least be reviewed. The two who failed will be retested soon to settle the matter. But as the arrow catch had already been scheduled, it was not possible to assemble everyone necessary to host another *dan* exam beforehand."

Yoritomo jogged up, a Japanese long bow and quiver of blunt-tipped arrows slung over his shoulders. He bowed to the Master General, then smiled at Jonathan. "You did not think you could take this adventure without me, did you?" He said, then turned to Kancho. "May we be excused?"

Kubo waved them away and chuckled as the two ran happily off.

The teenagers didn't stop running and jostling each other until they reached the edge of the old *batjutsu* field, where a *dais* had been recently erected.

Yoritomo pointed at an oval of packed earth amid the tall grass. "That must be where the catcher stands." Marching off fifteen paces from the spot, he searched until he found a second patch of bare earth. "I think I found the archer's spot," he yelled.

Jonathan waited just outside the catch point as Yoritomo drew an arrow from his quiver and nocked it. "Are you ready?"

Jonathan waved.

His friend took careful aim. "Here it comes!" he yelled. The arrow flew from the bow. Jonathan calmly watched it sail past, wanting only to see what he was up against. On the next shot, he swept his hand across his body as the arrow was released but again made no attempt to grab it, just see if he could follow its trajectory and speed. As Yoritomo nocked and drew back his third arrow, he stepped into the oval and readied himself.

Jonathan stifled a wave of growing fear and locked his eyes onto the arrow's tip. As it sprang from the bow, his hand swung across his chest to intercept it, but a split second too late.

He eagerly awaited the next shot, fully expecting to succeed this time. His hand was right on target but only managed to slap the arrow aside, earning a loud "*Yatta!*" from Yoritomo. Now confident, Jonathan focused his eyes on the tip of what would be his fourth attempt. But although he was quick enough, he couldn't get his hand closed fast enough. And he did no better with any of the succeeding five shots. Each slipped teasingly through his grasp.

"You give it a try," he yelled. "My hand's too slow."

The two traded places and Jonathan quickly notched his first arrow. When he let it fly, Yoritomo swatted at it but wasn't even close. The next several shots ended exactly the same.

"Well that went well, didn't it?" Jonathan said as the two trudged gloomily back towards their dorm with far less confidence than when they had arrived.

"You must practice," said Yoritomo.

"What about you? I came closer than you did."

"They will ensure I pass. It will be the opposite for you."

A crisp, repetitive slapping sound punctuated the darkness. Jonathan lay awake on his *futon*, his hand opening and snapping shut, over and over.

18

Jonathan's eyes sprang open. He glanced at the faint gray glow filtering in through the side *shoji* and knew he had overslept. "No, not today," he hissed, rushing into his *gi* and running outside.

Dark clouds blanketed the sky. *That's not good*, he told himself as he jogged down a steep, damp trail. The arrows would be harder to see against the flat light.

When he reached the white-water stream that had served for years as his retreat and where he had brought Nanami for a day never to be forgotten, Jonathan dove into the frigid water and swam out to the rocky ledge. The stream, he had only recently learned, was the official demarcation between the upper and lower camps.

He knelt in *seiza* directly beneath the water fall, almost disappearing inside the splayed white chrysanthemum formed as the water struck the rocks. Closing his eyes, he filled his lungs with the moist cold air and held it. A minute or so later, he relaxed and allowed the now warm air to hiss slowly back out, sending out a white vapor with it. Steeling his body and mind against the pain and frigid cold, Jonathan meditated while the falling water buffeted his head and body and spirit.

Where others were content to meditate comfortably on *zafu* pillows and *zabuton* mats in the *zendo* hall, Jonathan had come to prefer a more active and challenging form. He might meditate in a tortured horse-riding stance, his thighs parallel to the floor and his arms extended straight out in front of him, staying motionless for a half hour or forty-five minutes. Or he might sit in *seiza*, his legs tucked tightly beneath him, until his legs went to sleep and screamed for relief.

In the beginning, he had done as *Kancho* had taught him, disassociate himself from his pain by dwelling on pleasurable thoughts – his parents or Nanami or Reiko or the stack of blueberry pancakes and hash browns his mother had made on Sunday mornings. But with time, he had moved far beyond mind tricks. As he sat beneath the falls that morning, awaiting the final test that would determine the direction his life would take from that point onwards, he blocked the pain with nothing more than the mundane sound of his own breath.

He breaststroked back to shore and climbed up onto the muddy bank where a swarm of flying bugs immediately enveloped him. When he swatted them away, they returned immediately in even greater numbers. Angrily, he snapped his hand out to grab one pestering his face. He missed. He locked his eyes on it and tried again, with the same result.

As the big bug darted in and out, up and down, he tracked it. When it was hesitated to hover directly in front of his face, his hand lashed out... and missed again. *How can you hope to catch an arrow if you can't even catch a bug?* he asked himself.

Shaking the tension from his arm and shoulder, he locked his eyes again on the elusive insect. In a flash, his hand snatched it out of midair. Then he set his sights on another and waited.

Yuso Yonai strode along the forest trail, his feet slapping rapidly in his stilted *geta* sandals. Yonai was a diminutive man, standing an inch or so less than five feet, but his *samurai* dress – indigo *hakama* and *uwagi* jacket and red breastplate – and the raised sandals, which gave him another four inches of height, made him appear much taller. In one hand, he carried a Japanese long bow; in the other, a scowling *samurai* facemask. Four full quivers were slung tightly over his shoulders.

"Oos, Yonai San," said Minne Kengoshi, stepping out from behind a cypress tree.

The archer bowed, a deep bow as befitted one more senior. *"Ohayo gozaimasu,* Kengoshi Sama. It is an honor to see you again."

"I need to speak with you about something of critical importance, a foreign infection that now places in peril the very soul of the Dai Kan and our ancient traditions."

Yonai nodded. "It worries me as well. But unfortunately, it is not within my hands to change." He bowed to leave.

"You are wrong. It is in your hands alone. And *giri* to this sacred institution transcends that to any misguided superior."

Yonai's eyes narrowed. "I am sorry but I cannot help you, *sensei.*" He bowed once more, then continued on his way.

"Then be gone!" screamed Kengoshi, his voice unrestrained rage. "And to think I once counted you among our true patriots!"

The sun had finally managed to burn through the layer of clouds and now flooded the field in brilliant yellow light. A row of stone-faced examiners knelt on the raised viewing platform, waiting for the archer to arrive and for *Kancho* to take his place. There was also the matter of the missing candidate.

Only four knelt at the edge of the field. Yoritomo sat at the head of the line. Next to him sat Yamagushi, who tried with limited success to stifle a yawn. The always serious and stalwart Kumagai was to his right. Then, there was an empty space between him and Murakami, who impatiently yanked up handfuls of grass, wadded them into balls, and tossed them away.

After pacing off the distance between the two dirt patches for a second time, *Kancho* stared disgustedly at the shoot point and the missing archer. His mood didn't brighten as the man jogged out of the trees and bowed in apology.

"Isogi," snapped Kubo. "You are very late."

The archer bowed again. *Kancho* spun on his heels and strode towards the officials platform, while Yonai quickly knelt in the center of the oval of packed earth and readied his bow.

"Are you prepared, Yonai *San?*" *Kancho* yelled. When the archer bowed, he trudged up the platform steps and took his place at the head of the row of examiners. After a final glance back up the trail, he nodded.

"First candidate!" called the Chief Examiner, Takayuki Uchida.

Yoritomo rose.

"*Yame!*" Kubo ordered, spotting Jonathan running their way. "Where have you been?" he demanded.

"I am sorry, *Kancho*. I was preparing myself."

"May we proceed?" asked the tall, gruff Uchida after Jonathan had taken his place.

Kubo nodded.

"First candidate, Kiyoshi Yoritomo, please come forward!"

"*Hai*," said Yoritomo, walking casually to the spot where the vegetation had been worn away. He bowed to *Kancho* and the judges.

"As established by Nishihara *So-shihan*, you will receive five shots," Uchida announced. "If you successfully catch one of them, the test will be considered over and the requirement met. Do you have any questions?"

Yoritomo shook his head.

"Then let the test begin!"

Yonai slid an ornate, blunt-tipped arrow from one of his quivers, nocked it, and drew the string to his chest. He held it for a second, then parted his thumb and forefinger, sending the bamboo shaft toward its human target.

Before Yoritomo could even flinch, it was past him. Fortunately, it had not been targeted at his heart as prescribed and passed safely to his left.

Yoritomo's flippant attitude was long gone as he nervously readied himself for his second shot. He teetered on the sides of his soles, more prepared to bail than to hold his ground. But there was no need. This arrow arced high and slow, forcing him to wait for it to arrive before plucking it easily out of mid-air.

Uchida bowed. "Welcome, Yoritomo *Sama*. You are now a Kami Kan initiate."

Yoritomo shrugged at Jonathan in embarrassment as he walked sheepishly back to his place in line.

"Next candidate, Daisuki Yamaguchi!"

Yamaguchi strode into position and confidently awaited his first shot, clearly expecting something like what Yoritomo had received. But he was badly disappointed. The arrow crossed the field and struck him in the chest so fast his hand barely moved.

Two aides ran to where Yamaguchi lay on the ground. The young man cried out as one of them pressed his hand against his chest. "Ribs are broken," called the aide. Kubo nodded and the men helped Yamaguchi to his feet and down the trail towards the main building. His test was over.

"Hachiro Kumagai, please come forward!"

As the square-faced Kumagai stepped into the oval and looked down field, Jonathan saw just a flicker of fear in his eyes and knew he too was nervous.

The first shot whistled straight towards the cadet's head. Kumagai frantically swept his hand across his face, deflecting it off target at the last instant. As the archer nocked his next shot, Kumagai stared at his feet, his face set, a serious conversation obviously raging inside him. He lifted his gaze and nodded.

The arrow took flight. Kumagai's hand swept across his chest. The two intersected and his fingers wrapped tightly around its shaft. Seeing it still in his hand, Kumagai's dark eyes opened wide and a rare smile spread across his face, but only for a second.

"Welcome Hachiro Kumagai," declared Uchida. "You are now a Kami Kan initiate!"

Kumagai bowed and stoically retook his place in the line.

"Next candidate, Jonason Lusk."

Jonathan jogged to the catch point and shook the tension from his catching arm and shoulder. He filled his lungs with the warm morning air, held it for a few seconds, then slowly let it back out. He gazed across the field and fixed his vision on the arrow's shiny broad tip. He would have to start his hand the instant it moved.

He nodded.

The arrow sprang from the bow. A fraction of a second later, Jonathan slapped it aside, stunning all but one of the examiners, *Kancho* Kubo.

The young American felt a wave of pride sweep through him but instantly cautioned himself. When he had practiced with Yoritomo, he had been equally confident, all for naught. So he readied himself as if he had completely missed the last shot... then nodded.

The arrow reached him far more quickly than the first had, but he still managed to get a hand on it, although not around it. His hand still wasn't closing fast enough. As the archer drew back his third arrow, he noticed that almost none of the arrow's shaft was visible beyond the bow, far less than what he had seen with his first two shots.

Not surprisingly, it was past him almost before he could get his hand moving. Something was wrong. He glanced at *Kancho* for an answer but he was watching the archer prepare his next shot. The bowstring had been drawn back so far it rested lightly against the cheek of the archer's mask, the bow stretched into a tight half-moon.

"*Yame!*" yelled Kubo. "The prescribed draw is two *shaku*. You are to draw it back no more and no less. Is that understood?"

The archer bowed in apology.

"The last shot was not correct," announced Kubo. "As such, it will not be counted. The next will constitute his third attempt."

Under Kubo's close scrutiny, the archer drew the string back exactly two *shaku* and took careful aim at Jonathan's heart. The instant the Master General's head turned back towards the catch point, Yonai jerked the string back its full length and quickly realigned its tip onto Jonathan's face.

The bow string snapped forward. The arrow flashed towards its human target.

Jonathan jerked his head back and slung his arm across his face in desperation, trying to ward off the arrow he could not see but sensed was there somewhere. His hand brushed aside the tail of the bamboo shaft but not before its blunt tip struck his forehead with bone-jarring force. Jonathan staggered back, then dropped to one knee.

"*Yame!*" yelled Kubo.

The masked archer snatched a sharp-tipped killing arrow from behind his breastplate and rushed it onto the string. He drew it as far back as it would go and leveled the tip onto the teenager's face. "For Sugiyama *Sama!*" screamed the archer.

The archer hunched violently forward, his arrow's tip burying itself into the earth a few feet in front of him. The man's hands clawed briefly at the arrow shaft protruding from deep inside one of his mask's eye holes before his body fell motionless onto the grass.

Kubo, his long bow at the ready, sprinted across the field to the downed archer. Planting one foot on the faceplate, he jerked his arrow free, then ripped off the archer's mask. Kengoshi's contorted face scowled in death much like the mask that had hidden it.

Kubo pressed two fingers against the side of the man's muscular neck. Finding no pulse, he ran back towards the catch point, where Yoritomo hovered helplessly over the kneeling American. On *Kancho's* approach, Jonathan struggled to his feet, only to stumble sideways.

"Please stand still and close your eyes," Kubo ordered.

Jonathan did as he was told but quickly reopened his eyes when he felt himself falling. Kubo turned him towards the trail and waved for an aide to take him back to the main camp. Jonathan spun out of his grasp. "I will finish the test first."

"You cannot stand with your eyes closed. You have a concussion."

"Then I will keep them open!"

"I cannot permit it."

"Will I be allowed to retest?"

"You have to, right?" Yoritomo asked. "It was not his fault."

Kubo looked questioningly at the examiners. No one seemed to know the answer. "This has never occurred before. We will have to schedule a meeting and discuss it."

"Then I demand my right to complete the test now."

"Get checked," said Yoritomo. "I am sure they will let you finish later."

"No. One encounter, one chance – you taught me that," Jonathan said to Kubo. "People have been trying to get rid of me since my first day here. If I don't finish today, someone will find a way to make sure it doesn't happen. I'm finishing now."

"You realize that by so doing you forsake any claim to retake the test at a future date?"

"*Hai.*"

"Very well," said Kubo, his voice heavy.

Aides removed Kengoshi's body and Yuuta Kouda, the backup archer, strode to the catch point, notched his first arrow, and waited.

Jonathan stepped unevenly into the dirt patch. He took a long minute to shake the tension from his arm and loosen the muscles in his catching hand. Then he fixed his eyes on the arrow's shiny tip and nodded. The arrow sprang forward. Jonathan's tenuous courage deserted him and he leapt away. Kubo and Yoritomo let out a loud, collective groan.

"Coward," Murakami scoffed.

Uchida's hard eyes fixed on the boy. "You utter another sound and your test is over!"

Jonathan fought to keep his rising fear from overwhelming him. His mind refused to empty, as he had trained it to do. It was not cold water he was facing this time. It was not pain. It was a raw, primitive fear, like what he had felt watching Sugiyama commit *seppuku* or his mother searching for him through the rubble at the Levys' house.

But what do you have to fear? he asked himself. There was nothing that could be taken from him that mattered any longer. If he failed, there would be neither a place for him to go nor anyone waiting when he got there. He had no life, no family, no home. He had lost contact with Reiko. So, he decided, he would face the catch as if he were already dead and let *karma* do to him whatever it wished.

As he stepped back into the catch point, he found comfort in the thought of death. Its dark silence had long appealed to him. He would open the door. If death was there to greet him, he would gladly accompany it to where his father, mother, and grandfather awaited him.

Taking a breath as deep as he lungs would hold, Jonathan held it a few seconds, then let it hiss out slowly, clearing his mind and unloading his muscles so they could move at maximum speed. He shook the tension from his catching arm and shoulder, then reached out and snapped his hand closed a couple of times, as if catching one of the fast flying bugs. He fixed his eyes on the arrow's tip, channeling all of his anger and frustration onto that one glistening point. It was his enemy. It was Dr. Makram, who had killed his father. It was whoever had murdered his grandfather. It was Murakami and all the other boys who had tormented him at the Dai Kan.

He nodded.

The arrow fishtailed out of the bow but quickly stabilized and raced straight at his heart. Jonathan's arm flashed across his chest. The bamboo shaft slide across his palm. His fingers grasped as it struggled to break free, his face contorting and his muscles bulging as he fought to keep hold.

He looked at his hand in disbelief. The arrow was still there.

"Welcome, Jonason Lusk," said Uchida. "You are now a Kami Kan initiate."

Jonathan bowed and returned to his place in the line, wanting to look as stoic as Kumagai. But his excitement, or self-satisfaction, or relief, or whatever it was couldn't be contained. A big grin swept across his face and filled his entire body.

"Next candidate, Yukio Murakami!"

Murakami sprang to his feet and jogged to the catch point. On the surface, he seemed his regular cocky self. But Jonathan noticed that his hand trembled as he awaited his first shot. When the archer let it fly, the teenager catapulted himself backwards and landed unceremoniously in the grass on his rear end.

He scrambled up and dusted himself off. "I apologize," he offered, bowing, but earning nothing from the examiners but cold-eyed stares.

Murakami pressed his lips firmly together... and nodded. The second arrow hurled towards him. His hand frantically swept across to intercept it but was off-target. The arrow's metal tip smashed hard into his chest, doubling him over and stealing his breath.

A medical aide quickly removed the teenager's *gi* top and inspected the injury site. "He has a broken rib!" called the aide.

"Please escort him back for treatment," said Uchida.

"If the *gaijin* can stay," croaked Murakami, holding tightly onto his chest, "I will stay as well."

Uchida nodded. "That is your right."

When Murakami retook his spot, he began acting bazaar, as if something had snapped inside him. He grunted like an animal, softly at first but it grew louder and louder. "*Rin! Pyo! To! Sha! Ka! Jin! Retsu! Za! Zen!*" he said, entwining his fingers in strange configurations, switching quickly from one to the other as he uttered each of the nine *mantra*.

"What's wrong with him?" Jonathan asked.

"It's *ninja* crap – *kuji-in*, they call it," Yoritomo said disgustedly. "They think it gives them more power. But the idiot's using *ninja* hand seals and *mudra* at a place created to destroy scum like him. I'm sure the judges are not impressed."

"I thought he was just going crazy."

"Well, there is that too."

Eventually, Murakami fell silent. He locked his eyes on the archer and nodded. As the arrow sprang from the bow, Murakami let out a guttural scream, putting everything he had into his attempt. He missed.

Huffing noisily and talking out loud, he tried to pump himself up. But for all the shouting and heavy breathing and secret finger configurations, he missed the next two shots as well.

With but one shot left, Murakami's behavior became even wilder, screaming the *mantra* at the top of his lungs and weaving his fingers and arms together in even more intricate patterns. When he finally nodded and the blunt-tipped arrow was released, he stunned everyone by jumping directly into its path. The metal tip smashed hard into his chest, knocking him back. But he managed to grab the shaft with both hands before it could reach the ground.

A huge smile lit up his face as he thrust the arrow into the air in victory. The examiners sat stunned, their eyes fixed on the blood seeping through his white *gi* top. Uchida spoke briefly with the panel before turning to Murakami, who was still celebrating his 'catch.'

"The original intent of this test was to demonstrate ones prowess on the battlefield. Had the tip been one used in battle, you would now be dead. As such, you have failed," Uchida said. "Please step aside."

Murakami erupted. "He got hit," he said, stabbing a finger at Jonathan, "and was allowed another shot. I demand the same right."

"He was hit due to an improper action by the archer," corrected Uchida. "All of yours were shot as prescribed. I will only tell you one more time. You have failed. Please step aside."

As Uchida strode towards him, Murakami broke the arrow over his knee and raised one end of a sharp half into the air like a dagger.

"You dare threaten me?" Uchida asked.

Murakami spun and charged, intending to stab Jonathan, but Uchida deflected his arm and wrapped a powerful forearm around his skinny neck in a tight rear choke. He wheeled, slammed Murakami onto the ground, then kneeled on the back of his neck as he dexterously bound his hands behind him with a length of short rope. Two aides hoisted Murakami up and lugged him away as he screamed obscenities directed at everyone present.

Kubo leaned back in his chair and glared at the now contrite former candidate, who stood nervously across his desk. "Lusk San and the Dai Kan have endured your bad manners far too long."

Murakami started to say something in his own defense. "Do not interrupt me!" said Kubo, cutting him off.

Murakami bowed.

"You were only allowed entrance because your father bribed my predecessor. As dishonorable as the act was, I allowed you to remain because the institution's word had been given. But your behavior today can neither be overlooked nor tolerated. You are expelled. Someone will help you gather your things and escort you to the front gate."

Murakami started to speak.

"There is nothing to be said. It was your actions alone that sealed your fate. Words cannot now unseal it."

"Please, *Kancho*, I beg you. At least allow me to stay long enough to graduate." Tears were pooling in Murakami's desperate black eyes.

"You made that impossible."

The door opened and two of *Kancho's* armed Kami aides entered.

"Also, Lusk San is not here," added Kubo. "If you attempt to search for him, you will find yourself in police custody."

A big-finned Cadillac slid to a stop in front of the Dai Kan entrance. One of the Kami gave Murakami a hard shove toward the roadway. The second tossed his suitcases onto the dirt. The Caddie's *yakuza* driver and passenger jumped out. While the driver picked up the suitcases and loaded them into the trunk, the passenger opened the rear door and bowed, *yakuza* style, as Murakami dashed inside.

Dirt flew from the Cadillac's fat rear tires. Tears filled Murakami's dark eyes as he stared longingly back at the Dai Kan gate. "The traitor Kubo and the *gaijin* pig will die for this, I swear it!"

19

Kagamura *Jo* had been home to the Tamashii Kami since Iyeyasu Shogun ordered the castle's construction in 1610. Its slender white peaked parapets and high white walls, keeps, and battlements sat perched atop a sheer, flat-faced mountain so high the castle often looked to be floating on clouds.

As Murakami was being expelled in disgrace, the Land Rover carrying the three honored Kami initiates – Jonathan, Yoritomo, and Kumagai – rumbled across the castle's wooden drawbridge before entering the massive inner grounds, which encompassed almost four square miles of training facilities and lush green forests.

A Kami aide escorted the initiates to their new rooms. Jonathan had expected all of them to be housed together in the same dorm. But each was assigned his own private room. His was bare and immaculate, about the same size and much like his old bedroom at his grandparents' house. But since it was the first time in many years that he had had a room to himself, it seemed enormous.

Before he could finish unpacking, his *shoji* slid open. "Please come with me," said one of *Kancho's* aides.

"Where are we going?"

"*Ofuro.*"

At the Dai Kan, there had only been a large general bath, where as many as fifty students and staff bathed at the same time. After reaching puberty, Jonathan had no longer felt comfortable there. The others stared so much at his body's new changes that he started bathing only at the least crowded time of the day, usually just before lights-out. The downside, however, was the water was luke warm and no longer as clean as it had been earlier in the day. Having private baths and hot clean water, as they did at the Kami Kan, was a special treat.

Sitting naked on the low stool, Jonathan lathered his body and head and scrubbed every inch with a long-handled brush. He had found the Japanese way of bathing odd in the beginning. In America, people got into the tub to clean themselves. In Japan, they cleaned themselves, then got into the tub. It made no sense until his grandfather explained that the stool and soap and bucket were for cleaning. The hot water was for soothing aching muscles and melting away the troubles of the day.

Jonathan eased his clean body down into the steaming water, scooped up a leaky double handful and poured it onto his swollen forehead. It burned but also felt healing too. So he poured a second. Resting his arms atop the redwood tub, Jonathan leaned back, closed his eyes, and let the hot water suck the soreness from his body like a powerful drug. Soon, beads of sweat dotted his forehead and face and reddened his skin. It was wonderful.

A warm joy filled his body and tingled his mind. It was the first time he could remember when he wasn't trying to get somewhere else. He was at the Kami Kan! There was no other place he would rather be.

The *shoji* slid open and he jerked upright, sloshing water over the top. A young woman in a short *kimono* stood in the doorway. She bowed low, her hands pressed tightly against her delicate thighs. "I am sorry if I disturbed you, young sir. I will wait until your bath is complete."

"What do you want?" he asked, covering his groin with his hands as if she could see through the sides of the tub.

"I am here to serve you, young master."

"Serve me how?"

"In whatever way pleases you."

"Thank you, but I do not need anything."

"Very well. I will await you in the dressing room." She bowed and backed out of the room, sliding the *shoji* silently closed behind her.

Jonathan forgot the bath. Her presence and whatever she had in store for him cast a dark uncertainty over what had been a wonderfully soothing experience. Not knowing what to do, he did nothing... for as long as he could stand it, until his skin grew pale and puckered and the heat made him light-headed. He had to get out.

His rubbery legs had barely hit the floor before the *shoji* slide open. The young woman was there, handing him a towel, then leading him into the next room. "Please lie down on the table," she said, bowing as she gestured towards the padded massage table in the far corner. "On your stomach, please, young sir."

He did as he was told. The towel didn't cover enough of him to argue. The young woman began massaging the muscles in his back. She found sore muscles in places he didn't even know he had muscles and painfully dug her surprisingly strong fingers deep into the center of each, burrowing a hard knuckle and twisting until the knot relented and let go.

When she was done on that side, she had him roll onto his back and began kneading the muscles in front. He opened his eyes a crack and watched her massage the tight waves on his abdominals, working her way methodically down towards his hips. The front flap of her short *kimono* loosened as she worked, giving him a clear view of one of her white breasts, which swung gently with each thrust. The towel across his hips began to rise and she smiled shyly.

"Thank you, that is sufficient," Jonathan said, sitting up abruptly.

"Please, do not rise," she said, pressing her palm against his chest. "Kenji San requests you remain here. *Domo arigato gozaimasu*," she said, bowing low before hurrying out of the room with a giggle.

Kenji the Healer was a rotund old man who, except for his hair, looked like the ubiquitous statues of Buddha. But where Buddha was always depicted as bald, Kenji's white hair hung well past his shoulders, like a lion's mane. The old man huffed as he leaned over Jonathan's face, his breath hot and reeking of garlic.

The healer's plump, sausage-like fingers traced the outer edge of the swollen lump on the young man's forehead. He pressed and poked the red mass as if it belonged not to a man but to some inanimate object.

He grunted, mumbled unintelligibly, then opened his bag and pulled out small leather bundles of dried herbs and thick, glass vials of various colored liquids, adding differing quantities of several – a little of one, a lot of another – into a small, stone bowl. Then he moistened the mixture with liquid from a couple of the vials as he ground the mass with a stone pestle, quickly converting it into a thick paste that smelled so bad it overpowered even the old man's breath. Jonathan cringed as the healer smeared it liberally onto his injured forehead and wrapped it in place with a length of white cloth.

"Keep this as it is for one hour – no more or it will burn your skin. Do you understand?"

Jonathan nodded.

"One hour. No more. No less," repeated the old man as he shuffled out.

Jonathan found a Kami aide waiting for him outside. "*Kancho* wanted me to tell you to rest and let your body heal. You will not begin instruction for several days. He also said your grandfather and grandmother would have been most proud of you."

Reiko would be proud too, Jonathan thought, as he strolled back to his room. He wished he could tell her that he had made it, become a Kami initiate, but all of his last letters had been returned.

20

A horn blasted from somewhere close by, jolting Jonathan out of his first sound sleep in weeks. He bolted upright and listened. It blasted again. "Assemble in the main yard, immediately. Assemble in the main yard, immediately," blared Aoshima's high pitched voice over the PA system.

Everyone was rushing out of the building, as if they were under attack. Jonathan piled into his clothes and followed them out.

Instructors, administrators, Dai Kami, Kami, Kami initiates, common staff, and even gardeners milled around in the courtyard. From the looks on people's faces and the hushed conversations, Jonathan gathered this was as big a surprise to them as it was to him.

"What's going on?" Jonathan asked Yoritomo.

He shrugged. "Nobody knows."

"*Kiite!*" commanded Aoshima from atop the raised *dais*, his high-pitched voice like the screech of a hunting hawk. Everyone snapped to attention as *Kancho* Kubo strode out of the donjon and mounted the *dais* steps. A collective gasp went up as a contingency of heavily armed Kami security men swept in from the training ground and encircled the assembled group. Jonathan's fascination quickly turned to apprehension when two of them marched through the crowd and stopped on either side of him.

Kubo huffed heavily through his bent nose. Jonathan had been around him long enough to know that this was not a good sign.

"I have for some time been aware," began Kubo, "that many among you do not feel you can support my leadership. As a result, a great disharmony now exists, which I can no longer tolerate. Aoshima Dai Kami will read the names of those whose service is terminated and are to leave Kagamura Castle immediately."

Aoshima unfurled a rice-paper scroll and read the first name. "Abe, Isao."

Abe, a hard-looking man with a burned face, stiffened as guards surrounded him, then escorted him to his quarters.

"Miki, Kengo."

Kengo Miki, an unusually tall man for a Japanese, threw down his clipboard. He stared at Kubo, as if considering going after him, until four Kami guards led him away too.

Aoshima read through the list of twenty or so names. Some of the men left defiantly. Some just left. One charged the *dais* but was tackled and dragged, screaming obscenities, into the security office.

After the last man had been led away, Kubo addressed those who remained. "As of this moment, the castle is sealed. No one will be allowed to either leave or communicate with anyone outside these walls without my prior permission. The reasons will soon be made known to you."

On Aoshima's command, the assembled men bowed in unison as Kubo strode away.

"Many high-ranking government officials will be on-site over the next several days," continued Aoshima. "We expect each of you to present yourself in true Kami fashion."

Jonathan and Yoritomo started to walk away. "Please remain here," one of the guards said. The young Kami initiates waited until the guard's walkie-talkie informed him that the last of the traitors had left the castle. Then, without a word, the two marched off, leaving Jonathan and Yoritomo alone.

"That was kind of scary," said Jonathan, relaxing.

"Welcome to my world," said Yoritomo, matter-of-factly. "Why don't we have a look around?"

Shortly after midnight, huge military cargo helicopters began flying personnel, supplies, and equipment into the old castle, awakening Jonathan from another sound sleep. Construction crews, with the seal of the Japanese defense department on the back of their coveralls, began work early the next morning and continued around the clock for almost three weeks. When they were finished, the castle and grounds had been drastically changed.

The delicate bronze lanterns that had lined the gently curving walkways and building walls, and which until recently were hand-lit each night, had been replaced with glaring, high intensity security lights. Key spots around the ancient walls and grounds now bristled with the latest surveillance equipment. Satellite dishes and ugly antennae fingers thrust skyward from atop the main keep. Against the classic beauty of the ancient 16th century structures, Jonathan found the new additions sorely out of place.

A modern infiltration course had been built in the old bamboo forest at the back of the enclosure. New instructors were testing their skills against the stone cliff, using pitons and nylon rope where, for centuries, others had used grappling hooks and steel hand-claws.

The room where foreign and coded languages had been taught by rote was now filled with private listening booths and libraries of language tapes. A communications center, crammed with the latest military-grade electronics equipment, had replaced the old calligraphy classroom.

After the last of the workers were flown out, everyone was again assembled in the courtyard.

"The Kami Kan is being brought into the 20th century," announced *Kancho* Kubo. "Everyone who wishes to remain on staff or continue as an active member will need to update their qualifications to a modern standard."

No one chose to leave. Even Kubo and the oldest of the old timers, 90-year-old *kenjitsu* grandmaster, Sho Shimananji, were dressed for training and on the field that afternoon. They began with weapons qualification – .45mm Browning 1911 semi-automatic pistols and AR-15 select-fire ArmaLite rifles.

Jonathan found that the intensity of the training more than lived up to the school's rigorous reputation. Their goal, according to *Kancho* Kubo, was to instill mastery, not just skill. "Skill," said *Kancho* on their first day of training, "is nothing more than the ability to execute an action or technique, usually under ideal circumstances. Mastery requires much, much more. A master of a technique has such great proficiency that he can tell his opponent what he is going to do to him and then successfully do it. He cannot be denied."

During the training, they mastered a wide range of martial subjects – the use of modern weapons (pistols, rifles, automatic weapons, grenades, mortars, and rockets); rappelling and mountain climbing; infiltration; amphibious assaults; and interrogation. Although they ate well at other times, when in training they were allowed little food and even less sleep, forcing each to "perform his best while at his worst," as Aoshima had put it.

Jonathan had always loved training in the ancient weapons arts – sword, bow, spear, and *naginata* – and found them challenging on many levels. But training in modern weapons was fascinating, even fun. He liked the game-like quality of creeping down a darkened hallway in the new indoor combat range and shooting at pop-up targets with a solid .45. At the new outdoor range, he got to shoot automatic and semi-automatic weapons – machine guns, automatic rifles, Uzi machine pistols, and sniper rifles – at pop-up and fixed targets.

The defensive driving course had made him apprehensive at first. It had been years since he had even ridden in a car and now he was being asked to drive one at high speed. But he quickly overcame his initial stiff hand at the wheel and the line of orange cones flattened in his wake and was weaving his way through the course at full speed, tires squealing, and another car in mock pursuit.

But it was the next course that worried everyone, even the old Kami hands – airborne parachute training. After what seemed far too few practice jumps from the new jump tower, Jonathan and a mixed group of initiates, instructors, and staff were loaded into a Japanese Air Force DC-3. Turbulence knocked the fat craft about like a toy as it lumbered noisily into the rough air. By the time they leveled off, most of the men had already thrown up or looked about to.

"Line up!" yelled the Assistant Jump Master. Everyone, even those who were sick, queued quickly up at the open hatch.

"Check your chutes!"

Jonathan rechecked his parachute for what must have been the twentieth time, hoping he hadn't overlooked anything.

"Clip up!"

He clipped his ripcord to the jump line.

"Go!" yelled the Assistant Jump Master, slapping the first man on the back.

One by one, the men shuffled to the hatch, awaited their turn, and leapt on command. Jonathan's stomach tightened as he moved closer and closer to the open door. But once he was there, his mind was so focused on the mental checklist they had drilled into him that he was out before he realized it.

Air whistled over his helmet's earholes as he fell, his heart thundering. The chute snapped open, jerking him to an abrupt halt, then eased him downward toward the green earth.

The view was breathtaking. Small villages dotted the steep green forest surrounding the massive Dai and Kami Kan grounds. A twisting white-water river and its tributaries splayed out like lightning bolts beneath him. One of those had to be his stream.

He had mixed emotions as the ground rose rapidly toward his feet. Part of him was sad it was almost over and another part thankful that he would soon be back on solid earth. As the ground grew close, his gut tightened. *You have to land on your feet, not your butt*, he told himself repeatedly. They had been told to fall onto their sides or rear ends when they landed. But the Kami had all scoffed at that and said they would land on their feet, like men.

Even at the Kami Kan, Jonathan was still *The Gaijin*. Everything he did was viewed under a microscope. In general, everyone treated him better than had most at the Dai Kan. But there was still something missing, a tinge of dislike beneath it all – for being an American, for being allowed entrance to the Kami Kan, or for being responsible for the expulsion of the group of seniors – he was never sure which.

When he saw most of those ahead of him, even many of the Kami, landing on their back sides, he ran down the short list of steps in his mind a final time. He pointed his toes and arched his hips, keeping his eyes fixed on the landing zone. As his feet were about to hit the ground, he yanked up on the shrouds and righted himself. But he came in a little too fast and was forced to take several quick steps to remain standing.

"That was not a proper landing, Initiate!" screamed the red-faced Jump Master.

Jonathan gathered up his chute and waited as the rest reached the jump zone. He noticed that the Jump Master said nothing to anyone else who also landed on his feet.

They were loaded into trucks, driven back to the runway, given new parachutes, and again sent aloft. Before the day was out, he completed ten jumps, intentionally falling and rolling as instructed on the remaining nine rather than landing on his feet – and being ridiculed for it, even by the Jump Master, who had told him to land exactly as he did. *Nothing changes*, he told himself, *even there*.

They jumped every day for a week, completing the sixty-five jumps required to earn their Paratrooper Wings before the weekend.

After a couple of days off to allow the trainees to recuperate and new experts to arrive, advanced training began under even more deprived and intensive conditions.

Mayu, the pretty young woman who had embarrassed him at his first bath, escorted Jonathan to the healer's office. Blood flowed down his face from a cut above his eyebrow.

"How did you injure your eye?" she asked after they had walked a ways in silence.

"Something stupid. I didn't cinch my helmet tight enough and it came off while rappelling," he said, smiling sheepishly, "so I used my eye instead to protect my head."

She tittered that high-pitched little laugh all the females in Japan seemed to do, causing him to laugh at her laugh, which made her titter even more.

"Are you going to become a healer like your grandfather?" he asked as they walked.

"He refuses to teach a woman, then becomes depressed about having no heir and taking his knowledge to the grave. So I told him a woman would be better than no one. But he is as stubborn as an old boar."

"What took you so long?" Kenji said, scolding his granddaughter. "A Kami Initiate is injured."

"It was my fault," Jonathan said, only to be silenced by an angry scowl from the healer.

Kenji grabbed his head. "Do not move!" he said as he roughly inspected the cut. "Needle and thread!" he commanded. Mayu found them in the top drawer, then watched closely as he stitched up the gash.

"Would you consider teaching me a few things about healing?" Jonathan asked.

Kenji yanked hard on the last stitch, jerking Jonathan's head around. "You do not already have enough work to do?" snapped the old man. "If not, I will inform Kubo *Kancho* you need more to keep you occupied."

"I have sufficient to do. But I came here to learn from the best. You are the finest healer in the world," he said, bowing and speaking in his most honorific Japanese, as if addressing the Emperor himself. "I would be most honored if you could find time in your busy schedule to perhaps teach me a little of your vast knowledge."

The old man cocked an eye and studied his face. Jonathan could see he wasn't fooling Kenji Okazaki. He had been around far too long not to recognize flattery or know its goal.

"You will find me a most diligent student," he added.

"Diligence is not enough! It takes insight, clear vision into the very nature of things. It is nothing like the crude arts at which you are rumored so proficient – striking as strongly as you can and hoping to incur sufficient damage to disable or kill. You must have a sensitive touch for healing. You must possess the mystical inner eye that enables us to perceive all through our fingertips, our eyes, our ears, and noses."

"If you possess this mystical eye," Jonathan pointed out, "then surely you can see into my mind and know if I have the necessary qualities."

Kenji scoffed. But he fixed his eyes on the young initiate nonetheless and studied him closely. Abruptly, his eyes darkened and turned away.

"What?"

"I must discuss your request with Kubo *Kancho*. If he orders me to instruct you, I cannot refuse, no matter how strongly I may be against it." He waved Jonathan off with a flick of his fingers. "Go!"

Kenji watched the young man amble happily out the door. As soon as he was gone, he looked solemnly at his granddaughter.

"What did you see?" she asked.

"Death," he answered. "He is surrounded by it. When I peered into the young man's future, I saw nothing."

21

A sprawling Japanese estate sat amidst a lightly forested hillside, sided by a rapidly running river. An ancient ten-foot wall of plaster and river rock completely encircled the compound, blocking everything within from view. But for the knot of armed *yakuza* soldiers milling around its entrance, it could easily have been the home of any number of wealthy Japanese businessmen or government officials.

The house's interior was an odd mixture of Japanese and European. The living room floors were matted in traditional *tatami*. But Murakami and his half-uncle, Zuma, lounged on lush overstuffed leather chairs. On the grass-papered walls, a Monet and a couple of lesser Van Goghs hung among Japanese block prints by Masanobu and Hokusai. Crackling oak logs burning in a cream-colored French provincial fireplace cast a warm glow that played on the faces of the two men and everything else in the room.

"With all due respect, *Oyabun*, that is out of the question!" Zuma objected. "Abducting a princess, a Kami, and a prince who is also a Kami would be most foolhardy!"

"Would-be Kami, both of them," Murakami corrected, an edge to his voice. In spite of his longer, slicked-back hair, finely tailored suit, diamond rings, and expensive gold watch, Murakami was still a pimple-faced teenager.

"It is not them I fear," insisted Zuma, "it is the army of real Kami who will come after us."

"A great reward requires a great risk, Father always said."

"There is not enough reward in the world to have made this risk acceptable to your father. If we survive, which is unlikely, we will spend the rest of our days in prison. If you had spent time in prison, as I have, you too would have no desire to return, especially to avenge some childish insult."

Murakami scoffed. "I trained with those you fear. I know their methods. Our risk would be next to zero."

"But they know this as well! They will begin their investigation with you!"

Murakami's face flushed. He thrust his hand almost into his uncle's face and spread his fingers. Firelight sparkled gold and a brilliant red off the ring on his finger. "You insisted I leave the Dai Kan to lead the *kumi*. Now, when I am here, you fight me! Am I *oyabun* or are you?"

Zuma bowed contritely, then held up his index finger, begging for a few seconds to think.

"I was approached last year by a Japanese Marxist," Zuma said, breaking the silence. "His name was Oyama or Oyata, something like that. He proposed a joint operation, a kidnapping of a corporate head to raise money for both our organizations. He was a strange fellow so I dismissed him."

"Can he be trusted?"

"They are idealists. They fashion themselves the saviors of the poor. Most of their kind would rather die than put their cause in jeopardy."

Four unkempt Marxists cautiously approached the compound's front gate, their hands gripping the waffled handles of the bulky US Army .45s protruding from holsters on their web belts. The small group was made up of three long-haired Japanese and one close cropped Arab. All were dressed in fatigues and combat boots with checkered *keffiyeh* scarves around their necks.

Armed *yakuza*, two deep, barricaded the estate's entrance with their bodies. As the Marxists drew near, a black-suited *yakuza* lieutenant stepped forward and reached out his upturned hand, demanding their weapons. The three Japanese immediately surrendered theirs but the Arab balked.

Broad-shouldered and standing well over six feet, the surly Asim towered over everyone, Marxist and *yakuza* alike. He glared down at the much smaller man with disdain until Ozawa, the oldest and obvious leader of his group, loosened Asim's grip, removed the pistol from its holster, and handed it over.

The four visitors were escorted along an inner walkway to the back of the house. "Enter!" came a man's voice from the other side of a door when the lieutenant knocked. The *yakuza* opened it, bowed, and waved the four inside.

Murakami leaned back in his executive's chair, propped his feet on an ornately tooled desk, and waited for their guests to present themselves.

"Thank you for agreeing to meet with us," Ozawa said, bowing to Zuma, who sat against the side wall along with three *yakuza* captains.

"I was only the acting *oyabun* when we last met," Zuma said. He gestured toward his nephew. "You need to direct your presentation to Murakami *Sama*, our *oyabun*."

The Marxists were clearly surprised when they realized their mistake. Two stifled snickers. The big Arab let out a belly laugh.

Murakami's face flushed. His captains sprang to their feet, hands reaching into their coats. "*Yame!*" Zuma ordered.

Ozawa quickly bowed. "I sincerely apologize for our comrade's rudeness."

Murakami sniffed the air disgustedly, then covered his nose with his handkerchief. "I was informed," he said, his voice muffled by the cloth, "that you had a proposition to make yet we, who pride ourselves on being extremely well informed, have never heard of your Red Brigade?"

Ozawa stiffened. "I can assure you we are known quite well in certain circles."

Murakami shrugged.

"Perhaps you remember the incident at Waseda University five years ago?" Ozawa offered. "Tatsuo Watanabe. Held by the Red Crane Society to expropriate funds to feed the people? That was us, before we changed our name to one more fitting."

"Ah yes, now I remember...Tatsuo Watanabe. That was you?"

"Hai," Ozawa said, bowing humbly.

"I heard the Red Crane Society was destroyed by the police during that operation."

"Many died...although not in vain. Much of the leadership survived, however, and have recently returned from a period of training with our Palestinian brothers. We believe the time is ripe to...."

Murakami cut him off. "Frankly, we do not care what you believe, Mr. Ozawa. Our concern is that you advocate the destruction of everything we value."

Zuma and his three aides jerked their heads around in unison, clearly caught by surprise.

"We would be fools," continued Murakami, "to support such an operation. And as Japanese, we refuse to even discuss such an act. The kidnapping of members of the Japanese Imperial Family is unthinkable." He stood up. "We have nothing further to discuss."

"You realize our percentage of the ransom would be 360 million yen?" Zuma said. Murakami's eyes flared, sending a shudder through the other *yakuza* in the room.

"If that is not acceptable, we would be open to discussing it further," Ozawa added quickly.

"I made my position quite clear!" spat Murakami, staring straight into his half-uncle's eyes. "Please leave us, Ozawa San, and take our former 'acting' *oyabun* with you!"

Zuma shot his nephew an angry glare. "If that is how you feel after all I have done for you and this *kumi*. I go gladly!"

"Togo!" yelled Murakami. The door opened and the flat-faced ex-sumo wrestler's massive body filled the doorway. "Get these people out of my sight!"

Togo and his crew quickly hustled Zuma and the Japanese Red Brigade out of the room. As soon as the door closed behind them, Murakami pushed the button on his intercom. "Did we get everything?"

"*Hai*," his secretary answered.

"Have copies made of both the tape and the photos as quickly as possible." He turned to his three aides. "I want word passed throughout the *kumi* that Zuma is no longer a member of this family. No one is to speak to him or aid him in any way. Do you understand?"

The men bowed solemnly.

Zuma and the Marxists were rousted around the outside of the house and out the front gate, where Togo shoved his former boss into the street.

"This is my reward for lifting you from the gutter, a drunken has-been wrestler, and giving you your honor back?" Zuma demanded. Togo only glared at him.

The ex-*oyabun* turned and stomped angrily away but after going only a few steps something occurred to him and he went back. "Will one of you at least give me a ride home?"

The men glanced at the *yakuza* lieutenant, who shook his head.

"Isamu. I paid for your mother's surgery or she would now be dead," he said to one of the men, who clearly wanted to help but was stopped by the cold stare of his dark suited superior. "What about you, Riku? If I had not hired the best lawyer in the country, you would still be rotting in prison." The man turned away.

The dark clouds overhead finally opened and poured rain as they had threatened all morning. Zuma ducked his head and trudged down the road, toward where the Marxists were loading into their van. He jogged up to the side window and knocked. Ozawa rolled it down a few inches and studied him suspiciously.

"I can do what our cowardly *oyabun* will not," Zuma said in a low voice.

"Which is?"

"I ran this organization for many years. I can supply safe houses, an intelligence network, time schedules, everything you need for success."

"What would your services cost us?" asked the Marxist leader.

"Half of the ransom, not a third, so I may begin my own *kumi*."

"And?"

"Two people, in addition to the prince and princess, must be abducted and eliminated."

"That would not be a problem – if you can, in fact, do as you say."

"If I cannot, then I receive nothing."

22

To graduate and become a full Kami, Jonathan thankfully didn't have to catch another arrow or perform anything else of an extraordinary nature. In fact, he had already fulfilled most of the requirements along the way. He had qualified at Expert Level, the highest attainable, in each of the required weapons as well as demolitions, surveillance, defensive driving, communications, counter insurgency, riot control, and a half dozen other skills. His only remaining obstacle was an internship with Kami Response Team III, stationed in Tokyo.

Some of the team's operations involved what turned out to be minor incidents. On his first day, the team raced to the residence of the Emperor's great aunt. The woman – in her mid-nineties – had been so hysterical on the phone that no one could make out what she was saying. Yoritomo had accompanied them since he was related to the woman. When the team arrived, the sweet, obviously senile old woman invited everyone in for tea. It took Yoritomo several minutes to determine that the emergency was her cat, Momo, who had gotten himself stuck up a tree. While the Kami sat in their Land Rover, talking and listening to the radio for a real call, Jonathan and Yoritomo climbed a tall pine tree, cornered the uncooperative Momo, then got him down the ladder with a minimum of clawed flesh.

But his second incident was very different. It involved an army veteran whom the team leader named Nambu because he carried a WWII sergeant's sword and Nambu pistol, standard issue to non-commissioned officers during the war. Nambu had taken a little American girl hostage on the grounds of the Imperial Palace. He threatened to kill her unless the government increased benefits to WWII vets. His original intent had been to take the Emperor hostage. But he had hardly gotten through the gate before an Imperial Guard noticed the outline of a long sword concealed inside one of his pants legs. Not buying Nambu's explanation that it was merely a leg brace from a war injury, the guard demanded he lift his pants leg. When he did, Nambu drew the sword and cut the guard down. As other guards were descending on his location, he grabbed the American girl, whose family had unfortunately been on the same Imperial Palace Tour, and fled into a gardener's shack.

For two hours, Tokyo Police negotiators tried to talk him out while the Kami waited nearby. Finally, the door opened and the man appeared with the little girl in his arms. He lowered her to the ground and held up his arms in surrender. "Come to me," Jonathan called in English. She ran to him as fast as her little legs would carry her.

"Put down your weapons and lie on the ground," demanded the Kami team leader.

"Please see that my father gets this," Nambu said as he gently laid his sword on the graveled pathway. Then calmly, almost nonchalantly, he drew his pistol from its holster, pressed the barrel against his temple, and pulled the trigger. A red mist sprayed from his opposite temple and his body collapsed gracefully onto the walkway.

For days, Jonathan couldn't rid his mind of the image, the casualness of the act, the almost sterile way in which it had occurred. It held none of the horror of Sugimoto's *seppuku* or of what he imagined death by gunshot would look like. No grimace or scowls, or empty staring eyes. The old veteran had left with a peaceful, contented look on his face. It was as if he had merely fallen asleep, as Jonathan's mother had done years before.

Over the next few months, Jonathan accompanied the team in twenty-three operations. Most were non-events by the time they arrived. A goodly portion of the others ended quickly when those involved saw who they faced and how heavily armed the team was. All but two simply laid down their weapons. Those who didn't were quickly overwhelmed. In truth, Jonathan was disappointed that everything had gone so smoothly. He had secretly hoped for an opportunity to test and prove his skills and, thereby, increase his chances for acceptance.

Underneath, there rattled around the thought that he would never be deemed good enough to actually be selected, that he was just kidding myself into thinking he would. He was the eternal outsider, *The Gaijin*. But at least he hasn't been rejected.

"Pack your things," his Team Leader said the next morning. "The selection committee wants to speak with you."

23

The Kami induction ceremony reportedly hadn't changed since Tokugawa Ieyasu's day. The Shogun himself had attended the very first and personally awarded *menkyo kaiden* – certificates of transmission – to each named a Tamashii Kami.

Dressed in stilted *geta* sandals and the black kimono and winged over-mantle worn by 16th Century warriors, Jonathan's normally sure feet wobbled as he made his way clumsily across the uneven ground towards the Hall of Ceremonies. The back third of the ancient temple-like structure extended out over Yahiko Canyon, supported by timbers that angled sharply into the granite cliff.

As he walked, Jonathan shook his head at the irony – of being selected because he was a *gaijin*. The board had decided his ancestry and citizenship would be an asset to the organization when dealing with American tourists and military, of which there were many in Japan, and in securing assistance from the American government when needed.

The ceremony was, as always, held in the dark of the moon. So the only light inside the small room came from a single candle burning in a bronze candelabra that sat atop a plain but sturdy table in the center of the room. In its warm, flickering glow, Jonathan could make out the silhouettes of a double row of Kami and Dai Kami sitting in *seiza* along the back and side walls.

In a position of prominence near the front wall sat an enormous bronze meditation bell. A soft breeze blew in through the open *shoji* and the candle's flame rose briefly, revealing the Tokugawa *mon* – three hollyhock leaves in a circle – inlaid in gold leaf on the bell's side. *The Shogun's Bell*, Jonathan realized excitedly. Every Dai Kan student knew the story of the Shogun's Bell. Commissioned by Ieyasu, it had been constructed by the legendary *Zen roshi* and mentor to war lords and *samurai*, Takuan Soho, at his monastery foundry. Jonathan was the first person he knew to have actually seen it.

The black-robed Kami chaplain shuffled across the wooden floor, the bell his destination. Jonathan had been told that the tiny frail man had once been a Kami but had renounced violence and shaved his head after some accident that took an old woman's life. When Kodo San reached the bell, he bowed reverently, picked up a leather-padded baton, and gave the side of the bell a single strike. A loud, deep-throated gong filled the room, vibrating the floor, walls, ceiling joists, and everyone inside for several minutes. Its tone swept through Jonathan's body, feeling as if it was synchronizing each and every cell, filling him with a complete sense of peace and harmony.

While the bell still pulsated, the chaplain struck it again. "*Kyoshin no kokoro*," chanted the assembled Kami and Dai Kami in a deep, throaty rasp. Hearing the words, *mind like a mirror*, Jonathan knew the ceremony had begun. He hadn't expected to be the only one inducted that night. Yoritomo hadn't yet qualified but he had no idea why Kumagai wasn't there. Perhaps each initiate was given his own ceremony.

Kancho Kubo, followed by Dai Kami Aoshima, strode formally in from a side room. They too were dressed in the old style. In their hands, Kubo carried a *katana* while Aoshima carried a tray, which he set delicately onto the table. On it rested several items – an antique mirror, a double handled rice-paper scroll, an open bowl of black ink, an eagle feather quill, a clay *sake* jar, and two *sake* cups.

The Master General lifted the sword in both hands and bowed to it. He drew its long blade and carefully positioned it, cutting edge up, on the table top. The two masters knelt formally, then gestured for Jonathan to do the same.

"Jonason Lusk, please recite our oath," commanded *Kancho* Kubo.

Jonathan had memorized the Kami Oath, the words by which every Kami was guided.

"I, Jonathan Lusk, hereby pledge my life and the honor of my ancestors to stand for the remainder of my days as an unquenchable light and immovable and ever vigilant sword, forever poised to defend His Majesty, our revered Son of Heaven, and his family against those who cowardly fight in the shadows for dark and despicable causes. I will dedicate my life to mastering the martial ways and never allow myself to be outdone on the field of battle or to cease in my struggle as long as there is breath within me. I so swear."

"The three relics of the Tamashii Kami are the sword, the candle, and the mirror," *Kancho* said, "the sword is the soul of Japan and the means whereby we protect those we are pledged to protect; the candle illuminates the darkness and those who fight without honor; and the mirror represents the secret of our system."

Kancho gestured towards the ancient mirror. "Please recite Chuang Tzu's gift to us." Jonathan picked up the mirror and held it so that he could see his own face. He had repeated the quotation hundreds of times in preparation for this night. Still, he stammered out the first couple of words before settling down. "The perfect warrior uses his mind like a mirror. It grasps at nothing. It refuses nothing. It perceives but it does not keep." The saying, he knew, was actually a paraphrase of what Chuang Tzu had said. It was rumored that Takuan had changed "The perfect man" to "The perfect warrior" as the mental state he described as that he considered the perfect mind for a *budoka*, a practitioner of the Way of War.

The Chaplain struck the Shogun's Bell. "*Kyoshin no kokoro*," mind like a mirror, chanted Jonathan and the assembled group.

"Please illuminate the darkness!"

Jonathan removed the single candle from its holder. Moving slowly, his hand cupped over its flame to prevent the wind whispering softly in through the open back *shoji* from dousing it as he circled the room, lighting candles along the way. When all were lit, he returned and knelt at the low table.

"As with a sword, a Kami must be sharp, hard, and deadly to those who would stand against him," *Kancho* said. "We are most honored that Ieyasu

Shogun left us with this, the most treasured of swords, created at the kiln of Masamune *So-Shihan*."

Aoshima unrolled a section of the two-handled paper scroll and pushed it over in front of Jonathan. It was half covered in small, uneven maroon smudges, each with a black *kanji* written on top of it. *Kancho* slid his finger along the sword's razor-sharp blade, then touched a blank spot on the scroll, leaving a red smudge. He gestured and Jonathan did the same. Aoshima blew the marks dry, then dipped the eagle's quill into the bowl of black ink and handed it to *Kancho*, who wrote his name over his blood smudge. Aoshima dipped it again and passed the quill to Jonathan, who scribbled the *katakana* characters for his name over his mark.

The chaplain struck the Shogun Bell and the three men rose to their feet. "Let me be the first to welcome Kami Lusk into our sacred group."

"*Oos!*" said the assembled group in unison.

24

—————

As he and Mayu strolled towards the infirmary, Jonathan cursed himself for letting her convince him to visit her grandfather and propose what she had. Not many people scared him but Kenji was near the top of that short list. Besides, it also seemed pointless. He had asked before and received nothing but a silent scowl in return.

"You look fine," snapped old Kenji when he saw Jonathan. "Why do you waste my time?"

Jonathan glared at Mayu. She nodded toward her grandfather, pressed her palms together in prayer, and mouthed "Please!"

"I once asked if you would consider teaching me some small amount of your vast knowledge," Jonathan offered, knowing some of his reservations had to be noticeable in his voice. "You never answered me."

"Perhaps that was your answer!"

"Was it?"

"Kubo *Kancho* did not speak against it."

"So? Yes or no?" Jonathan blurted out, more strongly than he had intended.

Kenji put his hands on his wide, round hips and stared directly into Jonathan's eyes. "When you appeared at the Dai Kan gates many years ago," he said calmly, but with a tinge of anger, "did you demand they allow you entrance?"

It took a second for the light to go on. Jonathan bowed his most formal bow. "You are correct, Kenji *Sama*. I have been most rude and disrespectful. You deserve the exact opposite. I humbly ask your forgiveness for my bad manners." He bowed again and turned to leave.

Kenji shot his granddaughter an exasperated look. "Do you not see your old grandfather and this Kami are in need of *cha*? You get more useless every day!"

Mayu smiled as she bowed and left to fetch tea.

The old man gestured for Jonathan sit and did the same, settling into *seiza* on the matted floor, his eyes boring deeply into the young American's. "Relax," said Kenji, "I am merely seeing what you already know so I may determine where to begin." After several uncomfortable seconds, he finally spoke. "For you, we must begin near the very beginning, far before what we Japanese take for granted."

Jonathan blushed, afraid the healer could, in fact, read what he was thinking – that what was coming would be nothing more than a bunch of mumbo jumbo. *Kancho* had once warned him, "When in combat, the most skilled of enemies can read your thoughts as if their minds were connected to yours. So you must hide your intent even from yourself." Until that day, he neither understood what he meant by it, nor believed anyone could do such a thing.

The *shoji* slid open and Mayu entered with a tray of hot tea. She knelt on the floor and served her grandfather, then the Kami.

"The human body is the most wondrous of machines," said old Kenji, his face apparently not knowing how to smile even when speaking of things he obviously loved. "It can return from harsh treatment, even severe injury, stronger than before."

The old man noticed Mayu still there and shooed her away. "This is not for the ears of foolish women. Go!" She winked at Jonathan as she slid the *shoji* closed behind her.

"Where were we?" Kenji asked, his eyes blank for a couple of seconds.

"The reason our bodies can return from harsh treatment stronger than before," Jonathan repeated.

"Ah, yes," said the healer. "Unlike any machine man can devise, we are capable of our own repair, one of the many gifts given us by the Gods. Do you know why this is so?"

Jonathan wasn't sure if Kenji was asking if he knew why the gods had given this gift to us or why our bodies were able to rebuild themselves. He had learned long ago that the Japanese weren't big on questions. It inferred the speaker had done a poor job at explaining something, so simply shook his head.

"Because we were created from the basic elements – earth, mineral, vegetation, water, and air," said the old man. "It is with these that we make ourselves well."

Jonathan had never heard the old man speak more than a couple of sentences. Now it seemed he would never stop.

"Unnatural substances, like western drugs, may bring about a temporary reduction in the illness. But it is merely an illusion. It will not alter the cause, only mask its symptoms, the signs of its presence. Unnatural substances remain within the body, where they can destroy that which was designed to help us build and grow and repair ourselves."

Kenji gave the room a quick once over, then leaned close to Jonathan's ear. "Do you swear never to repeat what I am about to tell you?"

"I do."

"When I was a boy, I saw with my own eyes, penned in the hand of Prince Ninigi, a 3000-year-old scroll written in the language of the ancient gods. It contained the instructions the Great Prince received from his mother, the Sun Goddess – what was best for him to eat, how he should treat his illnesses, his injuries, a guide to enable him to live long and healthy on this earth."

Jonathan flashed an amazed look, deciding it best not to ask how he knew it was written by Ninigi or how he had been able to read the ancient language, especially as a boy.

"It spoke of two critical steps," continued the healer. "The first was to carefully control his diet, ensuring his body was made strong and resistant to damage and block infiltration by illness and disease. The second was to keep his mind as strong as his body. It must be kept thusly to deny even the idea of vulnerability, which always precedes an illness, and often an injury as well. A disease cannot grow, cannot even exist, if the mind does not allow it to, does not suppress its defenses so it can find fertile ground in which to take root. If one is weak-willed and a disease does take hold, the Sun-Goddess said we must get to the root of the disease and not merely its leaves, its outward appearances. Here at the Kan, we properly control the diet so illness is seldom seen and disease does not exist."

Jonathan was skeptical.

"When you were a small boy in America," said Kenji, "did you ever have a cold, sore throat, the influenza?"

"Of course. Everyone did."

"How many times have you been ill since you came to the Kan?"

He had never thought about it before. He had had the chicken pox and the mumps, but that was before he came to Japan. As far as a cold, the flu, sore throats, he couldn't remember for sure whether he had ever suffered from any of those while he had been there. "I cannot think of any."

"And who cared for your health before you came to this place?"

"You mean like a doctor?"

"In the West, they call such people doctors. But they are little different from the bleeders and leechers who once believed they could rid their patients of illness by draining out what they considered the cause – bad blood. Much of their medicine is poisonous to a pure body because we possess many meridians, lines of power, which transport *ki*, the life energy. When one of these is cut or altered, physically or chemically, an imbalance occurs and the body can no longer repair itself along that meridian. For true healing one must follow the advice left us by the Sun-Goddess and use the curative herbs and teas, the healing touch, and mental healing."

"Mental healing?" That was a new one.

"It is most old and used to diagnose and rectify imbalances, even injuries."

"Bone-breaks, torn ligaments, and cuts?" he asked skeptically.

"*Hai.*" The healer nodded gravely.

"How can a mind move a broken bone back into place?"

"Some injuries and illnesses must also include physical correction, a healing touch, that is true. But even in such cases mental healing also speeds recovery."

"Can you teach me some of this?"

Kenji's face flushed red. Jonathan immediately stood and bowed deeply. "Please forgive me. I was not questioning you. If something like this exists, it would be extremely helpful to me as a Kami. But I should not have made such an unreasonable request."

The old man glared at him, his eyes burning coals. "I will forgive you this time, because you are *gaijin* and know no better."

Jonathan bowed to leave.

"So you no longer desire to learn?"

Now Jonathan was confused.

"Sit," said the old man.

"Close your eyes," said Kenji and he did as he was told. "Breathe as you do in *zazen*." Jonathan filled his lungs, held it, then let them deflate slowly. "If you were to point to where you resided," asked Kenji, "that part of you that thinks and views the world, where would it be?"

Jonathan touched his finger against the center of his forehead. He had been through similar exercises before.

"Move your consciousness from behind your eyes to the inside of your right ear." Kenji said, then waited a few seconds for him to comply. "While retaining your awareness as it is, expand it to include the inside of your left ear."

Struggling to split his consciousness and become aware simultaneously of the inside of both ears, he nodded.

"This time, expand it further until you are aware of every point within your skull." Kenji waited. "Good," he said, "you are not so stupid after all."

The old man's compliment, his first ever, caused Jonathan to temporarily lose focus and his consciousness recoiled back behind his eyes.

"*Bakayaro*! I spoke too soon," scolded the old man. Quickly, Jonathan expanded his concentration so that it again filled his entire head. "Better," Kenji hissed. "Now, imagine that the inside of your body is but a giant balloon. Fill it to its entirety with your consciousness, as if it were air filling a balloon."

Jonathan sat completely motionless as his mind flowed into every square inch of his body. It was what *Kancho* had been trying to teach him to do while performing his *kata*, a simultaneous awareness of the position of every joint and the amount of tension within every muscle, something he had yet to master.

"The injury on your left wrist, focus upon it."

Jonathan's concentration narrowed to the sore spot in his wrist.

"View the injury in your mind. See the fluid around it being pulled away, the swelling and puffiness reduced; see the fissure in the bone being strengthened, minerals gathering along the break and fusing the pieces together again."

After a while, Jonathan opened his eyes and flexed his wrist. "It does feel better," he said, surprised but unsure if it was due to Kenji's mental exercise. There was no way it could have mended itself in just a few minutes.

Kenji looked at him as if reading his thoughts. "Punch my nose," he said.

"I can't hit you. Why would I want to do that?"

"Because I ordered you to do so! Punch me or get out!"

"Are you sure?"

"Punch me!"

Jonathan snapped out a quick jab that connected lightly with the old man's flat nose. Blood soon trickled out of his nostrils.

Kenji flicked his hand towards his nose. "Look."

"I'm sorry..." Jonathan stammered.

"Shut up and watch closely!" Kenji closed his eyes and slowed his breathing. After a few seconds, he reopened his eyes and smiled stiffly.

Jonathan wasn't sure what was so funny, other than the sight of Kenji trying to smile, which made him smile too. Then he noticed it. Kenji's nose was no longer bleeding.

"*Oos*, Kenji *Sensei*," he said, bowing low.

25

Yoritomo and Jonathan ambled out of the main building and headed up the winding pathway toward the garden, *bento* box lunches in hand.

"Come with me. We can have some fun in Tokyo," said Yoritomo.

"I can't. Kenji *Sensei* will boot me if I miss."

"My sister will be there," Yoritomo added enticingly.

"And what about your father? Will he be there too?"

Yoritomo laughed. "Got me."

Jonathan wrapped his arm around Yoritomo's shoulders. "You know, if you could convince your uncle to reappoint the Kami to oversee his security, we could probably negotiate a deal where we could be together in Tokyo a lot."

Yoritomo smiled. "*Kancho* been grinding on you too?"

Jonathan nodded.

"I already told him I would be happy to speak with my uncle when I see him."

They found a vacant bench and sat down. Yoritomo opened his *bento*. "No, not *fugu* again!" he cried.

Jonathan glanced over to see if his friend had something different than he did, but both their boxes contained the same thing – *tofu* and pickled vegetables over rice. Yoritomo popped a piece of *tofu* into his mouth with his chopsticks, pretending to savor it. "Mmmm. I love *fugu*."

"When are you leaving?"

"This afternoon. The Imperial Guard is sending one of their limos."

"Will your..."

"No. I tried to get them to bring Nana with them but she has too much homework. They will pick her up on the way."

Jonathan nodded and returned to his lunch, his disappointment obvious. Yoritomo smiled and slapped his buddy on the back. "I'll make them bring her with us when they drive me back tonight."

Jonathan's face beamed. "Then I'll wait up."

"There you are!" said Aoshima, shoving the library doors open and striding to where Jonathan sat at a table covered in old Japanese newspapers. Their headlines all mentioned something about the murder of an American Ambassador. "*Kancho* needs you, *isogi*!"

Kubo stood in front of a brightly lit table, a map spread out in front of him. "What did Kiyoshi tell you about his trip?" he asked as Jonathan rushed into the new command center.

"Just that they were going to his grandmother's birthday. He wanted me to go with him but I had promised Kenji *San* I would assist him."

"A farmer on his way home from a night of *sake* claims he saw Arab terrorists force their limousine off the road. According to him, some in the car were shot and others abducted."

Jonathan felt as if someone had buried a hard front kick deep into his guts. His mind spun in a flood of thoughts and images.

"It was too dark to identify which," continued Kubo. "We have sent a team to determine if it is true and what occurred."

"Can't you just call the Imperial Guard? They were under their protection, right?"

Kubo scoffed. "We only learned of the incident because Prince Yoritomo called, hoping his son was still here. I had the unfortunate task of telling him he was not."

"Will we be allowed to debrief the witness?" asked Aoshima.

"He is in the hands of the same buffoons who lost them," spat Kubo. "They will not want us anywhere near anyone who could prove their incompetence."

The phone rang and *Kancho* snatched up the receiver. As he listened, his shoulders slumped and Jonathan's sank along with them. "They reached the site," he said after hanging up, his voice heavy. "The driver, security guard, and a member of the Household Agency were killed. Kiyoshi and Nanami are missing and presumed in the hands of the kidnappers."

26

After three days of fruitless searching, Prince Yoritomo fired the Imperial Guard and replaced them with the Tamashii Kami. Although they had been ordered to stand down during the interim period, *Kancho* and the Kami had not sat idle. His intelligence people had discreetly gathered information. Literally around the clock, he and his command team had proposed, debated, and discussed possible tactics and strategies they would implement as soon as the Imperial Household Agency was eventually forced to turn the search over to them.

Within minutes of receiving word of their reappointment, Kami were dispersed throughout Japan. Past favors were called in for repayment and leads investigated, no matter how unlikely. But after another two days, they had turned up little more than the meager information gathered by the Imperial Guard.

Jonathan stood hunched over a map, feverishly scribbling down notes, his pace in stark contrast to the three exhausted Kami who slumped in their chairs. Every idea and suggestion they had come up with had produced nothing. All they could do was wait to see if anything trickled down from their efforts.

Kancho Kubo, with Aoshima on his heels, burst through the door and surveyed the room. The men snapped to their feet. "Where do we stand?" demanded the Master General.

"We spoke with the *oyabun*, those who would speak with us. They promised to investigate the matter and pass on anything they might learn, in return for sizable 'finder's fee,' of course. We told them to name their price. So far, not a word."

"Did you speak with Murakami?" asked Jonathan?

"He was 'unavailable.' His secretary said she would pass our request on to him and he would get back to us if he so opted."

"And the freighter in Yokohama?"

"Our men searched it… and all of those nearby, in case the informant was mistaken. We turned up only a young couple who had gone onboard in hopes of getting the captain to marry them and bypass their families' objections."

An aide appeared at the door. "Excuse me, *Kancho*," he said. "Yukio Murakami is on the phone. He says it is extremely important he speak with you."

The men looked at each other, then Kubo snatched up the receiver. He grunted in acknowledgement and listened. His face reddened. "That is not acceptable," he said calmly but his eyes blazed at whatever Murakami was telling him. "I will discuss it with my staff. Someone will get back to you." He slammed down the receiver and sat in silence for a few seconds. "He claims to have information about the Prince and Princess but will only reveal it to Jonason."

"Why Lusk San?" asked Aoshima, clearly surprised.

"I suspect to force Jonason – and us – to beg for his help," said Kubo. "If we decide to succumb to his blackmail, I want him informed that we will hold him personally responsible for Kami Lusk's complete safety. If anything whatsoever happens to him, and I mean anything, he will greatly regret it."

The next morning, a kitchen aide shuffled into the Command Center with a tray of food and a large pot of tea. Everyone who had been there the night before was still there. *Kancho* and Jonathan both waved off offers of food but accepted mugs of tea. As Kubo took his first sip, one of his assistants rushed in, bowed, and handed him a large manila envelope. "This was found taped inside a public telephone booth on the Ginza."

Kubo slid a photo and crudely written letter onto the table. He read through the note. "It is a list of demands from some group calling itself the Japanese Red Brigade. Do any of you know anything about them?"

No one did.

"Have someone gather everything they can on any group by that or any similar name," he told the aide, who quickly left.

Kubo studied the grainy photo. It showed a frightened, disheveled Nanami, her *kimono* torn and dirty and a copy of that morning's issue of the *Asahi Shimbun* in her hands. Her brother stood sullenly beside her. His left eye was badly swollen, his lip cut, and his nose bent and bloody. He glared intensely at someone just out of frame.

On the back of the photo was an inscription: "For their seven hundred and twenty million crimes against the people, the royal leeches of Japan have twenty-four hours in which to pay a 720 million yen fine or these criminals will become the first of many to be executed."

Jonathan snatched up the photo and studied it, tears filling his eyes faster than he could blink them away. "Set up the meeting with Murakami," he said, his jaw muscles bulging. "I will beg on my knees if that will get them back."

"As a representative of the Kan, you would also be begging for myself and the organization," said Kubo. "That is not acceptable."

"Then kick me out and I will beg for myself!"

Murakami sat at his desk, impatiently tapping the floor with his foot. His intercom buzzed and his hand flashed over and hit the call button. "*Hai!*"

"The *gaijin* is on his way," said his secretary.

A cold grin twisted Murakami's face. "Bring *sake* and join me."

The sound of *geta* clopped down the wooden outer walkway towards Murakami's office. The door opened and an ageless woman in pink mini skirt and revealing, low-cut top slipped out of her stilted sandals and flowed into the room, her feet no larger than a small child's. She set a tray onto Murakami's desk and carefully poured two cups of *sake*.

"This is a momentous day," he said, raising his cup in a toast. "Today, the past is to be made clean and the future secure for our *kumi*. *Kampai*," he said, downing the warm rice-wine in one gulp.

"*Kampai*," echoed Haiko, taking but a sip of hers.

"What time will he arrive?" he asked.

"Eleven."

"He must, of course, be kept waiting a proper amount of time, *neh*? Two hours would seem correct, would it not?"

"*Hai*!" she said, bowing.

From his middle drawer, he withdrew a thick manila envelope, opened the flap, and slid its contents – a stack of photographs – onto his desk. "Do you know what these are?" he asked.

"I do not, Murakami *Sama*."

"Bait to catch a mother-fornicating *gaijin*," he said, chuckling.

A Land Rover bearing the Kami Kan *kanji* logo on its doors, hood, and back hatch weaved its way up a steep, twisting mountain road, the jagged white peaks of the Japanese Alps stretching across the distant horizon.

Jonathan sat in the passenger's seat, lost in thought, as Hiro Kawano handled the wheel. Murakami had demanded Jonathan come alone. But *Kancho* wouldn't hear of it. Either he came with two team members or he wouldn't come at all. The two men had finally agreed on one. Hiro, who had been hand-picked by *Kancho*, was battle-seasoned and a senior Kami.

The spectacular scenery went unnoticed as other images played in Jonathan's mind – his last chat with Yoritomo; Nanami running from her father to console him at the funeral; their naked swim together; Hiroko pressing his and Nanami's hands together at the award ceremony and wishing them happiness. He could still feel the euphoric sensation of that touch, so soft it was like the faint, airy breath of a kiss or a whisper.

But it was not just his secret love of the young princess. Yoritomo was his best and only friend. When they first met, his enemies had become Kiyoshi's enemies. His battles had become Kiyoshi's battles. They had fought hard and bled together on the *dojo* floor and in the arrow-catching oval. They were blood brothers.

The thought of Nanami and Yoritomo in the hands of kidnappers and possibly dying filled him with a mixture of rage and remorse. Everyone who had ever become close to him had died. He couldn't help fearing they would pay the same price too and it would be his fault. Had he gone, as Yoritomo wanted, perhaps he could have done something to thwart the kidnapping.

They rounded a bend in the road and saw the Murakami compound up ahead. "Ready yourself," said Hiro. "We are here."

At the gate, they were greeted deferentially by a *yakuza* lieutenant and escorted into a reception room with all due respect. Inside, soft traditional Japanese folk music played over the stereo. Murakami's secretary offered them *cha* or *sake*, whichever they preferred, as well as rice balls and other snacks. Jonathan passed on everything, but Hiro passed only on the *sake*. He accepted the *cha* and ate every snack put in front of him.

Jonathan felt a bit guilty, thinking what he had about his former *sempai*. Yukio must have matured since they had last seen each other. But as a half hour passed, then an hour, then an hour and a half, Jonathan's anger grew to a boiling point and he cursed himself for being so naive. *People don't change.* He showed his wristwatch to Hiro. The Kami shrugged, then went back to the Japanese fashion magazine he had been reading.

At last, the intercom buzzed. "Haiko, please show Mr. Lusk in." It was Murakami's voice.

"You may go in, Lusk San," said the secretary. "I must ask that Kawano San remain here, as agreed."

"Could you bring more of those rice cakes?" Hiro asked as Haiko led Jonathan out of the room.

"Welcome, my old *kohai*," said Yukio, rising to shake his hand, the western gesture not lost on Jonathan. "I am sorry to keep you waiting so long, but this matter with the Emperor's family...a most difficult case to track. Please," he said, gesturing toward the chair across from him.

"What do you have for us?" asked Jonathan, his voice sharp and his face still flushed from the long wait.

"Did you bring the promissory note?"

Jonathan reached inside the breast pocket of his fatigue jacket and removed a folded piece of parchment. "How much? Your secretary said only that we needed to be prepared to meet your expenses."

"Our expenses on this were, as you might appreciate, unusually high. After all, it would be insulting, would it not, if the lives of two members of the Emperor's personal family were only worth a paltry sum."

"How much?"

"Please understand, all monies go to outside informants. We are only too happy to be of assistance to the Emperor and the Kami Kan. We keep nothing for ourselves."

"How much?!"

"500 million yen."

"500 million yen!" said Jonathan, sitting abruptly up. He had expected a million, two million tops.

"As I said, it was an expensive case to track. Informants understandably feared for their safety and required a substantial amount in compensation. But if you cannot afford...."

Jonathan scrawled in the amount and unceremoniously tossed the promissory note across the desk. He had been instructed to pay whatever was asked.

"Where are they?" Jonathan demanded.

Murakami inspected the note carefully, then quickly tucked it into his top drawer and pulled out the manila envelope. Jonathan started to reach for it but Murakami laid it on the desk in front of him. "It is a very bad thing, taking the Emperor's nephew and niece – bad for Japan and bad for the Kami Kan. The Prince was within the organization's charge, was he not?"

Jonathan thrust out his upturned hand. "If you are so poorly informed that you don't even know that he was under the protection of the Imperial Guard, then I want our check back."

"You are right," said Murakami. "Placing blame will not get them back, only action. Hopefully we can help you redeem yourselves."

"Do you have something or not?"

"*Hai*, I do, in fact, have something," said Yukio, sitting up. "Here are the ones you seek." He opened the envelope and pulled out several grainy, black and white 8x10 photos. He glanced at the top one, then threw it in front of Jonathan. "This is Masayuki Ozawa." Jonathan turned the picture around and studied the man's face. "He is the one who planned the abduction. He leads a group that calls itself the Japanese Red Brigade."

Yukio tossed over two more photos. "The second is of the house where we are told Yoritomo and his sister are being held. Unfortunately it is difficult to see clearly as the pictures were taken after dark and from a distance.

The third photograph shows the terrorists getting out of their van. As you can see, three are Japanese, one a desert *gaijin*."

"Where is this house located?" Jonathan asked, studying the photo of the stone-and-log structure.

"Not too far, near the north coast, just south of Fukui, on the road between Ayu and Takefu. You will pass a thatch-roofed stone house with a stone lantern in front, then, one half kilometer further, cross an old stone bridge. You will see the dirt road that leads to the farmhouse on the right."

Jonathan snatched up the photographs and got to his feet.

"This woman, I am told, assisted in the kidnapping," the young *oyabun* said, casually removing another photograph from his drawer and tossing it across his desk.

Jonathan picked it up and gave the grainy shot a cursory glance. The clock was ticking and he was eager to get going.

"It may not be of much use as they intend to kill her today... if they have not done so already."

Murakami's eyes studied Jonathan's face as his former *kohai* glanced at the photo, stifling a smile as the American's eyes flared in recognition.

"What did you say about them killing her?"

"She is the loose end, as you Americans say."

"Where is she now?"

"Still at the house, I would imagine."

"Can you call *Kancho* and tell him what you have told me? Our radio is out of range."

"Of course. How could I not help my former comrades?"

As Jonathan strode towards the door, Yukio pushed the button on his intercom. "Haiko, I need to speak personally with *Kancho* Kubo at the Kami Kan," he said loudly, then waited until Jonathan was out of his office. "Are they gone?" he asked his secretary.

"*Hai.*"

"Cancel that call. Instead, call Yasuo. Tell him 'the boar cries for its sow.'"

"Yes, sire."

27

Reiko knelt on the closet floor, one hand shielding her swollen eyes from the sudden light while her other tugged at her torn, soiled kimono in a futile attempt to cover herself.

Asim grabbed her arm. He yanked her up so hard that she cried out in pain, attracting Zuma's attention from the next room. "Control your animals!" he hissed at Ozawa. "If she dies before he arrives, you receive nothing! Not a single yen."

"Release her," ordered Ozawa.

Asim reluctantly let the woman drop to the floor, where she lay moaning.

Hiro slowed to negotiate a tight hairpin as Jonathan keyed the Land Rover's radio yet again. All he got was a hiss of static. "Still nothing," he said. "Hopefully he made the call."

"You should have called from his office yourself."

"I was afraid it would take too long to explain," Jonathan said, remorse heavy in his voice. "Plus I knew *Kancho* would surely have questions that only Murakami could answer."

Hiro scoffed. "Now we do not know if backup is coming, which means it will take even longer."

Jonathan didn't need to be reminded. He had been stupid to trust Murakami. But when he recognized Reiko in the photo, time had become his only concern.

Dusk was falling as the Land Rover approached the first structure of any kind they had seen in miles. It was a thatch-roofed house and there was a stone lantern of sorts in front. At some point in the house's obviously long history, the landlord had converted the lantern into a mailbox.

Soon, as Murakami had noted, they crossed a stone bridge.

"This has to be the place!" said Jonathan.

Hiro pulled off the road and hid the SUV among the trees and foliage. He snatched up the mic and keyed it. Still nothing. Quietly, he opened the door. "There was a light in the house. I will run back and see if they have a phone."

"I'll scout out the hideout," Jonathan said, jumping out.

"No! You will wait here. They may not..." But his words fell on deaf ears. Jonathan was already lost among the trees.

Asim squatted on his haunches in the corner, smoke curling up from the cigarette dangling from his thick lips. His dark eyes burned into his two superiors, Ozawa and Zuma, who had looked in on the woman again as they double-checked to make sure everything was in readiness. The instant the two men headed outside, the big Arab flicked his cigarette away and stood up. "Leave us," he said to Aki.

The Japanese rolled his eyes. "Not again, Asim. It will fall from your body like a wilted branch if you take her again."

"We depart soon," the Arab answered, his eyes fixed on Reiko, who cowered on the closet floor. "In Lebanon, there will be no one to love but camels, sheep, and our hands. Besides, she will soon be dead. I am only allowing the poor woman to die in bliss."

As Aki left, Asim crossed the room and shoved a battered and defenseless Reiko onto her back.

With his submachine gun at the ready, Jonathan pushed his way through the thick underbrush. His arms and face were webbed with bleeding red lines by the time he came to the edge of an old sweet-potato field, gone to seed and overgrown with weeds. Across the treeless bowl of land sat the stone house in the photograph.

From his hiding place behind a rocky outcropping, Jonathan focused his binoculars on three men chatting just outside the front door. Two dressed in military fatigues listened to a third dressed in suit and tie. All were well armed – two AK-47s and an Uzi. He swept his binoculars across the front of the house, then the field and surrounding forest, but found no additional men. Behind him, a sound. He dropped his binoculars and snapped the muzzle of his weapon around, only to see Hiro.

"He never called," Hiro said, "but they are now on their way."

"Sorry, I was so stupid," he offered, getting only a disgusted stare from the Kami. Jonathan shouldered his weapon and started toward a lower outcropping. Hiro grabbed his coattail. "We can't just sit here!" Jonathan pleaded.

"Without backup, we WILL sit here. That is an order!"

A man shrieked. A split second later Reiko launched herself through the open side window, clearly not caring that she landed on her chest and face in the dirt. She sprang to her feet and ran as fast as her short, strong legs would carry her. When she emerged from around the side of the house, she saw that Zuma and his henchmen had spotted her.

Yanking up the bottom of her torn kimono, Reiko raced between the trees, bullets kicking up furrows of dirt beside her bare feet and sending bark flying. She turned abruptly and sprinted down the hill and into the fallow field. An automatic rifle rattled from somewhere behind the rocks to her left and she slid to a stop. She started back to her right but bullets from the house cut her off. She froze.

"Over here!" Jonathan yelled from behind the outcropping. "It's me, Jonathan."

Tears of joy poured down her face as she ran toward him and he toward her, while Hiro lay down covering fire, keeping their attackers at bay.

When they met in the middle of the field, Reiko tried to hug Jonathan but he latched onto her wrist and rushed her towards the rocks. As they scurried for cover, Ozawa peered over the top of the hip-high grass.

"*Isogi!*" Hiro yelled, pinning down their attackers again with a long burst, so long that his clip emptied and the bolt clanged open.

The battle-seasoned Ozawa reacted instantly to the sound. He sprang to his feet and rushed off a shot at the runners' legs. His first went wide. But his second struck the woman's calf and she went flying, pulling Jonathan down with her. He tried to lift her but she was thrashing about so violently that it was impossible. Jonathan waved frantically to Hiro, then opened fire on their attackers as his partner left the safety of the rocks and zig-zagged through the grass toward them.

A shot cracked from the far end of the valley, somewhere in the trees. Jonathan spun and unleashed a mass of bullets into what he guessed was the sniper's position. The bolt of his SCK clanged open. As he flattened himself to switch clips, he caught a glimpse of Reiko, who was now barely moving, her eyes glazed, shock setting in.

"Hiro!" he yelled. Getting no response, he craned his neck up and looked over the top of the grass. Nothing.

"Your comrade is dead," yelled Zuma. "You have fifteen seconds to give yourself up or the woman will also die."

Jonathan slid his arms under Reiko's armpits, intending to drag her to cover. But the sniper fired again, sending up a spatter of dirt beside his feet. They were both clearly in the man's sights.

"You now have ten seconds. The next bullet goes into her head," said Zuma, before fixing his eyes on the sweep hand on his watch. "Five, four, three, two, one. Shoot her!"

Jonathan stood and raised his hands. He had no choice. She was all the family he had left. "She needs help!" he called, hoping his fears about their goal was wrong or that *Kancho* would arrive soon.

Zuma dusted the dirt and leaves from his tailored suit as he and the Marxists strode through the tall grass, their weapons trained on the American. "Do not forget," he said in a low voice, just loud enough for Ozawa, Sadao, and Aki to hear, "we kill the woman first, in front of the *gaijin*. Then, he dies."

"If he is to die as well, why not just kill them both and be done with it?" asked Sadao. "The longer it takes, the more we are put at risk."

Zuma shot him a look. "Because that is what I want!"

"Help her," Jonathan pleaded as Sadao jerked his rifle out of his hands.

The *yakuza* boss sidled up beside him. He yanked Jonathan's .45 from its holster, tossed it into the grass, then held a photo up next to his face. "It is him," he confirmed.

A wave of his arm brought the shirtless *yakuza* sniper running down from the trees, his muscular arms and bare upper body covered in tattoos of dragons and masked *ninja* warriors. With everyone momentarily distracted, Jonathan's eyes searched the grass for his pistol. It was behind him and to his right. When he looked back around, Zuma was staring him in the eye. "The pistol," the Japanese said to his underling, who picked it up and slipped it under his belt.

The sniper slid behind Jonathan, torqued his arm into a painful hammerlock, and wrapped his forearm around his throat. The man's grip felt odd. His little finger and part of his index finger were missing. A *yakuza* who failed a mission would often cut a joint from one of his fingers and present it to his superiors in apology. This man had obviously failed several times. Unfortunately, it didn't look like he would lose another joint on this mission.

Zuma squinted as he studied the young American's face. "I did not notice it in the photo. It must have been taken long ago. But looking at you now, I see much of your grandfather in you," he said. "Of course," he snickered, "the last time I saw that old coward, Eli, he was screaming like a little girl."

Jonathan bristled, causing the *yakuza* to leverage his arm higher, hunching him forward. The *yakuza* boss turned his attention to the woman, who lay on the ground moaning faintly as blood poured from the jagged wound in her calf, turning the loose earth black.

Nonchalantly, Zuma pressed the muzzle of his automatic rifle against Reiko's temple and braced himself for the recoil. Jonathan back-kicked the *yakuza* behind him, so hard that the man's knee shattered. In one smooth motion, he spun behind the man and yanked his .45 from his belt.

"Move away or he's dead!" Jonathan yelled, jamming the pistol's barrel against the base of the sniper's skull.

With no sense of urgency, Zuma took careful aim at the center of the sniper's chest. Jonathan didn't budge, knowing he was safely behind Zuma's own man. But he was wrong. As Zuma's finger flinched, Jonathon twisted sideways, contorting his body as he had during the arrow catch. The bullet passed through the *yakuza's* chest and crackled just past his own. Jonathan snapped up the barrel of his .45 and fixed it on the *yakuza* boss, who aimed his weapon at him, along with the three Marists. It was a crumbling, lopsided standoff and Jonathan knew it.

A pistol fired from the tall grass, pulling everyone's eyes onto its source. Asim, racked in pain and full of rage, stumbled through the grass, his pistol in one hand, his other covering his left eye. As he got nearer, blood and a clear fluid could be seen leaking from between his fingers. "Where is she!" he demanded.

Zuma's head snapped back around in time to see Jonathan sprinting towards the rocks. He and the others opened fire but the young American zig-zagged erratically, as he had been taught, and their shots missed. Along the way, Jonathan snatched up his dead comrade's automatic weapon before diving behind the outcropping.

He scrambled back into position and fired. Zuma, Ozawa, and Aki hit the deck. But behind them, Sadao was directing Asim to where Reiko lay in the tall grass. The Arab staggered over and shoved the barrel of his pistol into her mouth.

"No!" Jonathan yelled, rushing off a shot that hit the Arab in the stomach. As Asim hunched forward from the impact, he squeezed the trigger.

Bullets peppered the stone outcropping, forcing Jonathan to duck away. He swung around to the other side of the rock. But when he looked again, Zuma and the terrorists were running toward the house, half dragging Asim behind them.

With part of him still clinging to hope, Jonathan sprinted toward where Reiko lay, not seeing or hearing anything else, including what had sent his attackers running – the faint whopping sound of helicopters. "God, please," he prayed as he ran, "you've taken everyone else. Please don't take her too."

He dropped to his knees and pressed two fingers against Reiko's carotid artery, desperate to find a pulse. But there was none. Tears poured down his cheeks and fell onto Reiko's bloody, swollen face. At that time and in that place, Jonathan shed all the tears Hiroko had forbidden him to weep for his mother and his grandfather as he straightened Reiko's *kimono* and tenderly removed grass and dirt from her hair. Leaning over, he cupped her battered face in his hands and kissed her goodbye. "I hope God lets you eat *fugu* every day," he said.

Anger soon overpowered his sorrow. He readied his weapon and ran toward the ancient house, no longer caring whether he lived or died. All he wanted was to kill those responsible for murdering Reiko and apparently his grandfather too. But as he drew nearer, he remembered something important – Nanami and Yoritomo might be inside.

Jonathan flattened himself against the front of the house and peeked in through a gap in a wooden shutter. The front room was empty. Silently, he twisted the ancient wrought-iron handle, then kicked the front door open and lurched into the room, the muzzle of his submachine gun swinging left, then right. The room was clear.

Two trails of blood crossed the wooden floor. One, a series of dried drops, seemed to lead to a back bedroom. The second, a continuous red line, led to the house's ancient kitchen, across its packed-earth floor, and ended in front of a warped pantry door that stood slightly ajar.

Jonathan nudged the door open with the barrel of his rifle. There was nothing inside except a couple of apples so old they were little more than black marbles. When he pressed the end panel with his hand, it swung inward, revealing a dark tunnel.

Aki and Sadao struggled to maneuver Asim's large, lanky body through the narrow tunnel fast enough for Zuma. The *yakuza* boss finally blew. "We should have left him in the field, like I said! That would have sent the Kami after the desert *gaijin* instead of us!"

"We do not leave our men behind," responded Ozawa, who brought up the rear. "Would you also prefer I not set the devices to save time?" Ozawa asked sarcastically. "Or would you like to rush on and leave our rear unprotected?"

Zuma waved disgustedly. Ozawa knelt and clinched his penlight between his teeth. His obviously well-practiced hands quickly strung a thin trip-wire across the tunnel and attached it to a pack of explosives he buried under a nearby rock. Moving a few feet deeper into the tunnel, he set another.

"Be warned!" said Zuma. "I DO leave behind men who are too slow. Either leave him, move faster, or find your own way out!"

Jonathan rushed through the tunnel. He had no intention of allow-ing those who had murdered Reiko to escape unpunished with Nanami and Yoritomo. But the tunnel soon divided, with branches and drag marks heading in three directions, forcing him to stop and make a closer inspec-tion. They were obviously covering their route. He headed up one branch. Ten feet in, the marks stopped. He double-back and followed the second, aware that valuable time was being rapidly consumed. It too was a false lead. To make up time, he almost ran up the third branch, heading at full speed towards Ozawa's booby trap.

28

An olive-drab Huey helicopter swooped in fast and low. It crossed the length of the small valley before disappearing over the tree tops. Four more heavily-armed Hueys raced in from north, south, east, and west, then hovered, their guns trained on the structure below. Ropes dropped and men rappelled from the crafts' bellies, where they quickly formed into small combat units. As they relayed their way to within thirty feet of the stone structure, a small executive helicopter, carrying Kubo and Aoshima, landed in the fallow field. The master general scanned the scene with his field glasses, then nodded to Aoshima, who gave the signal for the assault to begin.

A Kami team laid down heavy covering fire while three of its members crawled beneath the stream of tracer bullets to the house. There, they attached explosives to the door and heavy wooden shutters.

"Slow down!" Jonathan heard someone yell from deeper into the tunnel. As he ran, moving as fast as he could while hunched over, his mind laid plans for what he would do when he caught up with them. He was lost in thought when his flashlight beam reflected off a silver wire directly in front of him. A jolt of fear yanked his lead knee higher in mid-step. But his body was angled forward and committed. His full weight landed heavily onto his lead boot, where he froze, waiting to learn if he lived or died.

When nothing happened, his flashlight revealed how close he had come and how dangerous his position still remained. He was astride the wire. Any misstep and it would detonate. He took a deep breath and let it out slowly, gathering his wits. Delicately, he eased his rear foot up and over.

He would have to move more carefully, he lectured himself. If he missed another trip-wire, he'd be of no help to anyone. But Ozawa had coated the second wire in mud. So Jonathan's flashlight beam revealed nothing as he approached the second device. Just as his foot was about to make contact, an explosion shook the tunnel and startled him. He jerked around, afraid the first device had detonated.

Dust, finely shredded stone, and chunks of old wood roiled out of the house's front door and windows, filling the air with the pungent odor of cordite. On the team leader's command, tear gas canisters sailed through every opening.

Eye and lung-burning clouds of white smoke soon billowed out of the house. The light breeze caught it and moved it toward where Kubo and his command staff stood. All but *Kancho* turned away to shield their eyes. His remained locked onto the hazy doorway. "Hold your fire!" he yelled.

Gagging from smoke and gas, Jonathan staggered out into the welcomed breeze. "Inside!" he yelled. "An escape tunnel!" Still coughing, he ran back into the house, followed by Kami in gas masks. "Be careful! The tunnel's booby-trapped after the first fork!"

One after another, the men crawled into the dark hole. Jonathan grabbed the sides of the trapdoor to follow but Kubo latched onto the back of his belt.

"Nanami and Yoritomo are down there," Jonathan insisted.

"You saw them?"

"No, but…"

"These men are experts and far more experienced than you. Besides, I need you here for debriefing."

Reluctantly, Jonathan turned away from the tunnel. He ignored the sting and the tears streaming down his face as he led Kubo to the back bedroom, where he showed him the pool of blood.

"Tell them they are likely transporting someone very injured," *Kancho* told one of his aides. "That should slow their escape."

As soon as the two moved outside, a medic faced Jonathan into the wind and rinsed his eyes with water.

"*Kancho*," said Hayashi, one of the senior Kami, peeling off his gas mask. "My men came upon something odd, a dead desert *gaijin*. He had a deep puncture wound in his left eye and a high caliber gun shot to the gut. Unless you desire otherwise, they will extract his body upon their return."

"Leave him. Have they found anything that would help locate the tunnel's exit?"

"Not as yet. It forked into three directions. Each fork divided again and again, branching throughout the entire mountain, it seems. With more men, we could search more quickly."

"What about the Yoritomos? Any sign of them?"

The Kami team leader shook his head. "No clue."

"It is likely the prince and princess were never here," said Aoshima. "I suspect this was merely a ruse to entrap and murder Lusk San."

"That may be true," said Kubo wearily, "but we cannot risk proceeding on that assumption. Send two more squads to find the exit and one more below. And find out who owns this property."

The team leader bowed and jogged back towards the house.

Kancho turned to Jonathan. "Show us the bodies," he said.

As Aoshima checked on the property's ownership, Jonathan led *Kancho* to where Reiko lay in the flattened grass. "I am sorry for your loss," Kubo said. "It is most odd they would be holding this same woman from your past, *neh*?"

"The prefectural clerk said its ownership of record is a front company for the Kichida Kumi." said Aoshima, rejoining them.

"I thought they were inactive?"

"For the last ten or so years. Their entire upper staff died when their heater supposedly malfunctioned and destroyed their headquarters with them in it."

"Hiro *San* is over there," Jonathan said, pointing at a spot in the tall grass near the rocks. The men headed towards their fallen Kami brother. On the way, they passed the dead sniper. Kubo knelt and checked the man's hand. His little finger and the tip of his index finger were missing. *Kancho* held the man's hand up for Aoshima and Jonathan to see. "*Yubitsume*," said Kubo. He turned the man over and searched for his wallet. There was none. "We will have to run his fingerprints."

"I know him," said Aoshima. "His name is Satou, Uyeda Satou. I had occasion to interact with him many times while attached to the national police. He was a member of the Momochi Kumi."

"*Kancho*!" hollered the communications operator. "A call! A member of the Imperial Household Agency."

Kubo jogged over to the communications tent and took the call. "The Household Agency just paid the ransom," he told Aoshima. "They believe they will soon learn where to find the prince and princess. But we both know that unlikely. I want a rapid response team standing by, nonetheless, to respond if and when they give us any actionable intelligence. Perhaps Jonason should accompany them as he knows both very well," said Kubo, looking around. "Where is Jonason?"

29

The Land Rover, its lights and motor switched off, coasted down the mountainside. It wasn't just that *Kancho* wouldn't approve, that he would want to think it all out first and gather more proof; he was legally restrained from acting until he had done those things. Acting alone, Jonathan was free to follow his gut.

When he figured that he was beyond earshot, he fired up the engine, turned on the lights, and raced downhill through the moonless night as fast as the Land Rover could go and still remain on the roadway.

After several miles, he came to a small mountain village and stopped when he saw the lights on in a tiny grocery store. He hurried inside and quickly returned with a bag of items.

The Land Rover flew around trucks and slow moving cars, passing anything that got between him and where he thought Yoritomo and Nanami might be held hostage, or where there were people who knew where to find them. *Better to die than fail again*, he lectured himself. He had failed Reiko. If he also failed Yoritomo and Nanami, he could never live with himself. This time, he would leave everything on the field of battle.

A half hour later, his headlights lit up a long row of motorcycles and cars parked bumper-to-bumper on both sides of the two-lane roadway. Five *yakuza* chatted and shared a bottle in front of Murakami's front gate.

Two of them glanced around briefly as the Land Rover sped by, before returning to their conversation.

As he crossed the bridge just beyond the Murakami compound, Jonathan flicked off his lights. He turned sharply off the roadway, flattening bushes and small trees as he hid the boxy vehicle among the thick foliage that lined the fast flowing river.

He stripped off his clothes and jumped out. Naked, he waded into the frigid white-water river, where he lathered himself from head to toe with the bar of soap he had bought at the market. He dunked beneath the rushing water and rinsed away the sweat and dirt and teargas, purifying himself for death. After he was dry, he cut off the traditional lock of hair and placed it, along with some fingernail clippings, into an envelope. All that remained was his death poem.

From the shopping bag, he took out a notepad and pen and, in as neat a hand as he could manage, wrote down the *kanji* for the poem he had composed many years earlier.

"Winter rain glistens on spring blossoms, releasing my soul to the long waiting arms of mother and father." He signed it, "Jonathan Lusk, Kami." He slid his death poem into the envelope, sealed it, and wrote "To Kancho Kubo, Kami Kan," on the outside, then hid it under the seat.

Taking a deep breath to focus his thoughts, Jonathan Lusk, Kami, stuck his pistol and extra clips into his web-belt and headed toward his destiny.

A scratchy version of Jerry Lee Lewis' *Great Balls of Fire* rose from the direction of the house as Jonathan made his way along the river bank. By the time he reached the rear of the large, enclosed grounds, the song had been restarted and the volume cranked up painfully loud.

He pulled himself up high enough to get a look over the top of the eight-foot stone wall. He had hoped to see a guarded structure where they could be holding Nanami and Yoritomo. But there were no buildings between him and the house, just a quarter acre of elaborate gardens.

On the positive side, the profusion of trees, shrubs, flowers, walkways, ponds, streams, arched bridges, and miniature pagodas would hide his approach. On the negative, they would make it far more difficult to navigate rapidly if he were discovered.

Lacking a likely target, it would have to be Plan B – break into Murakami's office and search for something that might say or indicate where they were being held. Should that fail, he would have to move on to Plan C – find Murakami and "convince" him to reveal their location.

Besides having to cross the obstacle-course of the garden, reaching and entering Yukio's office could also prove a challenge. Inside, a party was raging. People everywhere. Drunks fighting. Partially clothed men and naked women leaned out or ambled past the open windows.

Hooking a leg up, he started over the top. A nearby thumping sound flattened him against the cool stone. It didn't take long to find its source. Togo, the giant ex-sumo wrestler, and a tiny woman were making love about ten feet to his left.

Silently, he eased himself down onto the other side. As the big man reached a thunderous climax behind him, Jonathan was creeping through the garden toward the house.

"Where do you think you are going?" said Togo, in his gruff, booming voice. Jonathan froze. "Again," said the huge man. In seconds, the thumping sound resumed.

With the bright lights inside the house, the deafening blare of a new song, Jerry Lee Lewis' *Whole Lotta Shakin' Going On*, the wild pounding of dancers' feet on the wooden floor, and the raucous, drunken laughter pouring through the open doors and windows, Jonathan hoped everyone would be too occupied, too deaf, or too blind to see or hear him as he picked his way across the yard.

Luck, stealth, or great training was on his side. He snatched a peek through a rear window. Beautiful and not so beautiful girls danced naked with *yakuza*, while others danced alone in drug and alcohol-induced stupors. An entire table was covered with bottles of whiskey, sake, and champagne. Another with crystal bowls of pills and powder. A group of tattooed *yakuza* sat shirtless on the floor, drinking heavily and playing cards.

A bald *yakuza* leaned his tattooed head out a nearby window. Jonathan froze. The man took a deep final drag off his cigarette and flipped the glowing butt into the yard. His head turned towards where Jonathan stood motionless. The zing of a sword being unsheathed drew the man back inside, where it was quickly followed by the crunch of bones, women screaming, men yelling insults, and furniture crashing.

Jonathan readied his pistol. Delicately, he placed one foot onto the wooden walkway, shifted his weigh slowly onto it, then repeated the process, moving in slow motion towards the office door. Ancient houses had been deliberately constructed with squeaky boards built into the halls and elevated walkways to act as an alarm system. Like everyone else at the Dai Kan, he had been made to practice the *silent walk* many times through the years, moving back and forth across rice paper until he no longer tore the fragile sheets.

He tried the door handle, expecting it to be locked. It wasn't. He eased it open a crack and peered into the darkened room. Seeing no one, he slipped quickly inside and closed the door softly behind him.

Crossing the room, his penlight in one hand and pistol in the other, he opened Murakami's top desk drawer. Finding only pens and pencils and notepads, he rummaged through the second. Something inside caught him by surprise. He set his pistol down and reached in to grab it.

A noise. His hand went for his pistol as he fixed his light on the far corner, where a naked woman cowered on the floor. Not feeling his .45's cold metal handle, he swept his hand across the desk top. It wasn't there.

"Well," came a familiar voice out of the darkness. Jonathan spun, coiling his body to attack. The light clicked on. "Looks like we caught ourselves a sewer rat." It was Murakami, a huge .44 magnum in his hand and wearing only an unbuttoned white shirt and loosened tie.

"You know who I am and why I'm here," said Jonathan.

"You came to thank me for my help, armed and in the dead of night?"

"You're the one who kidnapped them, or ordered it, just like you murdered Reiko and tried to murder me!"

"I was right here. Ask anyone," said Murakami, his eyes flicking briefly toward the door. But it wasn't as if he was expecting help. It was as if he feared who might come through it. *He doesn't know I'm alone*, Jonathan realized.

"One of your people had a photo of me, shot at the Dai Kan. No one else could have taken it!"

"Everyone hated you! It could have been anyone!"

"Aoshima San ID'ed one of the dead *yakuza* at the scene. You'll never guess who he worked for!"

Murakami shrugged. "It had to have been someone who left with my half-uncle, Zuma. He and some Japanese trouble makers approached me a couple of weeks ago. I have photos and a tape of the meeting. They proposed a crazy plan, the kidnapping. I kicked them out of my office and expelled my half-uncle for considering such a thing. He swore to get even with me."

"He tried to implicate you to a man he was about to kill?"

"If I wanted you dead, I would have killed you myself!"

Jonathan scoffed. "If you could have, I would have died years ago. How long did you know it was your people who murdered my grandfather?"

Fear flashed across Murakami's narrow eyes, but only for a split second. He chuckled coldly. "I suppose you also believe me responsible for the assassination of your President Kennedy and Inejiro Asanuma?"

Jonathan snatched a stack of letters, held together by a rubber band, out of the desk drawer and shoved it at Murakami's face. They were his letters, the ones stolen from his Dai Kan foot locker. "How do you explain these?"

Murakami fumbled for an answer.

"Did you always know my grandfather sat on the tribunal that tried your father?"

"My uncle, the one I kicked out," he added quickly, "told me after I decided to leave the Kan."

"And you decided to kill me, Reiko, Yoritomo, and Nanami to gain revenge for your father being executed like a common criminal?"

"He was a patriot, murdered for following Imperial orders!" yelled Murakami angrily.

"The Emperor ordered him to cut the heads off his captives? Takes a real man to murder defenseless prisoners," said Jonathan. "How many *yakuza* scum did it take to throw an old, bound and unarmed diplomat off a building?" He held out his empty hands, palms up. "I'm unarmed too. Why don't you try the same with me?"

A loud cheer went up from the living room, where the party was obviously still raging. Murakami's eyes narrowed. The young *oyabun's* magnum started up. Jonathan parried it aside, grasped Yukio's bony chin with one hand and the back of his head with the other, then pivoted sharply, snapping Murakami's thin neck. As he did, the pistol discharged with a deafening boom.

The forgotten young woman screamed as Yukio crumbled to the floor and lay motionless, his eyes fixed and open. Jonathan stared in disbelief at the large bulge on the side of Murakami's neck and the odd angle of his head. It didn't seem possible that he could be alive just a second ago and now was dead.

He both heard and felt the floor-pounding sound of people running his way. Jonathan snatched up Murakami's magnum, slung the door open, and leaped across the walkway, hitting the soft earth on a dead run. Bare chested and naked men poured out of the house. Fortunately, it took a few seconds for their eyes to adjust to the darkness, giving Jonathan a head start. But not for long. Someone called out a warning and armed men poured off the walkway and into the garden.

Bullets crackled past Jonathan's head and kicked up dirt and water around his feet. He leapt the fake streams and ran through shallow *koi* ponds, zig-zagging erratically. As he angled his body and slipped through a stand of tall juniper shrubs, the hazy outline of the wall came into view. But just when he thought he would make it, a large rounded bush shifted over, blocking his path. It was the massive Togo, his tiny, naked girlfriend peeking out from behind his wide belly. Jonathan shifted over to get around the giant but the ex-sumo shifted too, surprisingly quick and agile for a man his size. The *yakuza* were closing fast and would be on him in seconds. He had to do something, and quickly.

Jonathan sprinted straight at the hulking giant. The man spread his arms to grab him. At the last instant, the young Kami leapt into the air, laid his body back, and thrust his legs out, driving both boot heels into Togo's full moon face. The big man stumbled backwards, tripped over his tiny girlfriend, and fell, slamming the back of his head against the stone wall and landing on top of the frail woman. She let out a death scream.

A sharp pain drilled straight through Jonathan's lower abdomen as he jumped onto Togo's head, dove over the wall, and landed on the other side. Behind him, he could hear the woman's wail and the mass of armed, drunken *yakuza* trying to scale the wall. Blocking out the pain, he ran as hard as his legs would carry him.

The Land Rover's engine roared. Dirt and rocks flew from its tires as it shot backwards out of the brush. He screeched to a stop in the roadway. In his rearview mirror, he caught a glimpse of a long line of headlights flicking on. He floored it.

Jonathan's hand went to the front of his shirt, where the sharp burning pain was centered. It felt wet. He held his hand up into the light of the rapidly closing cars. It was covered in blood.

The faster pursuit cars raced up behind him, two abreast. One tapped his rear bumper to distract him while the other tried to sneak alongside. Jonathan swerved to the middle of the dark, narrow roadway, leaving too little room on either side for another attempt.

He snatched the radio mic from its cradle. He wanted to let *Kancho* know where he was and what had happened, but all he got was a frustrating mixture of silence and static. "Lusk to base," he yelled, hoping it was just a weak signal. "I just left the Murakami compound. I'm heading east, with strong pursuit. I've been shot." He waited, praying for an answer. Nothing.

A shotgun blast shattered his rear window. He reached back over his shoulder and returned fire, backing his pursuit off... but only briefly. The roadway widened and a big Cadillac tried to muscle its way around him. He cranked the wheel over but the Caddie was too heavy to veer off course. The two pressed hard against each other, metal scraping as the Caddie inched its way towards his side window.

A narrow stone bridge loomed up ahead, just wide enough for one. At the last instant, Jonathan cranked the steering wheel to the left, a split second before the Caddie tried to do the same. Abruptly, the Cadillac's headlights froze in his rearview mirror and grew rapidly smaller behind him.

A tangle of cars quickly collected around the wreckage and Jonathan seized what he knew would be but a brief respite. He pressed his handkerchief tightly against the bullet hole. Then, as Kenji had taught him, he split his mind, visualized cells coagulating along the bullet's path, not sure if he was doing it right or even if Kenji's mental healing had any merit. But he had no other options. Although he could block out the pain, he could still feel blood pouring from the wound and himself growing weaker.

He wasn't afraid of dying. But he didn't want to bleed out before he could apologize to *Kancho*... and he had a lot to apologize for. He had been stupid at every turn, beginning with the first time they had met, when he thought he looked like Chimpie, his stuffed toy. Many times over the years, he had cringed at that thought. *Kancho's* flat face, bent nose, and mop of black hair had become beautiful to him and the man himself the strong, constant, ever-honorable rock in his life. One day, if he were allowed to survive and grow to manhood, he would be proud to be even one-tenth as good a man as *Kancho*. But his survival was rapidly becoming doubtful.

The thing that bothered Jonathan most, of course, was failing Nanami and Kiyoshi. His impatience may have cost them their lives and that thought was more crushing than the bullet hole in his gut.

Soon enough, a pair of cars managed to get around the wreckage and close the gap. Jonathan did his best to fend them off but knew it was only a matter of time.

A Buick tried to pass. Jonathan swerved over to cut it off but an unseen motorcycle raced out at the last instant from behind the big car. Its driver took aim and fired but only managed to shatter the passenger window behind him. The Land Rover swerved into the bike and it disappeared into the darkness.

But the move allowed the Buick room to swing onto the soft shoulder and angle its broad nose into the Land Rover's rear quarter panel. The SUV started into a spin. Jonathan cranked the wheel the opposite direction and it righted itself. But its brief, erratic route allowed the Buick to pull up beside him. A muscular *yakuza* thrust his arm out the side window and aimed his revolver at Jonathan's head. A quick bump against the car's door sent the man's pistol skittering down the roadway.

The *yakuza* grabbed hold of the SUV's broken side window. The jagged glass cut into his fingers but he refused to let go. The man began pulling himself across the ever changing gap between them. Jonathan swerved away. But instead of freeing him of the man, the move yanked him through the Buick's passenger window, leaving him hanging from the side of the SUV. The Land Rover's speedometer swiftly climbed to over 80. The *yakuza*, his knees held tight against his chest to keep his feet away from the blur of roadway beneath them, shimmied in through the window.

234

In his rearview mirror, Jonathan watched the *yakuza's* thick, tattooed body slip the rest of the way into the back compartment. He reached over his shoulder and fired, the pistol blast temporarily deafening him.

A muscular forearm snaked around Jonathan's neck. As he had been trained, he immediately turned his chin, keeping the bone of the man's powerful forearm off his windpipe. "*Yame*! Stop!" the man growled.

Jonathan aimed his pistol at where he thought the man's head would be and fired again. But the *yakuza's* grip didn't weaken. He pulled the trigger once more but got nothing. His pistol was empty. The man laughed as he squeezed tighter. "*Yame!*"

He had to do something quick. If the man pulled hard or long enough, the choke would cut off blood flow to his brain and he would lose consciousness. Jonathan hammered the man's bloody hands with his pistol butt. Nothing. Desperate, he stabbed in the car's cigarette lighter. A couple of seconds later, it popped back up. Jonathan pressed the glowing burner against the man's arm. Putrid smoke curled up from the burning flesh as the lighter sank deeper and deeper. The *yakuza* cried out and, for a second, relaxed his grip.

Jonathan slammed on the brakes. The man catapulted over the front seat and smashed head-first into the windshield. Reaching over, Jonathan flipped open the passenger door and shoved the man out with his foot. But the powerful *yakuza*, high on something, clung to the doorjamb, screaming as his feet bounced against the roadway. Jonathan nudged open the door a few inches, then jerked it closed on his fingers.

A quick glimpse into his mirror revealed the muscular man tumbling down the middle of the pavement behind him. The trailing car slammed on its brakes, trying to avoid hitting their own man. But the second car couldn't stop fast enough and piled into the first, knocking it over him.

Jonathan put distance between himself and his pursuers. But the pain in his gut was growing worse. He felt as if his life was leaking out. Again, he imagined the blood vessels along the bullet's path closing and the flow slowing.

A pair of brilliant white headlights raced up behind him. A Jaguar XKE, its top down. The two raced through a series of tight turns, bumper to bumper.

The Jag's passenger laid a shotgun on top of its windshield and aimed at the Land Rover's rear tire. Jonathan hit the brakes. The Jag bumped hard into his rear bumper, then backed off. But not for long. The *yakuza* re-aimed and rushed off a shot. The rear tire blew and the SUV jerked hard to the left. Jonathan spun the wheel to the right. The vehicle listed onto two tires, teetered, then flipped and rolled over and over before coming to a stop on its roof.

The *yakuza* jumped out and ran towards the wreckage, shotgun at the ready. He dropped onto his belly and looked in through the flattened driver's window at the motionless American, hanging upside down from his seatbelt. He eased the barrel of his shotgun through the narrow opening and pressed it against Jonathan's temple.

Headlights raced up on the other side of the overturned SUV and stopped. The *yakuza* shielded his eyes, trying to see who had joined them.

30

Kancho Kubo paced outside the stone farmhouse. A team of Kami were still in the tunnels, another was gathering evidence at the scene. Everyone else had descended on the Murakami Estate as soon as they received word from an informant that Jonathan had apparently killed the young *oyabun*.

Aoshima stuck his head through the flap of the communications tent. "The Katsuyama Police Chief is calling! He asked to speak with you."

Kancho pressed the receiver to his ear. His face softened and melted into a tired smile as he listened. He hung up and turned to Aoshima. "The prince and princess were found drugged and bound in a culvert outside Katsuyama. They are being checked medically. Get a team there, Code Three, and debrief them as soon as they are able."

"Excuse me, Aoshima *San*," interrupted the radio operator, holding out a radio mic. Aoshima snatched it out of his hand. "*Hai?*" he said, listening. He glanced gravely at Kubo. "They found Lusk San. He is injured. He crashed his vehicle while trying to escape."

"Badly?"

"They requested a medivac."

"Seal off the hospital!" Kubo demanded. "I want only trusted Kami to accompany him on the helicopter and remain by his side at all times.

237

They are to check anyone, and I mean anyone, who has access to him. They will surely follow him there."

The hospital corridor reeked of disinfectant and teemed with heavily armed Kami. Hospital staff grumbled at having to negotiate the crowded passageway and be subjected to repeated checks of their credentials.

The two stone-faced Kami guarding the private room stepped aside to allow Aoshima entrance. "You did not check my papers!" scolded Aoshima. The two men blushed, then bowed.

He pushed open the door to Jonathan's hospital room and found himself staring briefly into the barrel of *Kancho's* submachine gun. Aoshima bowed and held out a large, black and white photo. The Master General took it and glanced at the grainy image of Jonathan. It had obviously been taken by a security camera at Murakami's house. He read the *kanji* written along the bottom with a felt pen. "Only ninety million yen," noted Kubo. "Far less than I would have guessed. Perhaps they are glad to be rid of Yukio. Zuma is a far wiser man and used to being in power. Perhaps he intentionally baited and then allowed Jonason to escape at the farmhouse, hoping he would remove his replacement."

"It is difficult to understand the thinking of dishonorable men."

Kubo nodded tiredly.

"Would you like me to remain with him so you may rest?" asked Aoshima, fatigue raising his already high-pitched voice even higher.

"No... but thank you. I will remain by his side until he either recovers or leaves this world."

The Dai Kami bowed. "Kiyoshi Sama and his sister have requested permission to visit."

"That would not be wise at this time, *neh?*"

Before Aoshima could answer, a shrill, constant tone jerked the men's eyes onto Jonathan's heart monitor. "Get the doctor, *isogi!*" yelled Kubo. Aoshima bolted from the room.

Within seconds, there was a commotion outside. Kubo, his automatic rifle at the ready, jerked the door open to see his guards scrutinizing the papers and equipment of an older Japanese doctor and his assistant.

"It is okay," said Kubo, grabbing the doctor's elbow and dragging him into the room. "Join us," he ordered one of the guards.

The doctor was clearly rattled by the presence of so many armed men – his eyes, already magnified by bottle-thick glasses, looked larger than an owl's. "His heart is out of rhythm," he concluded. "I need a defibrillator."

"Then do it!"

The doctor pressed a button on the wall, an alarm sounded in the hallway. A nurse's urgent voice announced, "Code Blue, ICU Room 36!" over the loudspeaker. "Code Blue, ICU Room 36!"

Less than a minute later, a guard opened the door. "He has been checked," he said as he stepped aside to allow another doctor to push a crash cart towards the door. Kubo stopped him.

"Did you check the cart?" demanded the Master General.

The guard shook his head.

Kubo turned to Aoshima. "Have it checked, and quickly!" His senior aide hurried out, only to return in several seconds.

"Rigged," said Aoshima. "They are checking one on the next floor and, if clean, will bring it immediately."

"What does that mean?" asked the doctor.

"It contained explosives that would have gone off when you pressed the button," *Kancho* answered, matter-of-factly. The doctor and his aide blanched. When Aoshima rushed another cart into the room, they both shrunk away from it.

"Get on with it!" ordered Kubo. "This one has been checked."

The doctor opened Jonathan's hospital gown. His aide gingerly held out the defibrillation paddles as if they were live grenades. The doctor took them with equal caution.

"Make no mistakes," said Kubo, his tone a clear warning.

The doctor looked even more shaken as he delicately positioned the paddles. "Please step back," he warned Kubo, his voice quivering. Kubo didn't move. The doctor nodded weakly. His assistant mumbled a brief prayer before flipping the switch. The machine powered up to a loud whine, but didn't explode, much to the obvious relief of the doctor and his aide.

"Ready," said the assistant, his confidence returning.

"*Hajime.*"

The aide pressed and held down the button. The machine crackled like an arc welder. Jonathan's body bucked, then locked in rigid tension.

"*Yame,*" said the doctor after a couple of seconds. His aide released the button and Jonathan went limp.

All eyes fixed on the monitor. The men collectively exhaled when they saw the blue line once more a steady wave of slow, well-spaced peaks and valleys. The doctor separated Jonathan's eyelids and shined his penlight into his hazel eyes.

"Will he survive?" Kubo asked softly.

The doctor shrugged. "It is too early to tell. I will return soon to check on him again."

After everyone had left, *Kancho* dragged his chair close to the bed, sat down, and leaned in close. "I do not know if you can hear me or not," he said in English, "but there is much I feel obligated to confess."

He took a few seconds to gather his thoughts. "The first time we met, you appeared all we believed of *gaijin*. Weak, soft, unmotivated, lacking all concept of proper etiquette and honor. I accepted your application solely because of our indebtedness to your grandparents. Secretly, though, I not only expected you to fail but wished it. I am honored to say you proved me wrong and left me ashamed to have thought as I did. I ask for your forgiveness."

There was a commotion on the other side of the door. Kubo sat up, his hand going to his weapon, his eyes to the entrance. The noise, however, quickly settled back down to its previous dull buzz.

"I too lived for a time as an outcast," he continued. "My former colleagues labeled me a traitor and supposed friends deserted me. Even now, as *Kancho*, many follow me but my position allows me no true friends. Like you, I am alone in the world. We are like two lone wolves, you and I, a young one and an old gray battle-weary fellow. So, please, Jona..." Kubo struggled to get his tongue to properly shape the difficult word, "...than, be strong and rejoin us."

He sat beside his bed throughout the long night, the only light inside the dark room the blue and green glow from the monitors.

When the door opened the next morning, Kubo sprang to his feet, the muzzle of his rifle jerking upward and fixing on the female figure in the doorway. The nurse flipped on the lights, noticed the gun, and froze.

"Identification!" commanded Kubo.

"I just showed it to the goon in the hallway," she replied dismissively.

"You will also show it to me!"

The woman angrily thrust her badge at Kubo's face as she started toward the bed. He snatched the badge out of her hand and shoved her back with the flat of his hand. "Stay there!" he said, comparing the photo on her badge to her face.

A quick check of the list of hospital staff pre-cleared by his security team showed the woman's name was not among them. The nurse's eyes were scanning the illuminated numbers on the Jonathan's monitors when he looked up. *Kancho* slid over, positioning himself between her and the bed, blocking her vision. "Your name is not on the list."

"The regular night nurse took ill," she said, a condescending edge to her voice. "You should be thankful I agreed to fill in for her."

"Step outside!"

"I am not going anywhere! My supervisor sent me here! I will not leave until she orders me out!"

He latched onto her shoulders and spun her around. "Out!" he ordered. The door swung open and two guards stood in the doorway, guns at the ready. The men almost carried her into the hallway.

"She is not to return. And I want her identity verified," Kubo said, then saw the doctor standing behind the men and waved him in.

The medic checked Jonathan's pupils with his pen light, then grunted. "What?" *Kancho* asked.

"They are responding. That is a good sign."

The doctor pulled down the top of Jonathan's hospital gown. He pressed his stethoscope against the teenager's cut and bruised chest and listened.

Bullets shattered the outside window. The doctor dropped to the floor like a stone while Kubo flattened himself against the outside wall and peeked around the window sill. Below in the parking lot, a firefight raged. Kami and *yakuza*.

Aoshima bolted through the door and hit the wall opposite *Kancho*.

"How many and how are they armed?" asked Kubo.

"Heavily. No count yet but looks in excess of fifty. More could be poised in reserve."

"Call in all available units. And make sure everyone inside the facility is on highest alert. No one is to be allowed above or below us, on any floor."

Aoshima did a double-take. He pointed at a *yakuza* who stood at the open trunk of a black Caddie parked at the far edge of the parking lot. The man snapped two thick tubes together, then reached into the trunk for something, coming out holding a large projectile.

"Bazooka!" yelled Kubo as the man slid the missile into the tube. He grabbed Jonathan's bed and wheeled it around, knocking over carts, chairs, and monitors in his wake. "Door!" he yelled. The guards opened it.

"Preparing to shoot!" warned Aoshima.

"Help me!" Kubo yelled at the guards, who tried to pull the bed through the doorway. It was caught on something.

"Missile away!" screamed Aoshima, diving away from the window just as Kubo threw himself on top of Jonathan.

An explosion rocked the room. Flames, concrete, and brick erupted inward. Dust filled the air. Fire alarms rang. Bits of stone, glass, and ceiling tile rained down on the bed and the Master General's back.

Aoshima pressed his handkerchief over his nose and mouth, then rushed back to what was now a huge, uneven hole in the concrete wall. In the parking lot, the *yakuza* was loading another projectile into the firing tube. "He is reloading!" the Dai Kami yelled. Kubo and the guards struggled to get the bed through the door but the tubes, wires, and sensors that connected Jonathan to the monitors and drug drips were fouling their efforts. *Kancho* yanked out his knife and sliced through the obstructions in big hacks. But it wasn't going fast enough.

Aoshima keyed his mic. "Behind the black Cadillac," he said to one of his team leaders. "Do not allow him to fire again!" His Kami disengaged from a mob of *yakuza* and focused on the man shouldering the bazooka.

But the *yakuza* regrouped and fought viciously to stop them, killing one of the point men in the process. Aoshima glanced around and saw that the bed wouldn't make it out of the room in time. "Rifle!" he yelled. One of the guards tossed him his weapon. As the *yakuza* below took careful aim, Aoshima did the same, steadying the barrel of his rifle against the window-sill. He rushed off a shot. It rang out a split second before the rocket left the firing tube in a whoosh.

The missile flashed through the air towards Jonathan's hospital room, trailing a stream of white smoke. Aoshima dove for cover and Kubo again shielded Jonathan's body with his own. They waited for an explosion... but one never came. Kami on the roof reported that it had flown over their heads and exploded harmlessly in the open field beyond the hospital.

When Aoshima looked back outside, the shooter lay sprawled on the asphalt.

Experienced hospital orderlies arrived and helped maneuver the bed through the doorway and into the corridor, where Kami instantly surrounded it.

Outside, the firefight between the highly disciplined Kami and the disorganized *yakuza* had intensified. One by one, though, the Kami picked off the gangsters until only a handful remained and they soon threw up their hands in surrender.

"If the missing nurse was a *yakuza* spy," said Kubo, "then they are aware he will recover. We must move him immediately."

"To where?" asked Aoshima. "They can reach inside even the most secure military hospitals."

"I do not know," said Kubo tiredly.

31

———

Six Kami astride motorcycles with armed cohorts in their sidecars roared up the paved roadway, two abreast. Close behind, a pair of army Jeeps, mounted with 12.7 mm heavy machine guns, followed. An armored car, on loan from the Japanese Treasury, stayed on their tail, with two more Jeep M151s and two more armed sidecar motorcycles bringing up the rear. In the sky above the convoy, two heavily-armed Huey helicopter gunships added a loud and intimidating presence.

Kancho Kubo sat perched on the edge of the front seat of the armored car, his dark eyes continually scanning their surroundings and the road ahead. In the back, beyond the steel wall that separated them, Jonathan lay unconscious on a stretcher, attended by an American military doctor. Aoshima and eight elite Kami sat in the jump seats lining the side walls, their weapons at the ready.

They had had no choice but to return Jonathan to Kagamura Castle, where a temporary hospital room was being hastily assembled and staffed as the convoy made its long journey. No other medical facility in Japan could be made sufficiently secure, especially on such short notice.

The intercom buzzed on the dashboard and Kubo snatched up the receiver. "He is having a seizure!" came Aoshima's voice.

Zuma took a long drag off his foul-smelling Japanese cigarette, then let it out through pursed lips. "As you know, an unprovoked and cowardly attack was made on the main house by a team of Kami scum," he hissed to the sixty, western-suited Momochi Kumi captains and lieutenants kneeling on the floor in front of him. "An unarmed Murakami Yukio, fourteenth honored *oyabun* in succession, was murdered by the despicable *gaijin* he had mentored at the Dai Kan. This piece of crap returned his kindness by getting him expelled, then murdering him in his own home. My entire being burns in rage, as I hope yours does as well! Neither I nor this *kumi* will rest until the *gaijin* who murdered our *oyabun* is made to feel the full tortures of this life!"

"*Hai*!" responded the group.

"I am asking that each of you devote yourself anew to your *kumi* as I have, to join together in seeing that this insult does not go unpunished. As you can see," said Zuma, holding up his hands and spreading his fingers, "I have never failed you. Please devote yourself, body and spirit, to ensuring that this body," he said, pointing at his own chest, "and this body," he said, spreading his arms towards the assembled group of men, "remain intact."

"*Rei*!" commanded Saito, his new second-in-command. The group bowed in unison, foreheads touching the floor as their new *oyabun* left the room.

"*Kobun* are to be sent to watch the Kami Kan," announced Saito. "If they attempt to move the *gaijin*, kill him, even if it requires your own death. Your families will be well cared for and lavishly compensated."

Jonathan was confused. The last thing he remembered was the Land Rover flipping and his head hitting the door, the center console, and the steering wheel. Events in his mind had passed seamlessly from being slammed around in the SUV to the new medical room. He was there, inside the cab, then he was here. It was a strange feeling.

"Welcome back," said a smiling but tired-looking *Kancho* Kubo, who stood at the foot of his bed. Jonathan tried to sit up, to get to his feet and bow. But a web of straps, wires, and tubes crossed and crisscrossed his body, securing him to the bed.

"Remain still," said the Master General.

"I am sorry, *Kancho*," said Jonathan, his eyes misting. "I failed completely. I gained nothing and fear I did Nanami and Kiyoshi greater harm."

Kubo's eyes hardened, sending a wave of fear through Jonathan.

"I do not support what you did," Kubo said, "and most certainly will never tolerate such insubordination again or I will expel you. But the prince and princess are free and your actions did nothing to interfere with their release."

Jonathan's face lit up. "They were released? How?"

"They are home and have requested permission to visit you. I could not allow it as it was not safe. But now that you are here and awake, we will see."

"Were they in the tunnel?"

"No. They were held in a boat off the coast. The house and tunnel were merely a ruse to get additional money out of us and murder you."

It seemed that there was much left unsaid but, for some reason, Kubo chose to hold it back. Jonathan wanted to press him but it would not be proper.

"Rest," said *Kancho*. "We will soon talk again."

His days were filled with pain. Every inch of his body ached, inside and out. The massive headaches never slackened – from swelling in his brain, the doctor had told him. But the good news was that the gun shot in his gut was healing nicely, for whatever reason. Kenji, naturally, had no doubt but Jonathan wasn't so sure – although he was still smart enough, even with a concussion, to keep it to himself.

A week later, the doctor declared him sufficiently improved for *Kancho* to question him in more detail about what had taken place at the Murakami estate.

"Please look through these photographs," he said, handing Jonathan a National Police photo album. "See if you can identify anyone who was involved in the kidnapping."

The pictures were a mixture of school photos, family portraits, newspaper and magazine articles, and booking photos. Jonathan examined each face carefully. On the fifth page, he spotted one he recognized. It was a publicity photo of Ozawa, clipped from a Red Brigade pamphlet. "This one seemed to be the leader of the non-*yakuza*."

"Ozawa Masayuki," said Kubo. "He is head of a Marxist group that now calls itself the Japanese Red Brigade. It is so small you probably encountered the entire *brigade*."

Jonathan continued to scan the images. A couple of pages later, his eyes hardened. He stabbed his finger at a photo. "This is the one who murdered Reiko."

"Asim Al-Massri. A Palestinian terrorist and psychopath, a well-known troublemaker who even the Palestinians wanted no part of. We found his body in the tunnel. He poses no more of a threat."

Jonathan flipped through the remaining pages. Before long, he found Sadao, and then Aki, but not their *yakuza* boss. *Kancho* opened an envelope and pulled out five photos, laying them out, side by side. "How about these?"

Jonathan's finger went straight to the old mug shot of Zuma. "He's the one in charge and also the one who inferred he had either killed my grandfather or been there when he died."

"Kazio Zuma," said *Kancho*. "With Yukio's death, he now heads the Momochi Kumi. He was General Murakami's half-brother and second-in-command when the general was convicted and hung. So he almost surely ordered Eli Sama's kidnapping and execution and may well have been there. He is not as ruthless and cold-blooded as his half-brother, but far smarter, making him more dangerous in some ways. This is why you must leave."

"What do you mean, leave?"

"The Momochi Kumi has offered a ninety million yen reward for your death."

"For me?"

"The sum is not as great as it might have been, especially considering the huge amount of money the *kumi* must have received from us and the ransom paid by the Royal Family. Although money alone will not send the best against you, with the prejudice of many of my countrymen, it will be sufficient to allow the act to be viewed as patriotic. Because of this, I think it best you leave Japan for a year or two."

Jonathan didn't want to leave. As soon as he recovered and the doctor released him, his life would be perfect again. He was a Kami, someone every boy in the country dreamed of being. Kiyoshi and Nanami, his closest (and only) friends, were members of the Emperor's own family. They were in Japan and thankfully now safe. Plus, even though he would never say it out loud, he secretly considered himself Japanese, or almost Japanese. This was the only home he had ever really known. There was neither anyone nor any place connecting him to America any longer.

"Are the Kami not strong enough to protect me against a bunch of gangsters?" he asked.

"You would, of course, he safe here, but only at the expense of assigning a large number of men to protect you, men we would not be able to employ elsewhere. With our new duties protecting the Imperial Family once more, this would strain us badly, would it not?"

"I suppose."

"You would also live here as if a prisoner," Kubo continued. "The wolves would always be waiting just outside our walls. If, however, you were to go to a place where they could not reach you, we would have more time and manpower to track down those who have targeted you. Then, you could return if you so desired."

Jonathan felt empty, cast adrift. "Where could I go that they could not follow me?"

"Travel in the United States is still somewhat restricted for Japanese. You would be safe there – if you followed the usual precautions. You once told me that you had planned to attend an American university. If you studied the right subjects while there, you would become far more useful to us and perhaps even qualified to instruct here. Which college were you considering?"

"Stanford, where my father and grandfather went."

"Stanford would not be a good choice. Harvard, where your father was an honored professor, would be better."

"What's wrong with Stanford?"

"There are far more Japanese in California than any other state. An assassin would not be as obvious there as he would in the rest of your country."

He shook his head. "I don't care. Both my father and grandfather said they wanted me to follow in their path. *Karma* is *karma*. If I am to die, then *karma* will lead them to Harvard as easily as Stanford."

Nothing more was ever said and Jonathan tried to keep himself busy, living for the day the doctor would return him to duty. The librarian had allowed one of their microfiche readers to be setup on a wheeled over-the-bed-table in his room. On it, he studied microfiche film almost around the clock – newspaper and magazine articles, government documents, and court records on his grandfather's death, the Tokyo War Crimes Tribunal, Zuma, General Murakami, the Momochi Kumi, and anything he considered even remotely connected with the murder. He was reading a detailed coroner's report when he heard the door open behind him. *Probably someone to take his lunch order*, he told himself. But the report had taken away his appetite. "Sorry," he said without looking up, "I don't want anything."

Footsteps shuffled up beside his bed. He glanced over to see Nanami and Kiyoshi.

"Then I guess we should leave," Yoritomo joked, giving him a quick man-hug. Nanami stood shyly back. She was even more beautiful than when Jonathan had last seen her.

"I'm sorry I... I'm not presentable," he said, running his fingers quickly through his hair and wiping the sleep from his eyes. "They won't let me out of bed even to bathe and clean up."

"We will hold our noses," said Yoritomo, "as we always do when around you."

Nanami swatted her brother's shoulder. "They kept refusing our requests," she said. "But we had to be with you while you were injured. So we kind of borrowed..."

"More like hijacked," interjected her brother.

"... borrowed our uncle's helicopter and requested..."

"Made."

"... requested the pilot fly us here."

An aide brought in chairs, tea, and snacks for the royal pair. Nanami pulled her chair next to the bed and clutched Jonathan's hand in her tiny, delicate ones. The slow rhythmic beep from Jonathan's heart monitor quickened, embarrassing him and making it speed up even faster.

"What are you trying to do, Nana, give him a heart attack?" said Kiyoshi, laughing.

"He almost died for us," she said, her voice breaking.

Jonathan blushed, uneasy in this new role. "What about you?" he offered, hoping to get them off the subject. "Were you hurt?"

"No. They treated us most politely," said Nanami. "Except for a brief time in the beginning, when they first took us captive... and the horrible desert *gaijin* was with them."

"Yeah," said Yoritomo, "he was a real dick. He tried to pillow Nana and the *yakuza* guys pulled their guns. They were all aiming at each other. I thought we were all going to die. Then the terrorist leader, this older guy, took him away."

"I still have nightmares about him," she said, tears filling her eyes.

"You needn't worry about him," Jonathan said, his anger flaring at the thought of Asim. "*Kancho* said he is no longer a threat to anyone!"

"Why? What happed to the asshole?" Yoritomo asked.

Jonathan had assumed that they, or at least Yoritomo, had been briefed on the incident. When he realized that wasn't the case, he was afraid he had already revealed confidential information and needed to change the subject, fast. "*Kancho* wants me to leave Japan," he said, "go away to college or something. He's afraid the *yakuza* will try to kill me."

A smile flickered across Nanami's pretty face. "I have been thinking of going abroad for college as well! I have no freedom here. If we went to the same college, we could see each other as often as we liked."

Jonathan's face lit up.

"Father will never allow you out of Japan," Kiyoshi interjected.

"I am a woman now! He cannot hold me against my will. It is against the law."

Yoritomo rolled his eyes.

The door opened and a man in a military uniform bowed. "Excuse me, your highnesses. We have been ordered to return."

"Tell Father we will return when we are ready!" shot Nanami.

"He cannot tell Father anything, Nana," said Yoritomo. "We will be out shortly," he told the pilot. The man bowed and left. Yoritomo patted Jonathan on the shoulder, then slugged him. "Next time you better be out of bed and on the *dojo* floor, so I can kick your ass for letting those *yakuza* trash do this to you."

"I'm kicking yours for letting them take you in the first place!" Jonathan said, punching his friend lightly in the stomach.

Yoritomo leaned over, gave Jonathan a quick hug, then headed for the door. "Come on," he said to Nanami, who didn't move.

"I will be out shortly," she said.

Yoritomo nodded. "You better not hurt him," he added, then laughed.

As soon as her brother had closed the door, Nanami ran her fingers through Jonathan's blonde hair, straightening it. She stroked his face with her soothing hand. He could smell fresh mint on her breath and knew his own must stink, like his body. He started to turn his head away so as not to subject her to it, but she took his face in her hands and kissed him on the lips.

"How soon will you be leaving Japan?" she asked, her voice airy and musical.

"The longer I remain, the more manpower must be assigned to my protection. So the sooner, the better seems to be their wish."

She smiled. "Then, I will begin my…"

A loud knock on the door. Yoritomo opened it. "Come on, Dad's pissed."

She kissed Jonathan again, this time a soft quick peck on the lips. The citrus, rosemary, and spice of her perfume wafted in the air and trailed behind her as she left. He lay back, savoring the long lingering aroma and sweet tang of lipstick.

Jonathan sank into his pillow and closed his eyes to better enjoy the happy images his mind painted of the two of them in the warm California sunshine.

The nineteen Kami seniors expelled by *Kancho* Kubo sat smugly, arms folded across their chests, on one side of Kengo Miki's living room. On the wall behind them were two framed photos, draped in the white cloth of mourning. One was of *Shihan* Sugiyama and the other of his adopted son, Minne Kengoshi. The former Kami suspiciously eyed Zuma and his four *yakuza* lieutenants, who sat on the opposite side of the room, like boys and girls at an elementary school dance. Their placement in the room was much like their social standing. Coming from opposite ends of Japanese society, their only common ground was their mutual hatred of the *gaijin* and *Kancho*

Kubo and their grudging respect for the relationship between the *yakuza* and the martyred patriot, General Shinji Murakami. This was the only reason the Kami seniors agreed to the meeting.

"We assume you wish to discuss the *gaijin* who executed..." started the battle-scared Isao Abe, the stiff, shiny burned side of his face causing his speech to slur.

"Murdered," corrected Zuma.

Abe kept his hooded eyes fixed on the *yakuza* in obvious disdain. "Call it as you wish. But our contacts informed us that he went there in an attempt to free the unforgivable kidnapping of an Imperial prince and princess. To be honest, he elevated himself in our eyes and you sank even lower!"

"That is a vicious lie!"

The former Kami were on their feet.

"I was not referring to you, Abe San," Zuma quickly corrected. "We had nothing to do with the kidnapping. Kubo and the *gaijin* are attempting to spread that lie."

Abe just stared at him with no attempt to hide his disbelief. "We understand you believe your lack of success is due to an absence of information about the changes made inside Kagamura Jo." He smiled coldly. "We can rectify that, then see how successful you will become."

Zuma bowed. "We will not fail you."

Abe and several of the ex-Kami scoffed. "You in no way represent or act in our behalf. If you should attempt to make such a claim, you will have reason to regret it."

Zuma nodded. He and his lieutenants rose to leave.

"We have been informed that Kubo intends to secretly shuttle the *gaijin* out of Japan," added Abe. "If you seriously intend to act, you will need to do it soon."

"Togo!" yelled Zuma, as soon as he got back to his office.

The wrestler lumbered in, all 450 pounds of him. A white bandage covered his thick left hand, angling sharply in where his little finger used to be.

"I want the approaches and terminals at Haneda and Tachikawa watched," said Zuma. "I have information they may attempt to fly the *gaijin* to another country."

"Who will protect you?" the big man asked.

Zuma cocked an eye. "You no longer desire to kill the *gaijin?*"

Togo's moon-face flushed. "More than life itself."

"Then stop arguing with me! It is disrespectful!"

The big man bowed. "I will not fail again!"

32

Jonathan bowed his goodbyes and climbed into the back of a U.S. Army helicopter gunship. The craft, with its side-mounted rocket pods and M-60 machine guns, looked swift and deadly. When *Kancho* had requested assistance from the United States Embassy for the grandson of former ambassador Eli Lusk, they had sent one of their state-of-the-art aircrafts and their very best to fly it, a highly-decorated pilot who had just finished his second tour of heavy combat duty in Vietnam.

Jonathan found himself surprisingly excited about the trip, about seeing America again after so many years. But as the chopper's engine fired up and he took his final look at *Kancho*, the Kami, and the Kami Kan, he felt sudden pangs of both sadness and apprehension.

The Huey's double-bladed propeller bit into the air, lifting the craft off the ground. "Hang on! We're leaving hot!" yelled the pilot. Jonathan gripped his armrests. The chopper's nose pitched steeply downward, then raced full-bore towards the castle's tall, main keep.

Jonathan's jaw clinched as the stone wall flew at them. Just when he was positive they would crash into it, the pilot tilted the stick back and the chopper shot straight up, climbing thousands of feet until it was completely encased in the black blanket of clouds.

The pilot eased back on the stick and the craft leveled off. Flying by instruments alone to stay out of visual sight of enemies on the ground, they headed for Haneda Airport outside Tokyo. There, a French jetliner would be waiting to carry him to Paris, where he would board a Pan Am jetliner for his flight to New York and then California.

The phone rang behind the dirty bar at the Old Chicago Club, a small cabaret near Haneda International Airport. It rang again, its bell barely audible above the building-rattling rush of an incoming jetliner. A thick hand, the little finger missing and its previous attachment point still stitched and raw, snatched up the receiver.

"What?" demanded Togo, his gravelly voice, like that of many ex-*sumo* wrestlers, the end product of too many punches and elbows to the throat. The big man grunted as he listened to the short conversation, then slammed the receiver into its cradle. "Contact the *kobun*," he ordered the bartender. "He is coming. They fail to pass a check point, I am to know immediately."

"Hai!"

Togo yanked an olive-drab weapons chest, the size of a small shipping crate, out from under the bar. "U.S. Army" was stenciled on top in big, white block letters. He lugged the chest outside and stuffed it into the trunk of a small Toyota.

The car almost bottomed out as Togo squeezed his massive body into the front seat, started the small engine, and pulled away from the curb.

The Toyota weaved its way through the usual heavy airport traffic, taking a hard right just before reaching the departure terminal up-ramp. The short journey ended in the employee parking lot, where ten *yakuza* soldiers awaited their new boss. Just fifty yards or so beyond them ran the cyclone fence that enclosed the airport grounds and separated the parking lot from the taxi way, where jetliners traveled to and from the runway and the main terminal.

As the big man wiggled out of his car, one of his men yelled a warning and nodded in the direction of the terminal. Three police vans, blue lights flashing, sped their way. The *kobun* looked to their fledgling lieutenant for instructions. The corners of Togo's mouth curved stiffly up into something like a smile. When he waved at the approaching vans, the others followed suit.

Two of the policemen stared oddly at them as they raced past and continued on to where an Air France 707 had just pulled up onto the apron and shut down its engines. There, they scrambled out of their vehicles and encircled the jetliner.

"Find out where that plane is going," Togo ordered his second-in-command.

"I already know," the man said, obviously proud of having anticipated his new lieutenant's wishes. "I checked personally on the destinations of all the planes leaving today. It is returning to Paris, France."

"Does it have a stop-over in the United States?"

"No. It is heading the opposite direction."

A Citroen limo flying French flags from its bumpers pulled up to the foot of the ramp. Four French dignitaries exited the car. As they climbed the steps and disappeared inside the plane, the faint waffling sound of an approaching helicopter ricocheted off the surrounding buildings, pulling *yakuza* eyes into the skies.

"There," said one of them.

Togo followed his finger to a dark spot in the distant sky. "Ready yourselves!" he ordered. "But do not reveal your weapons to the blue dogs until the last instant." He opened the Toyota's trunk. Inside the chest was an arsenal of the latest military weaponry. He snatched up two U.S. Army grenades and stuffed them into his coat pockets. Then he eased out a bulky M-60 machine gun. "Fire when I do," he told his *kobun*. "We have but one chance. Fail and you will wish the Kami had killed you."

All eyes tracked the craft as it descended lower and lower, heading straight for the airport and the *yakuza* position. Before long, the chopper began its final approach. As the pilot's pink face came into view, Togo tossed the massive machine gun onto the Toyota's roof, centered its sight onto the cockpit, and squeezed the trigger. Flames flew from its muzzle, its heavy barrel bucking up and down, battering the Toyota's thin metal roof.

The chopper's own M-60s returned fire so quickly that it was clear they were expecting an attack. Togo ducked as a double-row of bullets pelted the asphalt in front of the Toyota, then its hood, windshield, and roof. The big man pulled one of the grenades from his pocket and flicked out the pin with his finger.

The Huey shot evasively upwards, but at the expense of forward speed. As the fat fuselage was about to pass directly overhead, Togo heaved the grenade underhandedly with all his incredible might. The oblong ball climbed to its zenith, just beneath the chopper's belly... then started back down. "*Che!*" the big man swore.

The grenade erupted, spewing shrapnel down on Togo and the *yakuza* below. But more importantly, it also hit the chopper above it, shearing off its rear rotor. Without its stabilization, the craft began to spin, slowly at first, then rapidly picking up speed. It spiraled downward like a wounded bird before crashing hard on its side just across the fence.

Togo snatched the carbine from the chest and shouldered it. The small rifle looked like a toy as he pressed its smooth stock against his cheek. With the chopper lying on the pilot's door, the only way out was through its passenger side, which now pointed skywards. The big man squinted through the scope, fixed the crosshairs on the side hatch, and waited.

The hatch jiggled. Someone inside was trying to get out but the twisted metal was not making it easy. Suddenly, a boot kicked the hatch and it flew open, banging against the side of the fuselage. Two pale hands reached out and grabbed hold of the door jam.

Togo ignored the flurry of police bullets zipping past him and carefully aligned the carbine's crosshairs onto the top of the blond head. "For Murakami *Oyabun!*" he yelled. As he squeezed the trigger, a bullet pierced his left shoulder and snapped his body around, sending his shot wide.

The big man hit the deck as bullets punched holes through the Toyota's metal body and crackled overhead. He scrambled around and knelt beside the front wheel, putting the engine block between himself and his attackers. "Cover me!" His *kobun* directed a hail of bullets at the advancing line of police, sending them scrambling for cover.

Togo jumped up, took quick aim again at the blond head, and squeezed the trigger. The head snapped back, then was swallowed into the cockpit.

The big man knelt in *seiza* on the gray, pitted asphalt. He ripped open his shirt, unsheathed his *tanto* dagger, and pressed its tip against his massive belly. Lifting his dark eyes to the sky, he mumbled a prayer and drove the tip inwards. Hunching forward, he grit his teeth as he slid the razor sharp blade across, leaving an enormous, gruesome gash in its wake. Done, Togo settled calmly back onto his haunches and stoically waited.

But death did not come. He had only managed to slice open the massive fat layer encircling his midsection. Angrily, he snatched the *tanto* back up and stabbed more deeply into the already open wound. His face tightened in resolve as he ripped across, blood pouring from the incision.

Again, he laid his *tanto* on his thigh and waited. "Che!" he screamed as the death he sought once again evaded him.

He grabbed the dagger. But his hands and the handle were slick with blood and it took a few seconds to grasp it tightly enough. Just as he was about to drive its tip deeper into his belly, two policemen rounded the back of the Toyota. The first bullet hit him in the forehead, the second in the center of the chest. The huge man fell backwards and lay, his eyes staring at the same sky, on the dirty asphalt.

Across the fence, two policemen scrambled up and disappeared into the hatch of the downed chopper. Others gathered around and watched expectantly. One of the two inside reappeared, looked solemnly down at his lieutenant, and shook his head.

33

An indigo-robed monk leaned his body hard into the thick, frayed rope, launching a rough pine log into an ancient bronze bell the size of a small car. The earth vibrated with its deafening gong.

A thousand-year-old temple drum, carried on poles by four bent-backed monks, boomed as a fifth struck it to an ancient rhythm with a wooden bat. Behind them, a smoky procession, led by *Kancho* Kubo, inched its way down the winding, graveled path at the back of the Dai Kan grounds.

A team of Kami, flanked by saffron-robed monks, pulled a two-wheeled caisson across the arrow catching field, a pair of shroud-encased bodies resting on the wagon's flat bed. It stopped when they reached the center of the field, where a mound of dried twigs, logs, and branches had been stacked higher than a man's head.

Four of the Kami lifted the bodies of their dead comrades and carried them to the pyre. There, they gently laid them on two wooden platforms that had been built above the branches. The men bowed in unison and backed respectfully away.

Kancho separated himself from the assembled group of Dai Kami, Kami, and Dai Kan staff and students and approached the pyre, closely trailed by an aide carrying two wreaths of white chrysanthemums. The Master General placed one atop the Japanese flag that covered the smaller of the two bodies. He bowed, then tenderly placed the second on top of the shroud draped in the Stars and Stripes of the United States. The master's hand slid almost imperceptibly off the flowers and onto the young man's lifeless body. He stepped back, gave the two a final bow, then walked heavily away.

Nanami gently lifted the hem of her exquisite, pure white kimono and took her brother's arm to steady herself. Yoritomo tried to smile reassuringly as he led Nana to the pyre but his eyes moistened and he looked quickly away.

They pressed their palms together in prayer, then whispered their goodbyes. Yoritomo took his sister's elbow and the two turned to leave. As they did, his lip quivered, allowing a sob to escape. It wasn't much but it shattered the thread-thin rein she had obviously been holding over her own grief. Nanami jerked her arm free and collapsed on top of the shroud. Yoritomo picked up his tiny sister and carried her away, disappearing into the throng of Kami.

Their braziers swinging to and fro, four chanting monks encircled the pyre. As they perfumed the air with incense, two others thrust burning brands deep into the kindling. The fire quickly caught and clawed at the dry branches and platforms. White smoke soon curled up from the shrouds, then burst into flames. Yellow and red licked high into the sky above the pyre, engulfing the platforms and their dead, temporary occupants. The frail structures quickly gave way, releasing the two corpses into the inferno's blue center.

Smoke drifted eastward, carrying the spirits of the two young warriors, mingling their souls among the trees of the Dai Kan's forests. There, the Japanese believed they would remain as true *kami* or spirits, looking after and protecting the living Kami from misfortune.

The circle of life now complete, *Kancho* Kubo turned and trudged sadly, slowly away.

34

A battered orange taxi idled noisily in front of Wilbur Hall on Stanford University's Dorm Row. Jonathan stepped out onto the sweltering sidewalk and sized up the two-story stucco building that would likely be his new home for at least the next two years.

During his ride in from the airport, he had gotten a good look at the sprawling campus that encompassed over eight thousand acres. They had driven through expanses of grassy fields, dotted with ancient oaks, through fragrant eucalyptus groves and clumps of privet and manzanita, that reminded him much of the Dai Kan.

The dorm RA showed him to his room, in the middle of the second floor as Kubo had specified. Although it contained little more than a bunk, desk, and cabinet, it was twice the size of his room at the Kami Kan. In Japan, an entire family could have lived in such a space.

After unpacking the few things he had brought with him, he shuffled through his photos, propping an old shot of Reiko on top of his dresser. Next to it, he placed one of Nanami and a shot of him with Yoritomo, their arms around each other. Yoritomo had said something funny just as the shot was taken and they both wore goofy grins. It made him smile.

He came across an unopened package of pictures he had picked up from the photo department just before leaving. He leafed through them, stopping when he came to one of him among a small group of Kami in combat gear. He and Eiji Sasaki stood at the back of the group, where the photographer had put them because they towered over the others.

Jonathan bowed his head to the photo. *"Domo arigato gozaimashita, Sasaki Sama,"* he murmured, reverently. He studied the other faces in the photo, trying to figure out who the second Kami might have been.

Had he known anyone would die, he would never have agreed to the swap. After the chopper had landed as planned to refuel at the American Air Force Base and the crew exited to eat and visit the restroom, intelligence had come in from an informant inside the Momochi Kumi. Heavily-armed *yakuza* were taking up positions around Haneda Airport, their destination.

When the crew returned to continue their flight, Jonathan was not with them. He had been replaced by Sasaki wearing a short blond wig borrowed from the wife of an American Air Force officer. Jonathan felt like a coward as, following orders, he waited in the tower, watching the Huey lift off to continue its journey south.

A privately owned American executive jet had been diverted to the base, where it picked him up for the trans-oceanic flight. He was over the Pacific, enjoying his first American meal of steak, baked potato, and garlic bread since the age of seven, when *Kancho's* call came in. What he heard took his appetite away.

He had assumed that the ruse would be terminated before the chopper reached the airport. But *Kancho* had wanted it played to the end, although he didn't know it would end as it did. He had merely hoped to misdirect the *yakuza* into thinking Jonathan had flown to France.

Extreme ranges of emotion teared his eyes or flared his anger throughout the remainder of the flight. He felt guilty for the deaths. Had he not gone after Murakami, the pilot and two good Kami would still be alive. He also felt anger that people like the *yakuza* had gained so much power over his life that he had had to flee Japan. He offered to return and aid in bringing down the *kumi*, but Kubo denied his request. "An educated mind will be of far more benefit to us than another trigger finger. We have many of the latter and too few of the former."

One of the first questions that popped into Jonathan's mind went unsaid and unanswered, however. *Kancho* was talking about dead Kami and he couldn't bring himself to ask if Nanami and Kiyoshi knew that he was still alive. So he waited. But before he got a chance to ask, they hit a patch of rough air and were disconnected.

The jet landed at Moffett Field Naval Air Base in Mountain View, just down the road from Stanford. As soon as he was inside the small terminal, he called *Kancho* on one of their secure lines and asked.

He could tell it was a sensitive subject, one Kubo seemed embarrassed to talk about. "We could not risk anyone outside the inner circle knowing until you were safely away," said the Master General. "So, unfortunately, they became part of the deception to throw off any who would threaten your life."

"What deception?"

"We held a funeral ceremony the same day as your supposed death, before any but those who already knew could discover that you did not perish in the crash. But as soon as I received confirmation you were safely away, I informed the prince and princess. They were extremely relieved, although I may not be sitting comfortably for some weeks from the scolding the young princess gave me. She also requested I inform you that she would send you a telegram addressed to an alias, Mariko Tonai, to throw off her minders. She requested you anticipate it."

The telegram made it to Stanford before he did. When the RA unlocked his door and handed him his key, the yellow paper sat on the floor near the door, where someone had obviously slid it.

Kancho being chewed out by Nanami... the thought made Jonathan smile as he headed down the Wilbur steps, taking them two and three at a time. He was anxious to see where his classes would meet when school started in a couple of days.

His tour took him through White Plaza, past the coffee house, Tresidder Student Union, the old admin building, bookstore, School of Ed, and into the Quad. He ambled along the covered sandstone walkways, noting the names of the departments.

Two pretty coeds passed. They glanced back in unison, checked him out, and smiled to each other.

But Jonathan took no notice of them or any of the others he passed that day or any other day. The only girl that interested him was Nanami, who had assured him in her telegram that she would arrive at Stanford a week or two before the start of the second quarter... and life, for the first time, would truly be perfect.